"You are so very lovely."

He turned her slightly and lifted her hand to his mouth. It was a gentle kiss, nothing at all like the kisses he wanted to share with her. Now.

Her lips parted in surprise, and her eyes grew large. He could not help but notice the pulse thrumming at the side of her neck, and sensed that she would not refuse further intimacies.

The need to taste her, to feel her enticing, feminine body pressed against his was nearly overwhelming. He drew her away from the gallery, searching for a private niche or an alcove where he could show her how much he wanted her. He pushed through a closed door and found a staircase in a deserted back hall. Slipping into a small nook behind the stairs, he pulled her inside and took her into his arms.

"I've wanted to touch you from the moment I saw you."

Romances by **Margo Maguire**

THE ROGUE PRINCE
TAKEN BY THE LAIRD
WILD
TEMPTATION OF THE WARRIOR
A WARRIOR'S TAKING
THE PERFECT SEDUCTION
THE BRIDE HUNT

The ROGUE PRINCE

Margo Maguire

AVON
An Imprint of HarperCollinsPublishers

This is a work of fiction. Names, characters, places, and incidents are products of the author's imagination or are used fictitiously and are not to be construed as real. Any resemblance to actual events, locales, organizations, or persons, living or dead, is entirely coincidental.

AVON BOOKS
An Imprint of HarperCollins*Publishers*
10 East 53rd Street
New York, New York 10022-5299

First Avon Books paperback printing: May 2010

Printed in the U.S.A.

10 9 8 7 6 5 4 3 2 1

This book is dedicated to my very good friend,
Ellen Reid Monkman, with my prediction that
2010 will be a great year!

Acknowledgments

My absolute gratitude goes to Shannon Donnelly, who knows everything there is to know about horses and horse racing, without whose advice and suggestions I would have been lost. I'd like to thank Nancy Mayer for her unerring knowledge of regency-era law, and Delle Jacobs for knowing so much about sailing ships and sea travel during this time period. These lovely ladies provided me the information—any errors of interpretation are mine.

My thanks to my editor, May Chen, for her thoughtful insights on this and all of my work; and to my agent, Paige Wheeler, for her enthusiastic support.

The Rogue Prince

Chapter 1

London. Late March, 1817

Anguish, dark and intense, ripped through Thomas Thorne when he gazed at number nineteen Hanover Square, the location of his ignominious downfall. By now, he should be over the incident that had occurred there more than seventeen years before. But his hatred for his accusers still burned, still sizzled like a flaming torch, deep in his gut.

Murder would be a far simpler solution than the revenge he'd planned at great length all these years. And though it would serve his purpose, murder would be far too easy. It offered nowhere near the satisfaction he sought.

He remembered Marquess Shefford's sumptuous mansion as though he'd only arrived there that morning as a lad of sixteen. He'd accompanied his father from Suffolk to London with the six Thoroughbreds the marquess had purchased on a trip to Newmarket, and somehow it had all gone wrong from there.

While Thomas had helped to prepare the horses to be shown, someone had put several valuables from the house into his pack. It could only have been Shefford's wicked bull of a son, Leighton Ingleby, and the boy's milksop friend, Julian Danvers, for they were the two who had accused him and held up his pack with the silver bowls inside for all to see.

The house had not changed in the least. As Tom stood gazing at the site, he could almost hear the wheels of the carriages and the clop of horses' hooves on the street as they'd passed in front of number nineteen that day, and even the melodic calls of the street hawkers nearby.

But then the scars on his back began to itch painfully, and his wrists and ankles throbbed as he remembered the weight and shame of his shackles.

Tom inhaled deeply from his cheroot and looked around. It was dusk, and all was quiet now. The air was chilly, but he barely felt it, for his desire for revenge burned in his belly and warmed him far better than any coal fire could do. He did not know what he could possibly have done to offend the marquess's son and his friend, Danvers. But they had surely known what the consequences of their conspiracy would be. Tom would have been hanged or transported.

There were days Thomas wished he had hanged.

He reminded himself that everything was different now. It was a long time since Judge Maynwaring had sentenced him to be transported to a violent and filthy penal colony with its sadistic commandant, Major Foveaux. It was past time for his lying accusers, his indifferent judge, and all of their families to suffer as Tom and his family had done. He might not be able to send them to Norfolk Island, one of the hellish colonies where Tom had spent the seven horrifying years of his sentence, but Tom now had the means to make their lives a misery. He would make Leighton and Julian's families pay for his lost years in the penal colony, as well as his subsequent years of hardship and degradation after he'd received his ticket-of-leave.

They deserved no less than what he had planned.

Tom's men had orders to be exceedingly circumspect as they investigated Ingleby and Maynwaring, and the Danvers family, for he did not want to alert any of them to his presence or his plans. He wanted them to be absolutely vulnerable, to be taken entirely by surprise, just as he had been all those years ago.

Tom and his men had also taken on false, foreign-sounding surnames in order to carry out their deception, and they'd come up with a plausible explanation for why their English was better than it should be. Tom had no reason to think anyone would be suspicious of their story. Not when he possessed more wealth than a dozen kings.

He walked across the square and turned to look once again at the imposing edifice of Shefford House before returning to his hotel. He would feel no satisfaction, no contentment, until they were all destroyed as he had been. Until they suffered as his family had suffered.

Tom did not know if his parents and sister still lived, or where they might be. His father, a prominent Suffolk horse breeder, had been devastated by Tom's arrest. He had pleaded with the judge for lenience, to no avail. Maynwaring would not give Tom's father the time of day.

Some of George Thorne's letters had reached Tom aboard the prison hulk, but after his transportation to the South Seas, the letters stopped. Tom hated to think why his father might have stopped writing.

The burning hole of loneliness that had hurt more viciously than any of Tom's beatings returned full force. During the first few weeks of his incarceration, he'd missed his parents and sister to the point of despair. It had become a dull ache in the following months, and dwindled to nearly nothing as he'd fought to survive. But he felt it again, now that he was back. Seventeen years fell away, and he was the raw youth who'd been desperate for his father's solid presence and the comfort of his mother's touch.

A small boy suddenly burst from the front door of a nearby house, and rushed into the street. He was well dressed, but disheveled as a boy at play might be. As he ran full bore toward the center of the square, a fashionable barouche barreled into the street, moving much too fast. In an instant, Tom realized that the barouche was not going to be able to stop in time. The horses were going to trample the child.

Tossing his cheroot to the ground, Tom dashed toward the boy and grabbed him, gathered him in his arms, then threw them both out of the way just as the barouche sped past them and came to a halt some yards away. Thomas rolled to the ground, protecting the child as best he could, barely aware of the shouts and cries all around him.

He hardly dared open his eyes, afraid he might be missing a vital part, or that the boy had been hurt. Yet when he felt a hand on his arm and smelled the soft, feminine scent of roses, he cracked one eye open.

"Zachary!" cried the woman who dropped to her knees beside him. Her cheeks were flushed with color, her dove gray eyes bright with terror.

Her unabashed maternal concern touched a chord deep within him. She was entirely fresh, with no artifice about her, just an open horror at what might have happened to her child.

Her face was a perfect oval, with full, sweet lips and a deep dimple creasing each cheek. Her nose was unremarkable but for the pale freckles that skittered across it. A lock of wavy, dark brown hair had escaped the knot at her nape, but most enticing of all was her half-unbuttoned bodice. Her rush from the house must have interrupted her dressing. Or undressing. For the curve of her full, soft breast pushed against the gap in her bodice, and her apprehension for her son outweighed any semblance of upper-crust arrogance.

Thomas swallowed hard and sat up with the child in his arms. It had been many long years since he'd felt the punch of arousal so quickly, so completely. And it was absolutely unwelcome now. He had to remind himself that it was this spoiled aristocracy that destroyed his life as though it meant nothing.

"Are you all right, sir?" Her question contradicted what he knew of west end residents. She took the child from Tom's arms, then returned her hand to his forearm, even as she admonished the boy. "Oh, Zachary!"

Thomas extricated himself from her grasp and stood, shocked by the force of lust he felt from their slight contact. "Quite all right, madam."

He tamped it down and attempted to be furious with the boy for putting them both in danger. Yet the child's puzzled expression tugged at something inside Tom. An appreciation of innocence he'd thought long-buried.

"Maggie! Come away from there!" came a carping female voice from the direction of the boy's house. "You look like a . . ."

The young mother—Maggie—ignored the older woman, keeping her eyes on him as he gave her the regal nod he'd practiced so assiduously. He had to take his leave as quickly as possible. He could not afford another minute with this pretty lady, with her pulse thrumming wildly in her smooth throat, and each breath coming fast in the wake of her distress.

She was far too tempting. Her emotional intensity and state of dishevelment made his body yearn for impossible things.

The boy's nanny arrived, a plump matron in a gray gown and white apron. "I'll take him, my lady," she said, hardly able to contain her horror at what might have happened.

"No need, Nurse Hawkins. I have him now," said Maggie, never breaking her gaze with him. Her voice broke, but she did not weep. The woman might have backbone, but Thomas felt an overwhelming urge to draw her into his arms and hold her close. Provide comfort.

Perhaps he was more shaken than he thought.

"Please, do come to the house and . . . and . . . allow someone to see to your clothes."

"No harm was done," Thomas replied as several more people from the house started across the street toward them. "A quick brushing will suffice."

As she held her son close, a crease of consternation appeared between her softly arched brows, and when she bit her lip, he noticed a thin sliver of a scar that underscored it. The flaw only added to her appeal.

"Are you certain, sir?" she asked quietly. "I would be entirely remiss if I—"

"It was nothing, madam. All is well," he said, as the older woman with the harsh voice crossed the street along with the rest of them. Here was the well dressed, the privileged elite, all talking at once.

The distraction of their voices was exactly what he needed to remind him why he was here. "If you'll excuse me, I'll bid you good night."

* * *

Maggie Danvers was trembling so hard she thought her bones might break. Her precious son had nearly met his death out in the street, and there'd been nothing she could do to stop it, not with her lame leg and the slowness it caused. She thanked God for the presence and quick thinking of the tall stranger who'd saved him.

"Who was that fellow in the street?" asked her mother, the dowager Marchioness of Shefford. "I didn't recognize him." Beatrice had hardly changed at all in the two years since Maggie had seen her last.

A few silvery threads had twined themselves through her mother's bright red hair, and Maggie noticed several delicate crinkles about her eyes. Her waist was slightly thicker than Maggie remembered, but Beatrice had been a beauty in her time, and her features had not changed much with age. Maggie looked around the room where her three older sisters had gathered, and saw that they still favored their mother, while Maggie did not. She never had, much to Beatrice's consternation.

Her sisters were much older than she, belonging to some sisterly club to which Maggie was not invited. They'd had their assemblies and parties, their beautiful gowns and handsome suitors, while Maggie had stayed home with her nanny.

"I've never seen him before," said Charlotte, the eldest. Her red-gold hair was elegantly coiffed with pearl combs that matched the pearls at her neck. She was even more beautiful than their mother had been at forty, with two equally lovely daughters who would come out together this year.

"He's not a resident of the square, is he?" their mother remarked.

Lord Horton, Stella's husband, folded *The Times* open to display a picture on the second page. "Look here. The man himself."

Maggie's stepbrother, Leighton Ingleby, Lord Shefford, took the paper, and as Horton passed it to him, Maggie could see that the drawing was a perfect likeness of the man who'd saved Zachary.

"*Prince Thomas Johan of Sabedoria*," Shefford read aloud, his words clipped, as usual. He hadn't bothered to rush out to the square with the others, so he'd missed Zachary's brush with disaster. Horton took it upon himself to explain what had happened.

Shefford stroked his thick mustache. "What is Sabedoria? Some French district? Never heard of it."

"Nor has anyone in the foreign office," Lord Horton said.

"It's a country. Apparently," said Lord Crusley, Elizabeth's husband.

"They're all atwitter over the flaxen cloth these foreigners brought from their country," Crusley added.

"Flaxen cloth?" Beatrice murmured, obviously puzzled.

Crusley turned to face Lady Shefford. "It's used by the navy to make sails."

But Beatrice was glaring at Maggie. "A *prince*, Margaret!" she scolded. "And there you were, half-undressed, with your hair a mess and your—"

"I was hardly undressed, Mother," Maggie retorted. She'd been in London only one day, and her mother was already interfering, managing, criticizing. Judging. Beatrice was one of the primary reasons Maggie had kept to herself at Blackmore Manor after Julian's death. She and the rest of the family always got along much better when they were in different counties, unlike Beatrice and her other daughters. The four of them all fit so very well together, while Maggie was different. Not only in looks, for she'd had the misfortune of taking after their father. But Maggie had committed the unforgivable.

Her actions had caused their esteemed cousin, the Marquess of Chatterton, to hang himself.

Maggie hugged her son closer, so grateful to the man who'd saved him from certain death. Both her children were precious to her, and she vowed never to treat either of them the way Beatrice behaved toward her. Maggie would protect her children, no matter how horrible the circumstances.

"Zachary," she said firmly, "you must promise never to run out of the house that way again!"

"But Mama—"

"The boy needs discipline, Margaret," said Beatrice, her scolding opening the flood gates of sisterly opinions and declarations. Her sisters and their husbands each seemed to have something to say about Zachary and his unruly behavior, and they did not fail to leave out his little sister, whom they had decided was unreasonably bashful. Maggie could understand Lily's shyness around her opinionated aunts. She didn't blame her daughter at all for preferring the nursery in the attic.

Shefford was the only one who had little to say. He was not much taller than Maggie, but he was built like a bull, thick and strong. His hair was a sandy brown color, and he wore a thick mustache that was somewhat darker than the hair on his pate. The expression in his wily, dark brown eyes always seemed to be evaluating, or scheming over some new plot. Such looks never failed to make Maggie uncomfortable, especially now, as he eyed the newspaper drawing of the prince.

She looked away from him, wishing that the entire family, her sisters and their husbands, as well as her mother, would all just disappear. She had managed very well in the two years since Julian's death, in spite of her family's conspicuous absence from Blackmore Manor. She did not need their advice or disapproval now.

Besides, none of their admonishments were relevant. It had been four years since Zachary's last visit to London, before his second birthday. Though Maggie and Nurse Hawkins had warned both of Maggie's children against the dangers of the busy streets, it was clear that Zac had not understood. Everything in Town was so very different from the easy environment he was accustomed to at Blackmore Manor.

"Do you promise, love?" she asked him, above the din of voices in the drawing room.

"Yes, Mama. But at home—"

"You are not in Cambridgeshire, boy!" Crusley said abruptly.

"You're not helping, Crusley," said Charlotte.

"What do you know of raising boys, Charlotte?" Elizabeth, Lady Crusley, who was the mother of two sons, raised a sardonic brow.

Maggie felt a headache starting, and wished she had not found it necessary to come to London.

"Really, Maggie," said Beatrice, and the others finally fell silent. "You must try to have better control of the children. And your nurse. Why, she just allowed Zachary to run straight into the—"

"Nurse Hawkins has much to do, Mother, looking after both of the children."

Maggie lowered her son to the floor and stood, taking his hand in hers. "We're not accustomed to Town."

She did not stay to listen to her mother's retort. Instead, Maggie made her way through the crowd of unwelcome relations who'd finally seen fit to pay her this incredibly inconvenient visit, and upstairs to deal with Zac as well as Nurse Hawkins, who was sure to be distraught.

Maggie still felt shaken by the incident, and astonished by the actions of the stranger in the street. She could not help but wonder if any of the men of her family would have risked their own lives and limbs to save her son from a trampling.

She doubted it. Shefford hadn't even bothered to go outside when Zac had run into the street.

And yet a perfect stranger—a foreign royal, for heaven's sake—had rushed to Zachary's aid, even though he might have been seriously injured himself. He was truly a hero.

"Are you very angry, Mama?" Zachary asked as they climbed the stairs.

"Terribly. You disobeyed Nurse Hawkins and put yourself into a great deal of danger, young man."

"I hate it here! I want to go back to Blackmore Manor."

"It's not yours to decide what we will do, or when," Maggie said, though she silently agreed with him.

They climbed up to the attic bedroom that Zachary shared with his little sister. The room was large enough to accommodate a nursery and play area, with a bedchamber at the back for Nurse Hawkins. It was very different from the children's rooms at Blackmore Manor, and Maggie wished they were still there.

She disliked London immensely, and had lost her naïve desire to please her mother and sisters. It had finally become clear to Maggie that such a thing was not possible. Her mother and siblings would always hold her guilty for "carrying on" when Chatterton had assaulted her—he a man of thirty, and she a child of nine years. She'd been traumatized by his inappropriate advances, and he'd been publicly shamed to the point of suicide.

Hawkins was waiting when Maggie entered, holding Lily in her arms, looking pale and over-wrought. "I will tender my resignation immediately, my lady," she said, handing the little girl to Maggie. "I can give you no adequate excuse for—"

"Please, Nurse Hawkins," said Maggie. "I understand what happened. And I believe my son owes you an apology for disobeying you. Zachary?"

"Sorry, Nurse Hawkins," was the boy's petulant answer.

"Go on, Zachary," said Maggie.

"I'm sorry for running away when you told me to come back."

"Go ahead, then," Maggie said to him. "You are to sit here in your bedchamber and look at a book until I decide you may come out."

"But Mama!"

"No arguments, my dear young man."

Maggie closed the door behind her as she and the nurse left the room.

"He was so fast, my lady," said the woman who'd been with Maggie since Zachary was born. Hawkins had provided far more support than Maggie's own family after Julian's death, watching over Zachary and taking charge of six-month-old Lily, while Maggie recovered from the birth of her daughter and the shock of her loss. "No matter how much he runs and plays in the park, he wants more."

"I know," Maggie said. "He has enough energy for two boys his size." And when she and Shefford visited Julian's solicitor tomorrow, she would ask for funds to engage a governess for him. He was nearly six years old, and it was past time for him to begin his formal education. "We'll just have to keep the front door bolted from here on."

"Yes, my lady," said the nurse, so shaken Maggie didn't think she would ever again give Zachary a free moment in which to misbehave.

Maggie could not return to face her family just yet, so she retreated downstairs to her bedchamber and stood at her dressing table for a moment to compose herself. The danger to Zachary had been all too real, and the thought of losing him was unimaginable. She was embarrassed by the realization that it was far more distressing than actually losing Julian had been.

Her mad dash to the street had been unseemly. Even worse was the stab of longing she'd felt when she looked into the prince's deep green eyes. Her raw emotions had no doubt given him the wrong impression—and yet she'd been deeply aware of those broad shoulders and powerful male physique.

He seemed to be all strength and dependability, compared to her husband's continuous irresponsibility and frivolousness—which were the cause of his death, in fact. If only Julian had had a sensible bone in his body, he would not have gone boating on a November morning when storm clouds threatened. He would have considered the consequences of his actions.

Dolefully, Maggie pinned up her hair. Neither her mother nor any of her sisters had returned to

Blackmore Manor after Julian's funeral, in spite of Maggie's invitations. Not even Shefford had come up, and he was Julian's executor. Only her dear friend, Victoria Ranfield, had come, but her responsibilities to her own family had limited her to visiting only twice.

Still, it was more than her family had done.

Maggie had felt abandoned as a new widow, and had struggled to deal with her children and the management of the rapidly declining estate. It was clear now that she had not managed well, for there never seemed to be enough funds for all that was needed. Perhaps worst of all was that she'd had to face the truth about her family. After all the excuses she'd made for them since Chatterton's death, she'd finally understood how much they actually despised her.

There was too much to do for Thomas to linger in Hanover Square, harkening back to the darkest days of his life. And yet he regretted leaving the pretty young mother. He would have enjoyed looking into her velvet-lashed eyes a while longer, thinking about the future he might have had if he'd not been set up to take the fall for a robbery he hadn't committed.

He'd have married a comely Suffolk girl, and continued the horse breeding tradition of his forefathers. No doubt he would have had a cottage full of children by now, and a sweet, warm, feminine body to curl up with during the cold nights.

But the life that had been thrust upon him was

devoid of warmth. Hatred burned inside him, but it was an icy heat that had frosted the chambers of his heart. He had naught but disgust and revulsion for the life that he'd been forced into, and his only redemption was vengeance. Only when his accusers had been adequately punished would Tom find the peace he needed in order to move on.

He walked back to the place where he'd left his carriage and driver, and traveled the short distance to Limmer's Hotel, where sporting men were known to gather. During the racing season, it was at Limmer's that they would make their books and speculate among themselves on the year's best runners.

It was early days yet, and Tom's men were still gathering information on his foes. They'd learned that Danvers—Lord Blackmore—was dead, but that unlucky fact had merely changed the character of Tom's revenge. The man's family would pay dearly, just as the Thornes had paid.

Tom was a patient man. He would wait until he knew more about his enemies before he firmed up his plans and put them in place. And he would not be satisfied with anything less than a complete destruction of those who had hurt him so profoundly.

He took a seat and ordered a meal, then asked for a *Sporting Review*. While he sat and skimmed the journal, he listened to the racing talk, and learned which two-year-olds were the most promising, and what races were going to be the most exciting in the coming season. He heard rumblings about Paragon and Palmer's Gold—Shefford's two prime Thoroughbreds—which were said to be unbeatable.

So much the better.

Everything was falling into place, like threads on a weaver's loom. The destruction of his enemies' reputations and finances wouldn't be anything near the devastation Thomas and his family had felt when he'd been wrongly accused and convicted, but would go a long way toward balancing the slate.

Perhaps then, Thomas would be free of the dark memories that shaped his every thought and action.

Maggie would not apologize for leaving her family in the dining room of Julian's town house, partaking of the supper Beatrice had taken it upon herself to order. She had reconciled herself to the way her family regarded her. It was difficult enough being the plain, lame sister who didn't quite belong among them, but she'd crossed the line when she'd reacted with screaming terror to her far older cousin's attempted molestation.

In Maggie's opinion, Chatterton had been a vile lecher who preyed on young girls. To her family, Maggie had wrought the destruction of a "perfectly fine" nobleman, a man who would one day have become the Duke of Norcross. Equally important, he'd been on track to become the husband of her sister, Charlotte. On his death, the title had passed to some distant relative who had no allegiance to Maggie's mother or sisters. They'd lost a very powerful connection for the family.

And it was all Maggie's fault.

It had taken far too many years for her to grasp that *she* had not been the guilty party. She had not enticed Lord Chatterton in any way, other than by being small and lame, and isolated on the day in question. She'd been the perfect prey for the kind of man he was.

Of course no one had ever explained his assault, nor had they really believed her accusations, in spite of some vague rumors of other young girls falling prey to his aberrancy.

And yet his suicide had told the truth of the matter.

Maggie would have thought it undesirable to continue an allegiance with a man so twisted he would comport himself in such a perverse manner with a little girl. But her family had not agreed. Charlotte's betrothal to their older cousin had meant all, and they blamed Maggie for Chatterton's fall.

Maggie considered herself fortunate not to have fully understood the man's intent at the time, though she shuddered even now at the thought of the ugly gleam in his eye when he'd cornered her in the nursery and—

She would not think of it now, after so many years had passed. There were more pressing issues to consider, such as keeping her children

safe in Town. And trying to guess why her family
had descended upon her now. It was likely that
Beatrice had insisted they all come at least this
once, to avoid any appearance of a rift in the
family.

She decided that Beatrice could play hostess,
since Maggie had no interest in doing so. There
was only one reason she had come to Town,
and that was to see what could be done about
having her dower portion released. Shefford
was the executor of Julian's estate, but he had
not responded to her pleas for assistance, and
she'd been without credit in Blackmore for over a
month. She couldn't make the desperately needed
improvements in Blackmore's lands until she had
some money.

She sent Nurse Hawkins down to the kitchen
for her own supper, and picked up her daughter,
Lily. Keeping the little girl on her lap, she sat down
beside Zachary on a comfortable settee before the
fire in their cozy attic bedchamber. The children
had already had their evening meal and were ready
for bed, but it was Maggie's habit to draw them a
story before they went to bed.

It wasn't enough just to tell them a tale of adventure and exciting events. Maggie's habit was to
draw pictures of the pirates and highwaymen, as
well as the heroes and maidens who populated her
stories.

Her skill at drawing was just a silly hobby, certainly not the high art of her sister, Stella. But her
lack of talent did not bother her, for she'd never

wanted to do more than amuse, and sometimes instruct, her children with her meager abilities.

"That's the man who pulled me from the street, Mama," said Zachary, noting the likeness Maggie had drawn of the prince. He was as dark and seemed as dangerous as a pirate, and yet he'd performed the good deed of saving Zac from the racing carriage.

"Don't you think he should be the hero of our tale?" she asked her son.

"Well, he didn't fight pirates, did he?" Zac queried, rising up on his knees and leaning close to watch every line that Maggie drew.

"Well, of course I don't know for certain, but I believe he is fully capable of fighting pirates," she replied with a smile. The magnitude of the man's heroism mattered not to Maggie. She was just thankful he'd had exactly what was needed to save her son from disaster.

She wondered if he'd noticed his effect upon her. Her shock at Zachary's near death had been enough to cause her heart to thunder in her chest, but the prince's touch had stopped the breath in her lungs. She'd felt a quickening inside that had naught to do with Zachary, and everything to do with the man whose grass green eyes had looked at her as a man might look at a lover.

Not that Maggie had any experience in such things. She had felt awkward and unappealing during her one short season, and her sisters had scoffed at her flimsy attempts at flirting. Because of her lameness, she couldn't dance a creditable set, and she'd been too shy to be any good at conversation. Her season had been a disaster, which had made it quite easy for Shefford to pressure her into marrying Julian Danvers, his good friend.

There wouldn't be any other offers, her mother and Shefford had claimed, not when Maggie was still such a gangly, awkward thing at age twenty— with a lame leg, no less. The years-old Chatterton scandal had not helped, either, but Julian had been willing to overlook Maggie's shortcomings to know that he'd be getting a suitably innocent, biddable wife.

Lily took her thumb from her mouth. "Is there a bairn, too, Mama?"

"I hadn't thought of a bairn, love. Shall we give one to the handsome captain and his wife?"

"No!" Zachary protested. He got up from the settee and took up a fighting stance. "No babies, Lily! The captain must fight the villains on the sea!"

"Where on earth did you learn such a thing, Zachary?" Maggie asked, aghast.

"From Willy Johnston," Zachary replied with bravado. "We do boxing at home!"

"Come back here and sit down, young man," Maggie said. She wasn't quite sure what boxing was, but she had some idea that it involved two grown men throwing punches at one another. It was not something she wanted her son to be any part of.

If only he'd had a more conscientious father,

if only Julian had spent more time with his
son, perhaps Zachary would have a more even
temperament.

But Julian had always had more important
things to attend to in Town—estate management,
he'd said, and business affairs. Maggie would have
accompanied her husband on his trips to London
if he'd ever asked her, but Julian had wanted to
spare her, saying that his frequent treks to London
were wholly tiresome. There were solicitors and
managers and agricultural meetings he needed to
attend.

Maggie decided she could tolerate London for
a few more days. As soon as possible, they would
return to Blackmore Manor, where her children
would be safe from carriages racing through the
streets, and other unforeseen dangers.

And Maggie would be safe from the ridiculously
volatile reaction of her heart at the courtesy of a
stranger.

Chapter 2

Two days after the incident in Hanover Square, Thomas read through the invitations that his good friend, now known as Nathaniel Beraza, had left on the table. The two men were close in age, and they'd found it expedient to watch each other's backs during the years of their incarceration in the penal colony. It had been a dark hole of a place, rife with unthinkable hardship and violence. Survival in those first few months had been difficult, but between them, they'd managed to get by.

Nate had a handsome, open face. With his coppery hair and bright blue eyes, he could be a very engaging fellow when he chose to be, but he was not a man to toy with. Tom's friendship with him had grown throughout the horrific years they'd spent at Norfolk and in Botany Bay trying to survive, doing whatever was necessary to avoid the marines' vicious whips.

But it was Tom who'd watched over Duncan Meriwether, giving the old man a portion of his own food when others stole Duncan's, and protecting him physically from the fiercer prisoners on the island. It was to Thomas that Duncan had bequeathed the vast, ill-gotten treasures he'd stolen during his pirate days.

Duncan had been transported for life for his years of buccaneering, but he'd never told anyone of the riches he'd hidden away in a cave on an uncharted south Caribbean isle—not until Thomas. Duncan had called the place Sabedoria, after his Portuguese cohort who'd stashed his own treasures there before being killed in a raid.

The old pirate had quietly babbled about living like a king on a Greek isle one day, in spite of his life sentence. Tom had humored him until the old man's last brutal beating. Then he'd carried the bloodied, broken man away from the pillory. He'd taken Duncan into his own hut and placed him on his own raw pallet.

Tom remembered cringing at the sight of the cruel slashes in the old man's back, but there'd been nothing he could do to help him, nothing but offer him a few sips of water, and his own company.

Duncan had refused the water, taking hold of Tom's arm, squeezing as tightly as he was able, and insisting that Sabedoria and the treasure were real. Tom had known the old man would not survive that last flogging, so he'd humored him, letting him sketch a map on an old cloth with a piece of charcoal to show Tom the location of his treasure isle.

"It's on the south side. There are caves just under the water in a freshwater cove," he'd said. "Look there."

"Aye, Duncan," Tom had said. "I'll be sure to do that."

"Ain't easy to find, my isle," he'd rasped. "Ye must not give up when you get lost in the leeward isles, mate. Watch for the eagle. It's an eagle that will show you the way."

The old man had died soon after, and it wasn't until another three years had passed that Thomas and Nate had managed to get to Sabedoria. There'd been far more blood and water under Tom's feet than he cared to remember, and it had taken months of exploring the South American Antilles, searching for a gathering of eagles' nests before they'd finally come upon a small isle with a huge stone promontory carved by the elements into the shape of an eagle. After only an hour of exploration, they'd found that old Duncan's unlikely tales of riches beyond belief had been true.

Duncan's treasure could not ease the restlessness inside Tom, but they made all of his plans possible. It had been seventeen years since he'd known peace. Seventeen years since he'd felt any kind of contentment or satisfaction.

Until two days before, when he'd looked into the soft gray eyes of Zachary's mother.

He tossed aside the beautifully penned invitations from the scions of society and pulled on his coat. He was going back to Hanover Square. But not to wallow in his memories of past events at number nineteen. He'd put off seeing the woman again—Maggie—for too long.

He knew it wasn't prudent. She was married,

and he was a man with a mission that had nothing to do with any women at all, much less the flawed gray-eyed matron who'd touched his arm and sent a firestorm of awareness through him. She was no conventional beauty, but she was exactly the kind of woman who appealed to him. Unpretentious, and down-to-earth, her emotions had been heartfelt. She was no stuffy English noblewoman with the practiced airs of those he'd encountered since his return home, but a sweet woman with a hint of vulnerability lurking in her magnificent eyes.

Tom had not been able to stop thinking of the many pleasurable hours she must provide her husband in their bed, a ridiculously unproductive thought process.

"Tommy Boy?"

His nerves on edge, Tom looked up sharply at Nathaniel, who'd entered the room silently. He went right to the pile of invitations and picked up the one on top. "This one is it, my boy," Nate said, holding it up for Thomas to see. "Your moment is about to arrive."

"Aye," Tom replied quietly. It felt so strange to be back in his native land, under such changed circumstances. He'd shared his treasure with Nate, of course, and now the two of them were far richer than the prince regent himself. With an exceedingly careful orchestration, with flags and credentials and documents of authenticity, the English authorities believed he was a foreign dignitary who had treaties to be signed and a superior product to trade.

It was all a foil for the vengeance he would wreak against Leighton and Julian.

"This is the event we should attend," said Nate.

"I agree. Duchess Waverly's ball will give us entrée to the cream of society."

"Leighton Ingleby—Lord Shefford, now—will be there. You can make his acquaintance and begin to draw him into your web."

Nate harbored a deep hatred for the "toffs" who'd sent him away from London in chains, away from his pregnant sweetheart. Nate had learned that the poor mot, a rookery girl of sixteen, had died in childbirth only a few days after Nate's incarceration. So had the child.

Thomas understood Nate's hatred, for he harbored his own. And he had started on the only course that could satisfy his need to even the score. It was early in the season, and the Waverly ball was the most important event thus far. Shefford would surely attend a ball given by the most prestigious matron of society. That was where Tom would introduce himself to the man, and draw him into the trap he would use to destroy him. He only wished Julian still lived, and could be hurt as grievously as Tom had been.

He would like to send both his accusers and his judge to Norfolk Island to suffer the same pain and indignities Tom had endured. That was impossible, of course, but he could take away what was most important to them. He had the resources to make their lives hell.

"Has there been any word from Saret or Salim?"

Tom asked, using the fictitious names his cohorts had chosen for themselves. They were two former convicts who'd returned to England with Tom as part of his entourage. All of his men had been incarcerated for one offense or another, and each one had his own talents. In addition, Lucas Reigi, a former pirate, was in command of Thomas's three princely ships, all anchored near London where they could be seen, and marveled at, by incoming ships.

"Mark Saret is on his way up here as we speak. He said he has news. Sebastian Salim has already left for Suffolk, to look for your family." Nate gestured to Tom's coat. "You're going out?"

"Just to familiarize myself with the city," Tom said, deciding it was pure folly to visit Hanover Square. "Maybe I'll take a ride up to Hampstead Heath and look at Mr. Delamere's property once more." Anything to take his mind from fantasies of the lovely, disheveled Maggie, the wife of some damned nobleman.

Nate opened the door after a sharp knock, to admit Mark Saret. He'd been a Yorkshire man of business in his previous life, and his particular skills were of tremendous value to Tom. He was not a very tall man, but with his pale blond hair and fair complexion, he possessed enough charm to have bilked three different ladies out of their fortunes.

But that was years ago. Saret was no common criminal, but possessed a fair knowledge of the law, and was no mean forger when necessary. Thomas had provided Saret with a fortune of his own, so there was no need for him to beguile vulnerable young ladies any longer, or to falsify documents.

Unless Tom asked him to do so.

"You have Mr. Delamere's answer?" Tom asked.

"The transaction is complete," Saret replied. He produced the deed to Delamere's extensive estate, along with a key, which he placed in Tom's hand. "He could not refuse your, *ahem*, exceedingly generous offer. The man sold me the property late last night and we transferred the deed this morning. The old miser vacated the premises within hours of that."

"Oh dear," said Lady Victoria Ranfield, Maggie's very best friend from childhood. "I didn't want to be the one to tell you, Maggie, but neither did I want you to hear it at a soiree or at some other some public gathering."

Maggie's sketchbook and pencil slid to the sofa beside her, and she pressed a hand to her chest, as though she could eliminate the shard of pain that sliced through her faltering heart.

Dear God. Had she stayed at Blackmore Manor in Cambridgeshire, she never would have known, would never have had to face the truth about Julian. He'd been a negligent husband, but Maggie had never thought . . . She'd never dreamed . . .

She leaned back against the sofa, swallowing hard, feeling light-headed. Disoriented. As though the axis of the world had shifted.

As well it had.

"Are you all right?" Victoria said, reaching over to collect the drawing Maggie had started. "Oh, bother, I should never have told you."

Maggie thought back upon the day Julian had proposed to her, more than eight years before. She had hoped for a better match, but her mother and Shefford had insisted that Julian's would be the best—the *only*—offer she could expect. And Julian was Shefford's best friend, besides. So much the better, according to Beatrice.

Somehow, they'd made a decent marriage. They'd been content. At least, that had been Maggie's belief for all these years. Julian had had his shortcomings, as had she, of course. But, fool that she was, she had not guessed this.

She bit down on her lower lip in an attempt to quell its trembling. She supposed she should thank her good friend for informing her of her late husband's marital infidelities.

Yet she wondered if all her memories of Julian would now be tainted with the tinge of nausea she now felt. Would she look at her family and friends and wonder if they'd known all along that he'd sought the beds of other women during their marriage?

Had she been so inadequate in the bedchamber that he'd had to seek gratification elsewhere? Of course. She'd been a consolation wife, the girl no one else had wanted, and Julian had been too lazy to bother courting one of the more sought-after young ladies. Her heart sank to the pit of her stomach.

"Here. Drink this," Victoria said.

"No, thank you," Maggie replied, turning down the brandy her friend had hastily poured. "I must—"

She didn't know what she must do. Go, she supposed. Back to Julian's town house where her children waited. Back to the life that was a complete and total sham. She and Julian had never spoken of marital fidelity. Maggie had just assumed their vows meant something. Had *wrongly* assumed . . .

"Look here, Maggie. Not to put too fine a point on it, but Julian is dead and gone," said Victoria, Maggie's very proper friend. No doubt it had been immensely difficult, having to give Maggie such distasteful information. "It's been over two years since he drowned. And you've been up at Blackmore Manor ever since the accident. Nothing has changed now that you know. Julian cared about you—"

"Don't!" Maggie cried, her voice a ragged rasp of pain. She stood abruptly. "I—I know you mean well, Victoria, but . . . Please do not speak to me of caring." She shook her head, speechless now. With a husband like Ranfield, who was mad about his wife, Victoria couldn't begin to understand the depth of betrayal Maggie felt.

In a haze of utter shock, Maggie gathered her things and went to the front door, allowing the butler to help her with her pelisse. She refused Victoria's offer of her carriage or even a footman to escort her, and walked down the steps, barely conscious of her maid, who followed right behind her.

Absently, she rubbed her aching thigh, the site of the old fracture that had never healed correctly.

After the Chatterton debacle, Maggie had taken pains to please her mother, to be a dutiful daughter. And when Beatrice insisted that marriage was less about caring than it was about family alliances, titles, and fortunes, Maggie had squelched her hope for a match based on affection and perhaps even attraction. She'd married Julian and tried to be the best possible wife to him.

Apparently, it had not been enough.

Needing to walk and clear her head, Maggie proceeded forward like an automaton, completely unconscious of the discomfort in her lame leg, unaware of the carriage traffic on the street or the passersby who nodded and tipped their hats. She had been an exemplary spouse, managing her household, giving her husband children. She'd visited Blackmore's tenants far more often than Julian ever had, fretting over sickness and bad harvests without him, while he *tended to business* in Town.

Business, indeed.

She brushed away her tears of hurt and embarrassment as resentment and anger rose within her. Perhaps *she* should have an affair or two of her own. Or even ten! No one could argue that she had not been a virtuous wife, then a properly mournful widow these past two years. Now that she knew Julian had not respected their vows during their marriage, Maggie did not know why she should do so, either.

She did not understand how she could have been so blind. Julian might never have spoken of undying love, but she had thought they'd done well enough together. They'd had two children, for heaven's sake, and he'd spoken of wanting another after Lily's birth. Another son, he'd said.

And yet he'd shared intimacies with another woman. *Women*, if Victoria was correct.

She shuddered as disgust roiled through her. Who was Julian to soil their wedding vows? How could he taint the sanctity of their marriage with the obvious precedence of other women in his life, in his heart and mind? How could he come to her bed at Blackmore Manor and touch her after . . .

It should not hurt quite so badly, but it did. And it shook what little confidence Maggie had. All these years she'd fooled herself into believing she had satisfied her handsome husband, when in truth she hadn't possessed whatever it took—beauty, charm, sophistication—to keep him faithful. Or happy.

Maggie swallowed back her tears. If Victoria was concerned that she would learn of Julian's infidelities in some public place, then *everyone* must know. Her family and friends, the servants, maybe even shopkeepers . . .

Mortification flashed through her. Julian's disloyalty and dishonesty cut into her like a jagged knife. Her entire married life had been a lie.

Her vision blurred by her tears, Maggie tripped, and would have fallen, but for a pair of strong hands that caught her.

It was him. The prince.

"Madam, we meet again."

"Oh!" Maggie felt her cheeks go warm, and knew she was blushing bright red. She blinked away her tears and pressed one hand to her breast, feeling as sad and raw as a jilted bride. "Clumsy me."

"Not at all," he said. "There is a crack in the pavement."

He could have released her arm then, but did not.

Maggie took a shaky breath and looked up at him, into those lovely green eyes, and forced herself not to sniffle. She swallowed thickly. "You . . . You seem to be making a habit of rescuing my family."

"How is your son? He is fully recovered from his misadventure, I trust?"

She nodded, needing to escape, to find some private place where she could weep until she used up all her tears, but he continued to grip her arm. Somehow, she managed to answer the man. "But for a scolding and some time spent alone in his bedchamber, he is fine. Thank you for asking. And thank you again, for intervening the other night. If not for you—"

"Think nothing of it," he replied. And still he did not release her. Maggie took another quaking breath, her earlier upset complicated by the attentions of the man who had occupied far too many of her thoughts since his daring rescue.

"You are distraught," he said, frowning fiercely. He took her elbow and looked down the street. "Is there anything I— Perhaps you would join me for tea?"

"Oh, I really should n—" she began, but everything had changed. Her world had shifted in Victoria's parlor only a few minutes earlier, and her life would never be the same. She was a widow, no longer bound by the same constraints she'd known as a debutante or even a wife. There was no reason to decline an invitation from this man—a prince in every sense of the word. "Yes. I'd like that very much."

She sent her maid, Tessa, home, then stepped forward to place her hand in the crook of his arm.

He slowed his gait to match hers, escorting her to Blakeley's Tea Shop, then going inside to a small table near a window. He ordered their tea, then turned his full attention upon her.

Maggie felt her heart flutter, much as it had the night before, when she'd knelt beside him and taken Zachary into her arms. This time, her panic was due to her lack of experience. Her sisters had decried her as a failure at flirting, but it had not mattered. Before she was halfway through her first season, she'd married Julian, and any attempt at flirting had come to an end, for he'd seemed oblivious to her attempts to engage him.

Maggie was on her own now, in uncharted waters. If she were to have an affair of her own, she could not have asked for a more intriguing or attractive man to have it with. And yet she knew better to think he would even entertain such a possibility.

"I hope it is nothing serious," he said.

"What?" came her breathy response. Of course it was serious, just the thought of sharing intimacies with—

"Whatever has upset you." He removed his gloves, then leaned forward and lifted one hand, gently using the pad of his thumb to rub away the remnants of her tears. Maggie hoped no one noticed his intimate act, but every fiber of her being vibrated with awareness.

Attraction shimmered through her, making her breasts tingle and her womb tighten with expectation. She had to force herself to ignore the pebbling of her nipples and the heat at the crux of her legs, for she knew such sensations would bring her naught but an afternoon of feeling vaguely frustrated and ill-at-ease. That was how it had always been with Julian on the occasions when he'd taken his pleasure in her bed, and then left her feeling unfulfilled and unsettled.

"It's nothing. Only some strange news," she said. She did not think she could ever speak of her late husband's betrayal to anyone. It was bad enough, just hearing the few details Victoria had told her.

The prince seemed to understand that the subject was not open for discussion. "I hope you weren't too harsh with your son last night. Zachary, was it?"

"Yes, Zachary," she managed to say. "I fear I was much too lenient with him. I yield far too often to my softer side."

"He is a lucky boy, then," said the prince,

his voice low and seductive. He moved his hand slightly, touching Maggie's fingers with his own. It could have been an inadvertent contact, but she did not think so, not after he'd touched her face so tenderly.

His hand was large and square, with a sprinkling of dark hair on its back, his fingers long and blunt-tipped. Just looking at them caused a frisson of sensual awareness to shoot down Maggie's spine.

"My son needs discipline," she said quietly, "and a father's influence."

"His father does not provide it?"

"My husband passed away some time ago," Maggie said, aware that her statement might be construed as an announcement of her availability. She'd half intended it to be so.

But the prince said nothing, and Maggie lost heart. As her sisters had been pleased to point out, she hadn't the slightest idea how to attract a man, and it was obvious now that her marriage to Julian had not improved her skills. If anything, what few she possessed had become rusty during her marriage. He'd had little interest in her or the children, coming to her bed every now and then, whenever it suited him.

Maggie pushed back her chair, embarrassed at her own failures and her silly forwardness with this man, this stunning stranger who attracted the surreptitious attentions of every fashionable lady who walked past their little niche. "Perhaps I should go."

"Please don't." He placed his hand over hers. "I'm new to your city and I thought perhaps you might have time to show me some of the sights."

Maggie felt a sudden fluttering of butterfly wings in her stomach and hoped he had not spoken out of pity. He could not possibly be indicating an interest in pursuing something with her. Something dark and sensual, and entirely improper. *Julian* was the one who'd engaged in—

No. As a widow, Maggie was as free as a woman could be. And she was going to enjoy the attentions of this man for as long as they lasted, even if it was for one afternoon.

"What . . . Er, d-do you have anything in mind?"

She swallowed nervously, suddenly aware of how absurd it was for a weepy, country viscountess to be entertaining the kind of thoughts she was having about this striking man.

"None at all. What do you recommend?"

Maggie believed he must be allowing her to dictate their terms. She could choose to move quickly, or slowly, or not at all, depending upon her own preference. "London is not really my home," she said. "I've only just come into Town to take care of some business. But there used to be a gallery in St. Alban's Street—with wonderful drawings. And there are Lord Elgin's marble works, newly arrived in Town."

"I would very much enjoy visiting either one with you."

The prince rose and went to Maggie's chair.

She felt a moment of indecision, then stood, determined to pursue a path she'd never once considered before. If this breathless sense of anticipation occurred every time Julian had met his paramours, Maggie could almost understand how he'd been drawn into his illicit affairs.

As the prince helped her with her chair, his hand lingered on her shoulder a fraction of a second longer than necessary, causing rivers of sensation to course through her.

If she had the slightest misgivings about going with him, she squelched them as they left the tea shop. They stepped into the street together and his carriage pulled up at his signal. The driver jumped down and opened the door, and Maggie climbed in.

It had not occurred to Thomas that Maggie might be a widow, and the thought that she might avail herself of his attentions appealed to him more than it should. Yet he could not devote his complete attention to his business. There had to be some relief from the intensity and focus of his mission in London.

She wore the same subtle fragrance of roses that he hadn't been able to put from his mind since their encounter in Hanover Square. It wasn't just her scent that drew him, but a lush potency that was purely female—her full mouth and delicate hands drew him like a horse to clover. Now that he was with her again, it was no stretch of the imagination for Thomas to think of her lying naked, her body round and soft with promise, wearing nothing but her lovely scent, in his bed.

Thoughts of tasting her flooded his mind, and Tom forced himself to rein in his erotic fantasies. She was upset and skittish, and probably did not understand the depth of his desire for her.

She would soon know.

The sorrow in her eyes touched some primal nerve in him, long since buried. Someone or something had hurt her, and he felt an entirely irrational desire to make certain it never happened again.

"No need to be nervous," he said, taking the seat beside her. He'd made a point of learning everything there was to know about high society, so he knew it was not quite proper to take her into his carriage alone. And yet she had not protested. It boded well for his intentions.

He turned toward her and took her hand, which was lying in her lap. "I promise not to ravish you."

"Oh, but I—"

"As much as I might want to."

With her deepening color and sharp intake of breath, Tom saw an innocence in her, and knew she'd never engaged in any kind of seduction. She'd likely followed the usual course for women of her class, and married at a young age to a man she hardly knew. And now he was dead.

It raised all kinds of possibilities for the way he might proceed.

He lifted her gloved hand to his lips. "Tell me what is special about the St. Alban's gallery."

Her thick, dark lashes closed over her exceptional eyes, as though savoring the moment, and Thomas felt a distinct tightening in his groin. She would be pure voluptuous pleasure in his bed.

He removed her glove. Keeping her hand in his, he lowered his head slightly, as though he might kiss her. He wanted to, desperately. As the pleasing scent of roses filled his senses, he could almost taste her.

"St. Alban's is full of p-portraits and beautiful landscapes," she said quietly, her breath feathering his cheek. "And there used to be a number of Mr. Rowlandson's prints on display. Perhaps they are still there."

She looked up at him with parted lips, more alluring than anyone he'd ever known. He'd bedded a fair number of beautiful women, but perfection had a way of playing out much too quickly. He sensed untapped layers in this woman—layers that would be an immense pleasure to peel away. Perfection was immensely overrated.

"I've never heard of him," Tom said quietly.

"Well, you wouldn't if you're new to England." Her lips were barely an inch from his. "Rowlandson is an artist I admire."

"Then he must be very good."

The carriage rolled over some uneven pavement, jostling them, and she tipped her head away, perhaps realizing how close she'd come to touching his mouth with her own. She was clearly out of her element, and her reticence inflamed him as much as the raw emotions she'd already displayed in his presence. He wanted to pull her into his lap and

cover her with kisses. Yet, if Tom had learned anything during all his years away, it was to exercise
patience. He could wait for this woman to adjust
to his advances.

But not too long.

They soon arrived in St. Alban's Street and went
inside the gallery, where Thomas paid the entry fee.
It was a two-story building, divided into several
rooms, each with tall windows to maximize the
light. There were only a few patrons inside, wan-
dering from one display to the next. Tom touched
the small of Maggie's back, and they moved together toward one of the back galleries.

He felt a sharp pull of possessiveness, and with
that fleeting touch to her lower back, craved even
more. They stopped to admire the paintings on
the walls, but Tom's eyes were drawn to Maggie
far more often than to the pictures. His senses
were alive with her—the roses, the freckles scattered across her nose, her full, kissable lips. Even
her slightly uneven gait and the intriguing scar on
her chin drew him—to a lass who had not been
coddled and spoiled by her aristocratic kin. She
seemed to be a woman apart.

Her clothes were nothing special, her simple,
brown pelisse covering her completely from neck
to wrists, and down to her ankles. And yet it fit her
form so closely, he could not stop thinking about
peeling it from her body, the way he would peel the
soft down of a peach from its sweet, pink flesh.

He steered her to a quiet room where there were
no other visitors and walked beside her as she

wandered from picture to picture, until an intricate drawing of a pub brawl suddenly caught her attention.

"Oh look, here is Dr. Syntax," she said, pleased at the drawing. "He is one of Mr. Rowlandson's recurring characters."

Tom barely looked at the drawing, but touched a fine curl at the base of Maggie's neck. He felt her shiver in response, but she did not move away. Bending slightly, he touched his lips to the spot.

He felt her sigh, and when she tipped her head to give him better access, he obliged her.

"You are so very lovely." He turned her slightly and lifted her hand to his mouth. It was a gentle kiss, delivered to the thin kid glove she wore—nothing at all like the kisses he wanted to share with her. Now.

Her lips parted in surprise, and her eyes grew large. He could not help but notice the pulse thrumming at the side of her neck, and sensed that she would not refuse further intimacies.

The need to taste her, to feel her enticing, feminine body pressed against his was nearly overwhelming. He drew her away from the gallery, searching for a private niche or an alcove where he could show her how much he wanted her. He pushed through a closed door and found a staircase in a deserted back hall. Slipping into a small nook behind the stairs, he pulled her inside and took her into his arms. "I've wanted to touch you from the moment I saw you."

Tom kissed her lips and he felt a shudder course through her. Encouraged by her response, he encircled her waist and took full possession of her mouth.

She melted into him, returning the kiss with innocent ardor. He felt her breasts push against his chest, and the sensation was nearly Tom's undoing. He pressed his hips against hers, then slid his tongue across the seam of her lips, desperate to be inside her. He was hard and ready, and did not think he could wait much longer.

It felt like lightning shooting through her when his tongue touched hers. Julian had never kissed her like this, had never seduced her with his mouth and the low pressure of his manhood against her pelvis. He'd never called her lovely.

The ability to think escaped Maggie, and she let herself be caught up in the enticement of this man's arms, his mouth, his obvious arousal. He cradled her face in the palms of his hands, then touched her shoulders, and moved farther down. When he cupped her breast and slid a finger over her taut nipple through the layers of her clothing, she thought she might melt in his arms.

"Leave here with me." His voice was a purely male rasp that reached deep inside her core and stoked the intense storm that was stirring within her. She felt breathless and wobbly, and yet more powerful than she'd ever felt before.

"Yes," she said, hardly aware that she had spoken, but she wanted to taste more of what he offered, wanted to experience more of the sensations he wrought so easily in her.

He released her breast, slipping his hands around her and kissing her hard, sucking her tongue into his mouth while he ground himself against her. Maggie thought her knees would buckle with the excruciating pleasure of his touch.

Dear God, was this what she'd missed during all the years of her marriage?

"Come on," he said, breaking away abruptly. He took a few deep breaths, then stepped away from their private little alcove. Maggie tried to appear perfectly proper and composed, and she assumed he did, too. He quickly led the way back through the gallery and outside, signaling to his carriage. In less than a minute, they were inside the conveyance and it started to move.

The prince pulled her into his arms again, but Maggie held him in check, her hands against his chest, suddenly uncertain. As much as she wanted more, she was a staid and settled country widow, with no knowledge or experience of such wanton conduct. She ought to demand that he take her back to Hanover Square.

"I don't even know your name," she said breathlessly, her body betraying her better judgment.

He was already unfastening the buttons at her throat and pressing his mouth to her bare skin, moving lower and lower until her pelisse was gone and her bodice fully open.

"Thomas. Tom," he said harshly.

She should put a stop to his seduction now, but

reason flew in every direction when he pushed her chemise down, baring her breasts to his gaze. To his touch. And then to his mouth.

Maggie shuddered with the most exquisite sensations she'd ever known. She let her head fall back as he licked and sucked her breasts, feeling a desperate pull of pleasure deep inside. She slipped her fingers through his hair, and bit her lip to keep from crying out. Julian had never failed to leave her unfulfilled and vaguely aching, yet she could not believe the same would happen with Thomas.

He kissed her mouth, keeping one hand on her breasts, stroking, teasing her nipples with a light, feathering touch.

Maggie's breath caught when she felt his other hand at her ankle, sliding it under her skirts. The rough surface of his fingertips glided against her calf, then teased the back of her knee, climbing higher as her pulse pounded in her throat. She should grab his hand and stop him, but every cell in her body craved his touch, cried out for the completion he could provide.

Maggie nearly came off her seat when he reached her feminine folds. He touched her gently at first, then opened her and slid a finger inside, even as his tongue speared her mouth.

She did not recognize the whimper that came from the back of her throat, but clearly it was she who'd made the sound. Pure, carnal sensation thrummed through her, enlivening a part of her that had been unfulfilled all through her marriage.

Julian had never done such a thing to her. His

habit had been to press a few dry kisses to her mouth, then lift her gown and shove himself inside her. The process had been vaguely pleasant until he entered her, and then it became uncomfortable. Even hurtful. Maggie had come to dread their marital encounters.

Clearly, there was more to intimate relations than her husband had ever shown her. There could be tender caresses that perhaps only a lover would share. Not a spouse.

"Open for me, sweet," Thomas said, looking into her eyes, while his fingers continued their intimate caress. Maggie should have felt mortified, but the passion in his gaze held hers. "Ah, that's it."

And suddenly, she felt the breath sucked out of her lungs, and a burst of savage pleasure overtook her. Her womb contracted, and her internal muscles quivered in utter bliss. She felt as though she were coming apart, and only the strength of Thomas's arms kept her intact.

"Yes. Come for me, love."

Maggie could not have stopped the flow of feelings, even if she'd tried. She clamped her legs around his hand as the wild sensations flashed through her like a flood over a dam, and held on to his shoulders as though she would fall away into nothingness if she let go.

She went limp in his arms and spoke so quietly that Tom couldn't quite hear the words she whispered. Nor did he know if he was going to be able to walk once they reached his newly purchased house just north of Town. He tried to compose himself as he smoothed down her skirts, but his arousal continued to rage, the evidence of which was painfully obvious.

He let his hands drift to her breasts, his thumbs caressing their pebbled peaks while he tortured himself with the promise of an intensely carnal interlude with her in his bed. He leaned his forehead against hers as her breathing returned to some semblance of normal.

His own was still out of control.

"Are you going to . . ." she started dubiously, though Tom did not doubt she could feel him hard and ready against her hip. "Do you need to . . ."

"Bed you now?" he replied with some difficulty. "Not here in the carriage. We'll soon arrive at the house."

Tom pressed his hand against her mound as the last few shudders of her orgasm took her. Her breath caught, and her eyes were glazed. He could hardly suppress his need to be inside her.

"House?" she whispered, her eyes shooting open, her gaze suddenly clear.

"Yes. I bought a house yesterday. It's not far." *Thank God.* Because he didn't think he could wait much longer. He was ready to explode.

Her face went pale and she started to pull the edges of her bodice together. "Oh, but— I didn't think . . . I cannot—"

He kissed the side of her neck.

"We will be completely alone," he whispered, moving her hands away from the plump, feminine flesh she was attempting to cover. "There will be no servants there yet, besides Oliver. My coachman. But he—"

"It's not that. I . . . I've never . . ."

"Of course you haven't." He circled one of her pretty, pink nipples with his tongue, aware that she was as innocent as a virgin. She might have borne a child, but her husband had obviously never made love to her, for it was clear she'd just experienced her first orgasm.

He took her hand and placed it upon the placket of his trews. She pressed her hand against his hard length, sliding it up and then down, shivering, her nipples tightening even more than before. She seemed to forget her objections, losing herself in his kiss, but then breaking away suddenly.

"Thomas . . ."

She removed her hand from his swollen member and pressed it to her chest, and a mounting wave of pure frustration came over him.

"I'm not . . ." She closed her eyes and tried to gather herself. "I have an appointment this afternoon that I must keep."

She looked into his eyes, her disappointment and confusion clear. "But tomorrow. I will meet you anywhere you wish. Tomorrow."

Chapter 3

Maggie saw one of her stepbrother's footmen standing at the front door when she exited Thomas's carriage at the far end of the square. She did not want to face Shefford now, not with her obvious flush and disheveled appearance, for he would surely grasp that something had happened.

And she did not want to share any part of it with him.

What she'd just experienced was far beyond anything she'd thought possible, and she shuddered with an eager anticipation of her tryst with Thomas upon the morrow. She refused to feel any guilt at all.

Somehow, she managed to keep her legs working after entering the house. She walked quietly to the stairs, anxious to get to her own bedchamber, hoping to avoid Shefford and whatever reason he had for coming for her so early. Her stepbrother could just bide his time until they had to leave for their meeting with Julian's solicitor.

The house was quiet, but for the sound of voices in the drawing room, and as Maggie crept past the closed door, she heard Shefford's voice, in discussion with another man. She kept walking until his words stopped her cold.

"She never bothered Julian," he said. "Can't imagine she'll be a problem for you, either, Kimbridge."

"If only the old dog didn't insist," said Shefford's companion. "Then I wouldn't have to look for a wife just yet. Or ever."

"If I understood you correctly," Shefford said, "your father told you to get a *respectable* wife, or there would be no allowance."

Maggie tried very hard not to jump to any conclusions, but then Shefford spoke again.

"Look here," he said. "You need a well-regarded wife, and Margaret is just the thing. God knows she cannot refuse your fortune, and your paterfamilias will surely be satisfied with a decent, reputable, country widow."

"I'm starting to believe you have a point, Shefford."

"Of course I do. Margaret will be as biddable a wife to you as she was to Blackmore. And you know she's a decent breeder. Blackmore got two children off her in the few years they were married."

"Dash it all, Sheff. I know you're right. I . . . When shall I begin the courtship?"

Maggie felt the burn of bile rising to her throat. She did not stay to hear Shefford's reply, but hurried on to her bedchamber, her mind raging between shock and disbelief.

* * *

Tom's first nine years away from home had been an exercise in painful hardships. The forced labor and brutality of the island guards were the least of it. The prisoners had known hunger on Norfolk Island, and every other kind of privation. Illness ran rife among the weak, and Tom had taken a few of the more vulnerable convicts under his wing to protect them. He'd stood up to the bullies who would have taken Duncan's food from him, and buried far too many children who'd been too weak to survive their seven- or ten-year sentences.

After four years on the island, he and Nate had been transferred to the mainland where they worked for a free landholder. It was hard labor, but their masters were not as harsh as Major Foveaux and the guards on Norfolk Island. There, Tom's whippings had been less frequent, and when he and Nate finally served out their sentences, they'd signed onto a whaling ship in the belief that it was the only way they'd be able to earn their way home. They had not been able to turn their backs on Port Jackson soon enough.

Tom spent every waking moment thinking of the time when he would be able to return to Suffolk and resume the life that Shefford and Blackmore had interrupted. He and Nate worked the whaler, planning to make their way toward the Antilles where Duncan's island was located, for there would be no harm in seeing if there was any truth at all to the man's ramblings.

But their whaling endeavors ended when their ship was attacked by the pirate Jacques Butcher.

Tom could not help but question his luck at escaping with his life when he and Nate were taken as slaves on *Butcher's Blade*. His years in the penal colony paled compared to the horrors he witnessed during his captivity on the pirate sloop. Major Foveaux was a babe in arms compared to Captain Butcher.

It was two long, unspeakable years before Tom could take no more. He instigated a mutiny among the pirate's slaves, and somehow managed to rally all of them against Butcher. A long and bloody melee resulted, but Tom and the other slaves had prevailed, killing and tossing overboard the vicious pirate captain and every last member of his depraved crew.

During the first nine miserable years away from home, Tom managed to live through the agonies inflicted upon him only by dreaming of the day he would bring Shefford and Blackmore to their knees before him. When he finally located Duncan's treasure and realized the power it gave him, he'd turned his plan for revenge into reality, and mastered the skills he needed to carry it out. He'd cultivated patience, unwilling to act precipitously and ruin everything.

And yet the daylong wait for Maggie was proving to be a surprising challenge to his oft-practiced self-denial. She was no shrinking virgin, and yet she was an innocent, a woman who was clearly without knowledge of the pleasures of the bedchamber. Her husband must have been a fool.

Tom took a deep, tremulous breath as he

watched to be sure she entered the house safely, his gaze lingering on her retreating figure as she went inside. He'd learned how to put away his wishes and desires and turn his attention to the things he could control.

He finally forced himself to leave the square, but felt far too restless to return to his hotel. He decided to drive up to the Delamere property, just as he'd planned to do before happening upon Maggie in the street. He knew it would be much more productive to assess the floor plan of his new house before taking her there on the morrow, and be sure everything was as he wanted it. There should be a fire crackling in the master's bedchamber, a tray of refreshments on a table nearby, and a bottle of wine beside the bed when he laid her upon it.

It did not take very long to reach Harrow Road, and from there Oliver drove onto a side track that led to the house, a Palladian mansion, suitably ostentatious for a visiting prince. Saret had been authorized to pay Delamere up to twice the value of the property, just so that Tom would have the perfect location for his horses. It was close enough to London to make the trip easily, and there were more than enough acres to create the race course he needed.

At the time of his arrest, Thomas had had a promising future in breeding and raising thoroughbred horses alongside his father. The stables in Suffolk had been his life in those days, and he'd returned to his earlier vocation in recent years. He'd gone to America with Duncan's treasure, and formulated his plans while building up Thorne's Gate, his beautiful, sprawling horse farm in New York.

But no one in England would ever know that. Tom just had to convince them that Sabedoria existed—an isle in the South Seas, hidden within the clutter of islands north of Botany Bay. He was gambling that with his immense wealth and ostentation, no one in England would challenge his veracity.

Ollie pulled the carriage to one side of the massive front staircase of Delamere House, and when Tom got out, he was greeted by Nathaniel Beraza, Ted Careaga, and Mark Saret. They might be three of his most trusted friends and allies, but their presence made him realize he needed to plan his assignation with Maggie more carefully. There was no need to subject her to their scrutiny.

"Good. You're finally here," said Nate. "We've been looking over the property. Will you walk out to the stable with me?"

Tom put the morning's interlude behind him. Maggie was a distraction he desperately needed, but he could wait. And somehow, he would get her into the house and his bed without all of his friends taking note of their every move.

"What's happened?" Nate asked, scrutinizing his face.

"Happened? Nothing," Tom replied, clearing his face of anything but curiosity. "Why?"

"You have a look about you."

Tom figured it was no different from the expression worn by any number of sexually frustrated males. He shrugged as though naught was on his mind, and continued on toward the stable. "What needs to be done here?"

"Not much. A week's work, perhaps."

They walked into the stable and Tom examined the stalls, noting there was plenty of room for his own twelve horses, and another dozen, besides. "What about Arrendo?" he asked of the thirteenth horse, his champion. His ringer.

"There's a barn some distance from the house, with living quarters for a groom or two," Nate replied. "We'll keep him there."

"He'll be out of sight?"

"Aye," Nate said. "It's on the other side of a copse of trees near your huntsman's cottage."

"There's a huntsman's cottage?"

"Not that we'll have any use for it."

Perhaps not that Nate would ever know. The huntsman's cottage was a fine solution to the problem of how to bed Maggie without making all his friends aware of their liaison.

They left the stable and ambled toward the paddock where workmen were already repairing a few broken wooden slats on the fence.

"With the thick woods between Delamere House and the huntsman's barn," said Nate, "we can get Arrendo out early every morning and run him without anyone ever seeing him."

They walked across to Delamere's second stable which also had its own paddock. "We're ready to proceed, Tom. I've ordered enough grain for all the racers and the carriage horses. And Ted has already sent for Mickles and the rest of the sailors who will function as your house servants and grooms."

"What about riders?"

"We've got Arrendo's rider, but Saret and Careaga are looking up some old friends for the others."

"Excellent," Tom replied, aware that both men had connections in the racing circuit. "Send someone out to the ships and have Lucas Reigi bring them in. I want to get the horses settled as soon as possible. What about the race course?"

"I think we've found the best spot," said Nate. "It's out this way."

It was a short walk, past an elaborate garden of sculpted shrubs and stone pathways. They passed a stately row of poplars and eventually came upon a large, relatively flat stretch of land. Much of it was covered with low shrubbery and grass. Thomas looked it over and knew that Nate was right. This was the perfect spot for his race course.

"Excellent. I'd like to get work started on it right away," he said.

"I expected you would," Nate replied. "Careaga's already hired workmen to clear out the brush and shrubs, starting tomorrow."

"What about the house?" Tom asked, though he was far more interested in how well the huntsman's cottage would suit his more immediate purpose.

"Delamere kept a surprisingly small house staff.

They're already making the changes I requested on your behalf, but I'll pay them off and send them on their way tomorrow."

Tom nodded. "Have our trunks brought here from the hotel today, all but our clothes for the Waverly ball."

Tom reined in his preoccupation with Maggie and focused his thoughts on his first encounter with Shefford. That was his purpose there. A tryst with a desirable woman was not going to interfere with the execution of his plan. He would have to work around it.

If Maggie had thought her morning extraordinary, the afternoon was no less so. She twisted her hands in her lap, shocked, unable to credit what Julian's solicitor had just told her. It was too much, coming so soon after learning of her husband's mistresses, and then her astonishing interlude with a complete—*nearly* complete—stranger.

"You are saying that Julian . . ." she swallowed thickly, " . . . that he *mortgaged* the lands that were not entailed?"

Mr. Clements looked down his nose at her. "And the note is due at the end of the month, my lady."

Maggie turned to her stepbrother. "Shefford, you never said—"

"Margaret, it's not for you to worry about," Shefford said offhandedly.

"*I beg your pardon!* How is it *not* for me to worry about?" she demanded. "Blackmore Manor is Zachary's birthright! Not to mention our living!"

No wonder her monthly allowance had dwindled so dramatically since Julian's death. "What of my dower portion? My inheritance?"

"As your guardian, Lord Shefford agreed to a settlement on the occasion of your marriage, rather than a dower portion," said Mr. Clements. "And your husband borrowed against it. It's gone."

"Gone? I do not understand. The settlement was mine. *Is mine.*"

Shefford turned to her. "Maggie, Julian had to—"

"He had to give me what was rightfully mine! How could you allow this to happen, Shefford?" She pressed her fingers against her temples and tried to understand. As Julian's widow, she was entitled to some portion of his wealth. And Shefford should have safeguarded that portion.

"What of the tavern in the village?" she asked. Julian's father had leased it to the tavern keeper, and to her knowledge, that circumstance had not changed.

"Also mortgaged," the solicitor remarked calmly, as though Maggie's world was not coming apart, and all because of Julian's perfidy and gross negligence. She knew what he'd been doing on all those trips to London, and it had nothing to do with taking care of estate business.

"The paper mill?" she queried, though she already knew the answer. She felt like the worst kind of idiot. Naïve and foolish during her marriage, then far too trusting of her stepbrother, the man who now intended to push her into marriage with yet another scoundrel.

"Julian sold off his interest in the mill a few months before he died."

She could hardly believe her ears. The mill that had provided income for decades was no longer theirs. And there were a number of expensive improvements that needed to be made to Blackmore land. How was she to be expected to take care of her tenants and keep the lands in good condition for Zachary when he reached his majority?

"There is some jewelry in the safe at the manor," Maggie said, sounding quite desperate to her own ears. "It belonged to Julian's mother and I'm sure it must be quite valuable."

Shefford shook his head. "You musn't have looked there lately, then."

This could not be happening. "What do you mean?"

"Julian sold most of it," Shefford replied, "to pay his gambling debts."

If Maggie had felt ill while sitting in Victoria's drawing room and receiving the news of Julian's duplicity, there was no adequate description for what she felt now. Her husband had ruined them. She had hoped he'd gained some maturity after Zachary's birth, and accepted his responsibilities, but it was now obvious that she'd deceived herself during all the years of her marriage. Her husband had never changed. He was the same rash and reckless scoundrel he'd been in his youth.

"Shefford, you are Blackmore's trustee, how could you have let this happen?"

"Julian's debts had to be paid," he said simply,

and Maggie wondered if he had always been so lax about important matters. Shefford had never seemed to care much about anyone's interests but his own, but she couldn't believe Julian would name him as trustee if he'd known how little attention he would pay to Blackmore affairs.

Except that Julian had been just as careless about his own affairs. He would never have foreseen this, because he had been entirely lacking in foresight. Not to mention fidelity. Or reliability.

"What will I do?" Her breath caught in her throat. "How will we manage?"

"You are going to remarry. A rich man."

A cold chill crept up her spine as she thought of the conversation she'd overheard earlier. She told herself that Shefford could not have orchestrated this . . . this *debacle* . . . in order to put her into dire straits. Could he?

She looked into his cold eyes. Oh God, he *had*. He believed she had no choice but to marry his friend, Kimbridge, a man she had met on one previous occasion and had not been impressed. She wondered if Shefford had done the same thing when he'd pushed her to marry Julian. For what reason had *he* needed a pliable, biddable wife?

Obviously, it was in order to pursue his fast life in Town while he kept his plain, unsophisticated, unquestioning wife at her country estate where she wouldn't interfere with his amusements. He'd gotten his legitimate heir, and had talked of siring a spare—

Maggie quelled the scream that welled up in her throat. Julian had betrayed her in every possible way. Not only had he conducted affairs with women during his frequent visits to London, he'd gambled away Zachary's inheritance as well as their income. And Shefford was no better. As trustee, he had to have known about Julian's debts. Yet he'd done nothing to protect her rights. She'd trusted Julian and then Shefford to see to her interests.

Maggie realized she shared a good deal of the blame for her present situation. She had been the "biddable" wife while she should have been challenging her husband more often, demanding answers to the questions she asked him. When he sold off his horses just before Lily's birth, Maggie should have made him tell her what was going on. She should have paid closer attention when the ancient Blackmore sword collection disappeared, and when Julian disposed of a number of valuable paintings in the manor house, saying he could no longer abide them.

In every instance, Julian had clucked his tongue at her questions and told her not to worry, as though she had the brains of a child. Maggie would have smacked her head against Mr. Clement's desk if it would have changed anything.

"My lady, you still have your portion of the annuity from your grandmother, Countess Rilby," said the solicitor.

Her paternal grandmother had left her a modest sum, certainly not enough on which to live, or to raise two children. Or to maintain Blackmore Manor.

Maggie felt numb. Somehow, she managed to pull on her pelisse and gloves, fumbling as Shefford stood and assisted her. She might have bid Mr. Clements good day, though she was in such a haze of mental disorder, she wasn't even sure how she got herself from his office to the front door of the building.

She didn't know what was worse—Julian's marital infidelity, or his destruction of Zachary's birthright. She didn't think society yet knew about the state of her finances, but they soon would, just as Julian's indiscretions had been common knowledge in Town. Maggie wondered if any of them had been remarked upon in the society columns.

"Lord B, of Cambridgeshire, was seen leaving the Drury Lane Theater with the notorious Miss W."

Maggie's cheeks burned with humiliation. *How could Julian have done this to her?*

Now Shefford wanted her to marry another wastrel, Robert Kimbridge. Maggie had no intention of complying this time, although she did not know quite what she was going to do. Nor did she know who she could turn to for advice. Obviously not to Shefford, who'd convinced her to marry Julian in the first place. And Maggie had never cared for Mr. Clements, whose disdain for her was palpable in every word he spoke.

Every man she'd ever relied upon had failed her, starting with her own father, who'd died far too soon after the Chatterton incident. Maggie had needed him desperately then, since he was the only one who'd shielded her from her mother's anger. He was the only one who'd agreed that she had done the right thing in screaming for help when her cousin had attempted to harm her.

Her mother's second husband had barely taken notice of Maggie and her sisters, and after his death, Maggie had ended up with her stepbrother as her guardian. And if he believed Julian and Kimbridge were good candidates for marriage, then she would be better off with no guardian at all.

She had already decided that Shefford would have nothing to say about how she conducted her life from here on, but the day's revelations solidified her feelings. She was quite aware that she needed to figure a way to take control of her own life. Fortunately, with a widow's freedom, she could do as she pleased.

If only she had funds.

"I have a friend . . ." said Shefford.

"I'm sure you do," Maggie said angrily. Every man in London could go hang for all she cared. Not a single one was worth even a second thought. Except, perhaps one.

"He's wealthy and well connected—"

"And a lame, destitute country widow would suit him perfectly, is that it, Shefford?" She did not enjoy sounding like a petulant child, but there was a limit to what she would endure. She was a grown woman now, and if she was not mistaken, her prince had found her desirable. He might not wish to marry her, but she had no intention of agreeing to yet another marriage for the convenience of another young scoundrel.

The carriage came to a halt and Shefford took hold of her forearm. "You're in a corner, Maggie."

"Not as much as you might think," she said, pulling her arm from his grasp. She stepped out of the carriage and went up to the house, only to retreat in dismay when she heard her mother's voice. She could not imagine what Beatrice was doing there, unless it was to harangue her over some triviality.

Maggie closed her eyes and muttered a few choice words she'd never thought to utter in her life. If only she could just take the children and return to Blackmore Manor.

Nathaniel Beraza would attend the Waverly ball with Thomas as his Sabedorian "ambassador," along with his American cohort, Edward Ochoa, as his foreign minister. Ochoa was a former lawyer who looked like anyone's benevolent grandfather. Tom didn't know what crime Edward had been convicted of, but he'd practiced law in America, and now made a perfect Sabedorian minister, mature and erudite. Tom had already paid him handsomely to play his part, and had promised even more after Tom's crew of ex-convicts completed their undertaking successfully.

They'd decided to keep their fictitious background simple, for that made it far easier for all of Tom's associates to keep their stories consistent.

All but Ochoa had been imprisoned in one hellish place or another by the English crown, or as slaves on *Butcher's Blade*. Ochoa had his own felonious history, and each man had a mix of talents, all of which would be useful as Tom put his plans into play.

Nate came into Thomas's hotel room, already dressed for the Waverly ball. He'd grown up in a London flash house, and earned his way by picking pockets wherever the opportunity presented itself. He'd been especially fond of racing events, but he'd progressed to some serious larceny before being condemned to the penal colony at a young age. He was independently wealthy now, but his loyalty to Thomas was unquestionable.

"Don't we look like a couple o' royal bastards," he said, grinning, slipping back to the east London accent he'd worked so hard to eliminate. They'd all worked hard to perfect their roles, altering their speech slightly, becoming accustomed to fine clothes, and learning the customs of moneyed people and their servants.

Nate reached over to straighten the golden ribbon that hung around Tom's neck. It held a perfectly authentic-looking Sabedorian medal with a large emerald set in its center. Tom wore his formal suit of clothes—a black coat and trews, with a white waistcoat and neck cloth. Beneath the medal, lying diagonally across his chest, lay a scarlet sash. Over his dress suit, Tom would wear his specially made scarlet robes, the dominant color of the flag one of his men had designed for Sabedoria.

The play was about to begin, and Thomas felt ready. His assignation with Maggie had been postponed, which was obviously for the best. He could afford no distractions in his quest to destroy his enemies. Maggie, with her alluring eyes and velvet femininity, was a huge disruption to his composure. Though his desire for her had not dwindled in the hours since leaving her in Hanover Square, his common sense told him his energies were better spent focusing on Shefford, Maynwaring, and the Blackmore estates. His plan was complex, with many facets, and a failure of any part could threaten the whole.

Mark Saret entered the room and greeted them. "You'll have them falling over themselves to please you," he said to Tom.

"One can only hope," Thomas replied wryly. "You have some news?"

"Aye. Andrew Harland has managed to get himself employed as a footman in Shefford's house."

"Excellent," said Tom, appreciating Saret's talent for accomplishing what needed to be done. No doubt one of Shefford's current footmen had needed to leave the marquess's employ for some reason— likely relating to a generous monetary enticement. Now Andy Harland was in a position to learn all sorts of information from Shefford's household that might not otherwise be available to them.

"What of Maynwaring? Anything new there?"

"His Honor Judge William Maynwaring is now His Honor *Lord Justice* Maynwaring. He is still on the bench, and still rendering overly harsh sentences. He lives in a mansion in Kensington."

"Anything more on the Blackmores?"

"Julian left a wife and two children who live up at the family estate in Cambridgeshire. Shefford is the trustee of his estate, and guardian of his children."

"Which means he has control over their finances?"

"Correct."

It felt wholly unfair that Julian had died before Tom had had the opportunity to destroy him, and the disappointment still was a bitter draught to swallow. The years of dreaming, of hungering for the sight of a ruined Julian Danvers, falling on his knees in desperation at Tom's feet, were wasted.

He stalked to the window and placed his hands upon the sill. Looking out at the traffic below, he watched the dandies in their top hats and expensively cut suits walking to their various fashionable destinations. No doubt Lady Blackmore was the same kind of irresponsible snob that Julian had been. Tom was going to see to it that she and her children paid for Julian's misdeeds, just as Tom's family had done.

"Then whatever financial disasters we devise for Shefford—you still believe we can orchestrate it so that Blackmore's estate suffers along with him?"

Saret gave a quick nod. "We haven't as much information on Blackmore as we've got on Shefford, but I've got a man on it now."

"Good."

"Shefford has an estate in Oxfordshire, as well

as some property in Dorset—providing far less income than would support his extravagant lifestyle. He likes to live on the edge."

"Does he gamble?"

"Some, though he is not known as a great winner."

"He owns thoroughbreds."

"Recent purchases," said Saret. "And no noteworthy wins with previous horses in the past few years."

Which boded well for the horse race Tom had in mind, the one that would deliver the fatal blow to Shefford's finances. Tom intended to crush him. "What of the Waverly ball?"

"Ah. Something I can answer definitively!" Saret said with a grin. "Shefford will be there. Harland is assigned to accompany his carriage."

"Perfect. Now, see what more you can find out about His Honor *Lord Justice* Maynwaring."

"I will not hear of it, Margaret!" Lady Shefford's shrill voice cut through Maggie's mental haze. "The duchess is one of my closest friends, and now that you are here in London, she will consider it a slight if you do not attend the ball tonight."

"Mother, I do not care if—"

"Well, you should!" her mother carped. She took one of Maggie's old ball gowns from the wardrobe and placed it on the bed. "You are out of mourning and it's time you found another husband."

"But I don't wan—"

"Do you expect to stay a widow for the rest of

your life?" Beatrice paced back and forth in Maggie's bedchamber. "No woman was meant to be alone."

Or to protest when her husband depleted them of their income, not to mention made a mockery of his vows?

Maggie was not dim-witted. She knew that a wealthy husband would certainly solve some of her problems. But she refused to endure yet another marriage like her first. She would allow no man ever to have the power to make a fool of her again as Julian had done.

"No. I am not ready."

"You will never be ready at this rate, Maggie. I had thought marriage would have changed you. But you are still the willful hoyden you always were. Look at your hat. And your hair is still as untamed as ever." Beatrice took hold of Maggie's chin and scrutinized it. "Your scar has not faded in the least."

Maggie pulled away. "Miracles do not occur in our day and age, Mother."

"There is no reason to be snippy with me, miss. Get dressed. Wear the pink—"

"Even if I were to agree to go, the pink is perfectly horrid. I cannot believe you would even suggest one of my old come-out gowns."

Beatrice pinched her lips together with annoyance, and Maggie took her mother's arm and started to usher her out of the bedchamber. How she'd ever found herself up there with Beatrice in the first place was a puzzle.

"Mother, there is no reason for us to argue. I've only just arrived in Town and I—" She heard footsteps in the hall outside her bedroom. "Oh no, who can that be?"

When she heard Stella's shrill voice calling to their mother, Maggie remembered why she'd hidden herself away in Cambridgeshire for the duration of her mourning. She wished she could have remained there.

Maggie's sister pushed open the door and came into the room, dressed in sumptuous finery. Her maid was right behind her, carrying a long, sheet-draped parcel across her arms. Obviously, a gown.

"Stella! I am *so* happy to see you," said Beatrice, the relief on her face all too obvious.

"Not that I had a choice in the matter," Stella drawled, draping the gown across the bed. "Mother said you would need convincing. So, here I am."

"Don't bother, Stella," Maggie said. "I am not in a particularly submissive mood."

"Really," Stella said dryly and started for the door. "Then I should go. Horton will be waiting for me."

"No, no! I need you here," said Beatrice with panic in her voice.

Maggie felt Stella's exasperated gaze, and she felt resentment beginning to build. She should just pack up the children and return to Cambridgeshire now. Make do with what little they had.

"Talk to her, Stella," said Beatrice.

"What happened to your hair?"

Maggie didn't believe they ever thought about the way they treated her anymore. They'd gotten into the habit after Chatterton's death, and criticizing her seemed to amuse them.

She dropped her hat onto the dressing table. "I've been out all day."

"Mother wants you to come along with us to the ball, Margaret," said Stella, unwrapping the gown she'd brought. "We brought the carriage, as Mother requested. Horton is waiting for us downstairs."

"It'll be a good diversion for you," said Beatrice.

"What makes you think I need a diversion?" Maggie asked, uninterested in being the unwelcome companion once again. It occurred to her to ask her mother and sister if they'd known of Julian's indiscretions, but she had far too much pride. Acknowledging her wifely shortcomings would give them just one more deficiency they could toss in her face.

Stella ignored Maggie's question and rolled her pretty blue eyes. "I should have brought some face powder. Your scar hasn't faded at all. And those freckles—"

"Where's your maid?" Beatrice demanded.

Stella pulled the bell cord before Maggie could do anything but mount a weak protest.

"Stella, please. You don't want my company at Lady Waverly's ball any more than I want to go."

"Come now, Maggie," her mother said, ignoring her plea. "Let Stella's maid help you."

"At least you've finally filled out," said Stella

coldly as the girl unfastened Maggie's bodice, the very fastenings Thomas had closed for her, so regretfully, only a short while before. "It must have been the children."

Her sisters had developed full, lush figures early, and they'd teased a much younger Maggie for her knobby knees and flat chest. They'd described her hair as the color of mud, while they all had beautiful, bright, coppery tresses and lovely blue eyes, just like their mother.

"No doubt," Maggie said tightly.

Stella shoved the pink gauze gown aside. "No, not this one. Margaret, what could you possibly be thinking? It would be hideous with your coloring."

"I—"

"Here is the sapphire crepe that I wore once last year," she said, pulling the drape off the garment. "It should fit well enough, though I doubt you will fill it out."

In spite of Maggie's protests, Stella started to peel her dress from her shoulders.

"Luckily, it's not entirely out of style yet," said Stella. "And it actually lends a little color to your eyes. Your friend, the prince, will be sure to notice."

"Prince?" Maggie asked.

"The Sabedorian, of course. The man who saved your savage little son in the square, in case the incident has slipped your memory. You cannot be so countrified that you do not understand the importance of the prince's particular attention."

"Of course not, Stella," Maggie retorted, torn between chagrin and anticipation. She really did not wish to attend the duchess's or anyone else's ball. "I remember the prince very clearly."

"Well, Horton said he's expected to attend the duchess's ball tonight."

"Shefford thinks you should cultivate his favor," said Beatrice.

No doubt he would, Maggie thought as Stella's maid pulled the blue gown over Maggie's head. She was gratified to note that she actually *did* fill it out. Quite nicely, in fact.

Chapter 4

Thomas made the circuit of the ballroom with Nathaniel on one side, and the duke of Waverly on the other. They were approached by a number of men with prestigious positions in government and society. Introductions were made as Tom considered how he'd have felt to be in such lofty company seventeen years before. Never would he have guessed his life would come to this.

He did not know exactly how many millions Duncan's treasure was worth. What he *did* know was that it had given him the wealth and status to pursue his scheme for vengeance. Without it, he wouldn't have had the blunt to build Thorne's Gate in New York and develop his stables. He never would have been welcomed into the finest drawing rooms of New York and Boston, where he'd learned the standards of behavior for the wealthy and powerful while he worked on his scheme to entrap Shefford and Blackmore.

Fortunately, Thomas would not be stuck in this country, having to abide by the rules of the

English *haut ton* for very much time. He would be glad to leave as soon as he dealt with the obnoxious aristocrats who'd tossed him away as though he were nothing more than a bit of offal in the street.

Tom hoped that when Sebastian Salim located Tom's family and brought them to London, he would be able to convince them to return to America with him. His parents could live a life of ease on his estate, and he would provide a generous dowry for his younger sister, Jennie. When he'd seen her last, she'd been a sweet, pretty child, and he had no doubt she'd grown up capable of attracting the most eligible bachelors in New York.

Lucas Reigi had orders to keep Tom's ships ready to sail immediately after the horse race, and Tom intended to spirit his family onto one of the ships as soon as it was done. Everything was to be kept in readiness for a hasty departure.

"Your Highness, it is a true pleasure to make your acquaintance," said one of the white-haired lords, eyeing the emerald that rested on Tom's chest. "I trust your country and ours will find much common ground."

"I have no doubt of it, Lord Branford."

"Your English is near perfect, Your Highness," said Lord Waverly. "I cannot help but wonder how that is possible."

It was not an unexpected question. "A few Sabedorians learned your language under duress on the high seas, Lord Waverly, and brought it back to us. My own tutor was a man who'd been taken

in slavery by *English* pirates and kept for a number
of years."

Waverly covered his mouth as he cleared his
throat, and changed the subject. Tom believed the
less said about his command of the language, the
better, and he hoped the mention of Sabedorians
being victimized by English pirates would stem
further questioning.

New guests were announced every few minutes, and Tom controlled the urge to turn his head
toward the entrance with each one. He felt an eager
unease at seeing Shefford again. He remembered
the husky, dark-eyed boy well, and had bet all on
the probability that the man had become as mad
for horses as his sire had been.

It seemed that Tom's gamble had been dead-
on. Shefford had recently purchased Paragon and
Palmer's Gold, and Tom didn't think the marquess
would pass on an opportunity to race the two
Thoroughbreds in an unsanctioned contest. Tom's
American horses were far superior to any horse
Tom had ever seen, and his champion would deal
the final blow to Shefford's fortunes, as well as to
his reputation. Tom was counting on the bastard
drawing all his cronies into the wager. They would
blame him for their losses—profound losses, he
hoped.

"Lady Beatrice Shefford," the footman called
out, and Thomas could not help but turn. He
saw the older woman from Hanover Square—the
harpy with white-tinged red hair. A sharp feeling
of foreboding knifed through him when he real-

ized she was the same shrew who'd shouted at Maggie when she'd run out of a nearby house to see to her child.

The woman moved forward into the room and the footman announced the next guests. "The Marquess of Shefford, and Lady Margaret Blackmore."

It was her. Maggie.

He felt as though his belly had dropped to his knees. And yet the intense desire he'd felt when she'd left him returned full force, and battled with the reality of who she was. The only person who could be Lady Blackmore was Julian Danvers's mother.

Or his wife.

His mind raced as Waverly and Lord Branford continued discussing the issues that would soon be debated in Lords, and how Waverly intended to introduce a bill of alliance with the wealthy principality of Sabedoria. There would, of course, be mutual benefits, not the least of which would be Britain's exclusive right to trade for Sabedoria's highly superior flax.

Tom gave a noncommittal nod as he watched Maggie enter the ballroom on Shefford's arm. She kept her eyes straight ahead as she moved through the ballroom, following in the older woman's wake, and Thomas guessed that Lady Shefford was her mother.

If so, it meant that Maggie was Shefford's sister.

Tom refrained from jabbing his fingers through

his hair in consternation. But Good God, the woman he desired more than any he could ever remember was in the thick of it.

Maggie almost asked Lord Horton to turn his carriage around and take her home. But the thought of seeing Thomas had kept her firmly seated on the plush squabs of his carriage, in spite of Stella's disapproving glare and her mother's continued harassment.

Shefford was getting out of his carriage as they arrived, and insisted that Maggie take his arm to enter the ballroom. It was her first social event since Julian's death, and a fair number of people took note of her entrance and seemed to be whispering to their companions as they looked her over.

She hated this, feeling as though she were on display like one of the young debutantes, only this time, as the brunt of some harsh gossip. For once she was grateful for Stella's reluctant help. Dressed in her sister's lovely blue gown, she hoped everyone in the duke and duchess's ballroom would recognize what a fool Julian had been.

She tried not to be too obvious as she scoured the crowd for the tall, dark-haired man she intended to make her lover. On the morrow, she would know all that she'd missed—all that Julian had deprived her of—during her marriage.

It had been a taxing and bewildering day, and she should have stayed home that evening, if only to collect her thoughts. She was still angry with Shefford for his lack of care in agreeing to her feeble marriage agreement with Julian, and his subsequent poor stewardship of her late husband's estate. He couldn't have been more negligent if he'd tried.

And then there was Thomas . . .

She took her hand from Shefford's arm and moved ahead without him, her stomach roiling with nerves. How did one approach a man—a near stranger—who had touched her so intimately, setting her blood on fire in a way her husband had never done?

"Margaret!" called Victoria, Lady Ranfield, and Maggie was relieved to see her friend's smiling face.

"Hello, Victoria," Maggie replied as the young woman took her hand and drew her away from her family.

"Are you all right?" Victoria asked in a confidential tone. "I was so worried about you after . . . you know."

"No, no. You were right," Maggie replied in a confidential tone. "Julian's been gone two years. Whatever he might have done happened a long time ago and signifies naught anymore." In Mr. Clement's office, she had come to the realization that Julian's past infidelities were the least of her worries. Her family was essentially destitute. Somehow, she was going to have to turn Blackmore into a productive estate, or else Zachary was going to inherit a worthless title.

She knew little of agricultural innovations and not much of estate management, beyond her own paltry duties. The steward that Shefford engaged was supposed to have taken care of everything. And yet Maggie now knew that he had not.

"You're taking it rather better now," said Victoria.

"Yes, well. I've had time to think about it."

Victoria slid her arm through the crook of Maggie's elbow and started them toward the refreshment table. "So, you've begun your hunt for another husband?"

"Good heavens, no," said Maggie. "You sound like my mother."

"God forbid. Is she still throwing Chatterton in your face?"

Maggie shrugged. "If not for me, Beatrice would be the honored aunt of an eminent duke, and Charlotte would be his wife. As it is, she only got Aughton for Charlotte, a lowly baron."

"Bosh."

"Anyway, how could I compete for a husband here with all these debutantes? Young, innocent, beautiful, *rich* . . ."

"Maggie, you are—"

"I am going to take a lover, I think."

Victoria gasped with shock. Then her face broke into a smile. "Oh, you. Having a jest at my expense."

Maggie allowed Victoria to believe so. Her decision to engage in an affair with Thomas was probably best left unspoken. "Where is Lord Ranfield?"

"Hobnobbing with his parliamentary peers. They are all atwitter with this foreign prince."

"Of Sabedoria."

"Yes. Have you seen him?"

Maggie swallowed. She'd certainly seen him, touched him, melted in his arms. "He happened into Hanover Square two nights ago, and saved Zachary from being run down by a carriage."

"*What?*" Victoria said, pressing a hand to her breast. "You never said anything! Is Zachary all right?"

Maggie nodded, the shock of the incident having receded, replaced by a sense of anticipation and longing unlike anything she'd ever known. She couldn't believe she'd met Thomas only forty-eight hours ago. "Zachary is fine, but only because of the prince and his quick action."

"Good heavens, Margaret. I cannot believe . . ." She put a hand upon Maggie's arm and turned to look at the crowd. "You know that he is here?"

"Oh?" She hoped so, since it was the only reason she had decided to attend.

"It's said he is unmarried," Victoria remarked, bringing Maggie up short.

It had not even occurred to her to wonder if he had a wife and she was appalled at her own lack of consideration. After what she had just learned about Julian, it should have been her first thought.

"Perhaps he intends to take a bride back to Sabedoria with him," said Victoria.

Maggie swallowed. She'd been an utter dolt in her dealings with him. Having intimate relations with a man who was actively seeking a wife was obviously not a prudent course of action. And yet—

"It seems impossible that he doesn't already have a wife." Victoria clasped her hands to her breast and sighed. "He is Apollo with dark hair, Prometheus with gorgeous green eyes, Atlas with the weight of his country on his shoulders. I don't believe I've ever seen such a remarkably handsome man. And when he smiles . . ." She fluttered her lashes and rolled her eyes in a feigned swoon.

Maggie would have laughed at her friend's antics, but she caught sight of Thomas just then. He certainly was as beautiful as Apollo, and Victoria seemed to be right about the weight on his shoulders. A fierce crease split his brow, giving him the appearance of a man who carried a heavy burden.

She hadn't given any thought to his reasons for coming to England, but as he stood conversing with the most powerful men of the realm, Maggie knew there was a great deal more to him than the little bit—as earth-shattering as it was—that she'd experienced.

And she realized how foolish it was to think he would turn his entire attention upon her. She'd been reeling over Victoria's revelation when she'd encountered him that morning in the street, and he'd done nothing but attempt to comfort her. He'd been purely gracious at the tea shop, until she announced that she was a widow.

She took the proffered glass of ratafia and drank it down.

"Maggie, what is it? Are you . . . ?" Victoria asked, and Maggie realized her faux pas. Thank heavens her mother hadn't seen her gulping down the sweet, surprisingly potent drink, but she felt her cheeks burn, anyway.

"I'm fine," she said. "Perhaps a little rattled. I haven't been part of a crush like this in years."

"It's certainly crowded. There is naught to compare to a Waverly ball. I'm so glad you came."

"Here comes your husband," said Maggie.

Lord Ranfield arrived at Victoria's side, took Maggie's hand and made his bow over it. "Lady Blackmore, it's been much too long. I hope you are well."

Victoria did not give Maggie an opportunity to answer. "Are the gentlemen going to monopolize the prince all evening discussing the price of corn, Ranfield? Maggie and I would like to meet the man."

"The dancing will soon begin," he replied, smiling down at his wife, at her mockingly petulant tone. He had always been a thoroughly engaging man, and Maggie knew that her friend had married him for love. Hers was a very different history than Maggie's and no one would ever believe Ranfield strayed from his wife's bed.

He turned to Maggie. "Will you do me the honor of a dance, Lady Blackmore?"

"Oh, I . . ."

"Maggie doesn't dance, Charles," Victoria said quietly.

"I beg your pardon, my lady. Perhaps you'll sit with us at supper?" he asked, and Maggie warmed to him as he recovered seamlessly from his blunder.

He'd obviously forgotten about Maggie's lame leg, and she liked him all the more for it. "We would enjoy your company."

"Thank you. I would be pleased to join you," she replied. She knew how to dance, but her badly mended leg prevented her from moving gracefully, so she preferred to avoid dancing in public. It was bad enough having to walk with a limp before the elegant company here.

"The prince first, Ranfield," said Victoria.

"Yes, my love," said Ranfield, turning to scan the room for a sight of him.

"This way." He took his wife and Maggie on each arm and started through the crowd as the musicians began to take up their instruments.

"Perhaps we should wait until later," Maggie said, with a sudden shyness at seeing Thomas again. She feared she would somehow betray the private, sensual interlude they'd shared.

"Nonsense. You've already met him—in a strange way," Victoria said, then recounted the incident in Hanover Square for her husband.

Thomas towered over a buzzing hive of female admirers and their mothers who swarmed around him. His frown was gone, replaced by what seemed to be a tolerant smile for all the hopeful young ladies.

He looked past all his pretty followers and let his gaze rest upon Maggie, as though he'd sensed her presence without even seeing her. She felt the same shimmer of excitement she'd known at his touch. He started toward her, excusing himself as the women stepped aside for him. He came directly to Maggie and took her hand.

"Lady Blackmore," he said, giving her a nod, over which she knew the entire crowd would soon be speculating. She hoped her family would dispel rumors by relating their earlier meeting. Or perhaps she should just enjoy the novelty of the ton's admiration for the moment. "It's good to see you again. Your son is well, I trust?"

Maggie felt breathless, but managed to give him the same pat answer as she'd done when they sat together in the tea shop. He was poised and collected, betraying none of the pure, sexual heat they'd shared in his carriage. She introduced him to Victoria and her husband, and Victoria fairly gushed over him.

"Your Highness, it's *such* a pleasure to meet you. You are a true hero in our district! Thank heavens for your quick intervention with little Zachary."

"All that matters is that the boy is safe and sound." He looked at Maggie. "I have only to wait for an invitation from Lady Blackmore to meet him properly."

Victoria turned a pair of incredulous eyes on her. "Margaret?"

"Ah, y-yes. Perhaps at week's end."

"Does the boy like horses?" Thomas asked.

Maggie could only nod, unable to imagine what he was thinking.

"Then he might enjoy a visit to my stables."

"You have stables here?" asked Victoria.

"Yes. A bit north of the city," he said. "I bought Mr. Harvey Delamere's estate."

"*Delamere's* estate?" Ranfield exclaimed. "Why, the place is—"

"Yes?" Thomas asked, his tone pleasant, his dark brows raised.

Ranfield seemed rather discomfited. "It's fit for a king."

"I do enjoy the countryside," Thomas said simply. "And the place suits my needs."

The first dance began just then, and Maggie had no further chance to speak of visiting his stables. She had not thought of drawing her children into her affair with Thomas, although perhaps he believed that involving himself with her children would make their assignations easier to accomplish. Maggie did not see how that would be possible.

One of the pretty young women who'd remained standing on the fringes near Thomas moved forward, inadvertently knocking Maggie off balance. Thomas reached out quickly to steady her as the girl curtseyed. "Your Highness . . ." she said. "It's the first dance."

"Ah, yes. Miss . . . uh . . ."

Giggling, she reminded him of her name, and took his arm. Maggie watched as he—dare she hope reluctantly?—drew the girl away and blended into the group of dancers.

"Imagine that!" said Ranfield.

"What?"

"The Delamere place up in Hampton! It rivals Wynard Park for size and grandeur," he replied.

"The grounds are superb. And the stables—there are two or more, as I recall. We were there once, Vic, don't you remember?"

"We've been many places since our marriage, Charles," she said, slipping her hand through the crook of her husband's arm and leaning toward him.

Maggie felt an intense pang of pure longing at their exchange. She and Julian had never had any such affection or easy banter between them. But at least she'd cared for him as any wife should do, while he'd deceived her.

She looked toward the dancers, surreptitiously watching Thomas perform the steps of the dance, while she wished she could be his partner. If only she were one of the fetching young women here, a pretty girl who could flirt and step back ever so gracefully to look into his smiling, green eyes. Perhaps touch his hand when they moved close.

"Lady Blackmore! Margaret!"

She turned to see another old friend coming toward her, a young woman who'd married the same month as Maggie, to one of Julian's peers. Maggie had not seen her since the funeral. "Nettie, it's good to see you."

And it was. Nettie had spent a goodly amount of time beside Maggie at every dance that season, waiting in vain for dance partners to approach them. But Nettie had been a sweet girl who'd eventually attracted a quiet gentleman. She hoped her earl had done better for his wife and family than Julian had done for his.

They wandered away to catch up on the years that had passed since they'd seen one another, and Maggie was grateful for the distraction from her disordered thoughts. She was insane for thinking of pursuing anything further with Thomas—*His Highness*. What did a man like the prince of Sabedoria want with a woman who could not hope to compare to the pretty young thing who smiled up at him so blissfully on the dance floor?

Maggie feared it had been a mistake to come, to sit on the fringes of the ballroom with the old women and young matrons, so acutely aware of every move Thomas made, every smile he bestowed upon his eager partners. It only made her deficiencies more apparent.

"Have you met the Sabedorian prince?" Nettie asked.

Maggie nodded.

"They say his English is nearly perfect. That he learned our language from English pirates! What do you think?"

Shefford rudely broke in, interrupting her conversation with Nettie. "Come and dance with me, Margaret."

Maggie did not fool herself into thinking he was trying to do her a kindness, for he barely looked at her as he gave her the order to dance. And he was not gentle in taking her arm as he drew her away from Nettie.

"No, Shefford, you know I don't—"

"Just this once won't hurt you."

Loath to make a scene, she gave Nettie an apologetic bow and stepped away with Shefford.

"I understand the prince acknowledged you quite familiarly, Margaret," he said as they moved around the periphery of the room toward the dancers.

"I suppose so."

"And he asked if your son would like to visit his stables?"

"Shefford, I'm not sure we should make anything of—"

"Are you out of your mind?" he hissed. "It's fabulous! They say he brought his Sabedorian horses with him and he intends to race them."

"How can he possibly—?"

"Unsanctioned, of course," he replied, then spoke directly into her ear. "There is money to be made here, Margaret. Don't muck it up for us."

She pulled away. *"Us?"*

"Never mind. Just get a solid invitation for you and Zachary. I'll come along to chaperone you."

Maggie stopped in her tracks, bristling. "I no longer need a chaperone, Shefford."

He looked down at her as though she'd just grown wings. Or perhaps horns.

"Julian is dead, if you recall," she said quietly. "I am an independent woman now."

"But penniless. And the prince is stinking rich," said Shefford. "Mark my words, he is in England to do more than establish trade relations with us. Did you see that emerald hanging from his neck?"

Maggie had not noticed. She'd only seen his eyes

and the fine cut of his thick hair while she remembered the heat of his touch and the hunger in his kiss. And yet when she looked up just then and met his eyes, he was frowning again.

Maggie held back, feeling uncertain about joining the dancers. She was too clumsy to fare well on the dance floor, and Shefford knew it. She should have told him to go to the devil, along with her inheritance and Zachary's birthright, but she was still so angry—

"Try to smile," he said.

"Why? Who are you trying to impress? The prince, I suppose." Though she could not imagine how Shefford thought he could profit from Thomas's good opinion. Somehow, her brother intended to draw Thomas into a horse race. With his charm, perhaps. And he would do whatever it took to win.

"A dance with my sister isn't going to impress anyone," he said dryly as they joined the two lines of dancers.

As angry as she was, she found it difficult to keep even a neutral expression, much less smile at him. Thomas was at the opposite end of the line, his features transformed to a mask of indifference. He did not seem to be enjoying himself at all.

Maggie would soon be paired with him, would touch his hand and link arms with him. Her nerves seemed to shudder with apprehension, with expectation, while at the same time, the cunning expression in Shefford's eyes put her on edge.

"Try to enjoy the dance, sister dear."

How could she, when she suspected that Shefford had some nefarious scheme in mind?

Shefford circled around her, then they locked arms and made their promenade down the center aisle between the two rows of dancers. When they passed Thomas on Maggie's right, the music and all the rest of the dancers seemed to melt away, and she was alone with him. He did not speak to her, but his eyes followed her as she came to stand opposite him, or rather, opposite her partner, Shefford.

But Thomas was right beside him, and Maggie's skin prickled in response to his intent gaze. She wished they could leave the ball now, wished she could lose herself in his embrace, and follow up on her promise, now. Tonight.

She would not be the first woman in her circumstances to engage in an affair, but Maggie feared she did not possess the sophistication necessary to carry it off. She had no idea how to manage the logistics of it, and there was no one whose advice she could solicit. Surely not her mother or sisters. The very thought of it was ludicrous. But how could it possibly work? How could she get away from the house without her maid or a footman with her?

They continued the set, and when she looked down the line at Thomas again, she saw that his eyes were trained on her, their expression unreadable. Maggie hoped his gaze would have been somewhat warmer, given all they'd shared, all they intended to share. Unless he'd reconsidered.

And why wouldn't he, Maggie wondered with a

sinking heart. With such avid attention from all the sparkling ladies at the ball, Maggie's appeal could do naught but fade. She knew her limitations, and realized that Thomas must have thought better of it, now that the diamonds of society were paying homage at his feet.

The dance ended and the ladies surrounded Thomas again. He did not seem to mind their attention, and she was obviously forgotten.

Her stepbrother stood beside her, looking over at Thomas with frustration. "I want you to introduce me."

"Perhaps later," she said, her heart sinking. "He is well occupied now."

He clenched his jaw. "Maybe you ought to think of how you can be of use to this family for a change."

"Not now, Shefford."

The dancing was unrelenting, and Thomas could not imagine a more tedious way to waste his time. The dullness of his young partners was nearly as painful as a flogging, and the process of discouraging a few wayward wives from trying to seduce him was tiresome.

He was there only to gain entrée into society, and it certainly seemed that he'd managed it nicely. He'd received more invitations than he could handle in a month, and all the mothers had shoved their marriageable daughters into his path—without even knowing what kind of man he was.

Clearly, the prospect of wealth and status

trumped every other consideration, including the fact that he would obviously return to his own country at some point. Any one of these people would consider it a triumph if their daughters married a foreign prince and left home, never to return again.

Tom shuddered at the reality of that. He'd experienced it, and it was not a fate he'd wish upon anyone. Except perhaps the Marquess of Shefford.

Tom kept an eye on the man, Shefford's color rising as the marquess spoke in earnest to Maggie. Tom muttered a quiet curse as her complexion paled and her brother stalked away from her. Left alone, she turned abruptly and slipped out of the ballroom toward what had to be the servants' area.

He still wanted her with a passion that had not diminished in the hours since he'd last touched her. But he cursed the fates that had connected her so intimately with the objects of his contempt, and tried to reconcile his desire with what he knew he must do.

Nate returned to Tom's side after dancing with Waverly's daughter. "It's unbelievable." He gave a nod toward Maggie's departing figure. "She is the link between her husband and Shefford. Sister and wife."

"Aye."

"You can destroy their families in one fell swoop. Blackmore might be dead, but you can ruin his line."

Thomas swallowed.

"She is quite . . . striking, is she not?" Nate asked. "In an unconventional sort of way. She's not like the other women here."

"No," Tom said. "Not at all."

Nate smirked. "You can shred her reputation while we destroy the Shefford and Blackmore finances. You can witness Shefford's helplessness as his family crumbles before his eyes."

It was all true, and Tom knew he needed to adjust his point of view. Now that he knew who Maggie was, he had to view her as a mere means to an end, and nothing more.

Nate frowned. "What is it?"

"Naught," he replied. As he drew Shefford into his web, he could eliminate Maggie's respectable reputation with a very public exposure of their affair. And with Tom's sham investment schemes and the race, the Sheffords and Blackmores would lose their fortunes as well as their fine, upright standing in society.

Tom reminded himself that this was all he'd lived for, ever since his discovery of Duncan's treasure, which made everything possible. He could not let any twinge of conscience dictate his actions, not after his years of anticipation and planning.

"There is Lord Ealey, one of Shefford's friends," said Nate. "I'll just go and make myself known to him."

As Nate made his way toward Ealey, Tom exited the room, following in Maggie's wake. He went through the same door which exited into a dim corridor, and looked into each room until he reached the last, the only place she might be.

She was an intricate part of it all, as Shefford's sister and Julian's wife. The crux of an unholy triangle. Tom could not ignore the exceptional opportunity she presented. Resolved to do what he must, he stepped quietly into the room.

She whirled in surprise at his entrance. "Thomas!"

"You left the ball," he said.

"Yes, I . . ." She pulled her lower lip between her teeth, and Tom's breath caught. He wanted to taste those lips, wanted to feel them on his skin.

He slowed his breathing and attempted to regain some control.

"I needed some air."

Tom approached her. "Aye. It's quite a crowd back there."

"You shouldn't have abandoned your admirers."

Thomas touched the side of her face with his fingertips and her eyes drifted closed. "Are you not an admirer, Maggie?" He felt her shudder and knew her pretty nipples were already peaked and yearning for his attentions. He bent to kiss her and her eyes flew open.

"Someone might come in," she whispered, distraught.

"Not here," he said quietly, pulling her into his arms. "What is it? Have you changed your mind?"

"Oh lord," she whispered as he touched his lips to her neck. "No, I . . . But you cannot possibly want . . ."

"What, Maggie? Want you?" he whispered. She had no idea of her appeal, of the effect her sweet innocence had on him.

"There are so many young ladies who would suit you far better."

"They don't." He feathered kisses down her jaw, touching the scar on her chin. "They are bland and uninteresting. They have no fire inside."

Not like the woman in his arms, who responded so unreservedly to his sensual attentions. He captured her mouth fully, kissing her deeply, intruding with his tongue, hardening with her avid reaction.

"Touch me, Maggie." Ever since her explosive orgasm in his arms, he was desperate to feel her hands on him, and when she slipped her fingers through the hair at his nape, he groaned with pent-up need. He took one of her hands and lowered it to the placket of his trews where he was hard and straining for her touch.

With a tentative stroke, she slid her fingers over the length of him, and he could not hold back a quiet growl of arousal.

"I want to be inside you, Maggie."

She let her head fall back and he nibbled his way to the plump mounds of her breasts, partially exposed by the low cut of her gown.

"Tomorrow is too long to wait," he said.

"No, I—"

"I will come to you."

"No. There will be talk."

Her words jerked him back to reality. His mission, his purpose was clear. The intense lust he felt had no place in his plans.

At the moment, he didn't care. "It's all right. I will send for you at noon."

"Oh, dear God," she whispered.

"Can you get away?"

"I'll think of something."

"Aye."

Supper was unbearable.

Thomas broke protocol and took a seat beside Maggie, in spite of the butler's quiet insistence that he go to the head of the table.

"Thank you, no," he said simply, and the butler had no choice but to retreat.

Of course no one made any fuss over it, for he was a foreign dignitary, and couldn't possibly know every social nuance here. Besides, he seemed to possess more wealth than anyone in Britain—or all of Europe, for that matter. No one wanted to alienate him.

But Maggie knew there would be talk of the grand prince who supped beside a widowed viscountess. And quite possibly some remarks would be made in *The Times* for all to read.

Victoria sat on Maggie's other side, and leaned forward to address Thomas. "Tell us about Sabedoria, Your Highness. Where, exactly, is it?"

"It's a faraway land on the southern half of the globe," he replied, "and it's much the size of your own Britain."

His thigh settled alongside Maggie's as he spoke,

and she knew it was not accidental. She should have shifted to avoid his touch, but when his hand drifted down to touch her leg, she found herself powerless to move.

While he spoke of Sabedorian ships and sea-ports, flax plantations and trade opportunities, Maggie felt the heat of his body scorch through hers. He was priming her for their rendezvous on the morrow.

Not that she needed any more priming.

Chapter 5

If Maggie had been able to sleep that night, she might have felt better the following morning. It was early, and not even the servants were stirring. Yet she was wide-awake, and pacing the length of her bedchamber, her body still humming with eagerness for Thomas's touch. There had been no more kisses in the dark, remote rooms of the Waverly house, no further light flirtations in the ballroom.

It had been a complete and utter seduction.

Maggie feared she had become a wanton. Anticipation of her assignation with Thomas had become all-consuming. He'd filled her dreams, and during her many wakeful moments she'd been hot and trembling, impatient for his touch.

An affair was the least sensible thing she could possibly contemplate. She should be grappling with all the troublesome aspects of her life, not dreaming of a man who would eventually sail away from England's shores, leaving her behind. But the thought of a few hours' pleasure in his bed had robbed her of her common sense.

Maggie had never been the object of such single-minded attention or admiration, and it was exhilarating. She understood that he'd made her no promises, beyond the hours of pleasure they would share. But she could not think past the moment when Thomas would send for her, resolving to enjoy their time together while keeping her heart protected. He *would* leave, after all.

She curled up in a chair next to the fireplace and clutched her warm dressing gown around her. Noon, he'd said. But she had much to do before then.

Sometime during the night, she'd come up with an idea that might be at least a partial solution to her and her children's financial woes. They would always have Blackmore Manor, for the estate was entailed, and Zachary was Julian's heir. But the property was next to worthless. Of course they received rents, but the past few harvests had been poor, barely enough to provide sustenance for the tenants. As a result, the income from the land wasn't nearly enough to support all the staff that was required to maintain the manor house and grounds. Nor would it even begin to cover the repairs and improvements that were needed, much less provide a disposable income. Julian hadn't put any money into the estate during their marriage, in spite of Maggie's repeated requests. Now she knew that he'd sold his share of the paper mill and mortgaged the public house and all his unentailed property.

He'd squandered the wealth he'd inherited with his gambling.

She picked up the drawing she'd made the night before, when she couldn't sleep. It was a caricature of Thomas at the Waverly ball. Shefford's distasteful drooling after the prince's wealth had inspired the drawing, but Maggie had left him out of the picture. Instead, she'd placed a number of overzealous, well-known ladies around him, standing with their reticules open and their tongues hanging from between their over-full lips.

It was one of her better drawings, for she'd paid close attention to its composition and details. All that was needed was her signature, but Maggie could not own up to such a picture, not if it were made public. She finally signed it "Randolph Redbush."

She was very good at this type of drawing, much to her family's disdain. It was not real art by any means, nor did it begin to compare with what Stella could do with a paintbrush. But Maggie's drawings amused her children, and that's all she'd ever cared about. But she'd seen drawings like this many times before, and knew they were very popular. They were often made into prints and displayed in shop windows, commanding exceptional prices. With such a picture and more like it, Maggie hoped she had a solution to her financial problems.

Her family would, of course, be appalled that she would even consider trying to *earn* enough money to get herself out of debt. But she would do what she must, in spite of what they thought.

Carefully placing the drawing into a leather port-folio, Maggie waited for Tessa, who soon came to help her bathe and dress. She breakfasted with her children, admonishing them to behave for Nurse Hawkins, then donned her pelisse and a bonnet that obscured her features.

She told Nurse Hawkins she was going out for a while, then collected Tessa and slipped out of the house. They walked down to Bond Street where they caught a hackney cab and rode to the office of Mr. Edward Brown, editor of the *London Gazette*. He'd seen some of her drawings years ago, before her marriage, and had told her on the sly that he would be willing to pay her for such drawings.

"I'll only be a few minutes, Tessa," she said. "I've a bit of business to do here, but I'd rather no one learned of it."

"Of course, my lady," said the maid, and Maggie trusted her unreservedly. Tessa was infinitely more faithful and true than Julian had ever been.

Even so, it would be impossible to take Tessa with her when Thomas came for her later. That was a confidence she could not possibly share—with anyone.

Hoping no one recognized her getting out of the carriage, Maggie went into the building and sent her card up to the editor's office. His clerk came down presently and escorted her up the stairs.

Mr. Brown's office was paneled in a rich, dark mahogany. There was an enormous desk in front of a large window, and a worktable against one wall, piled high with stacks of papers.

"Lady Blackmore," the man said, rising from his chair behind the desk. "It's been a very long time since I saw you at Hanover House. Do you remember that meeting?"

"Yes, Mr. Brown," Maggie said, taking a seat in one of the chairs in front of the desk, keeping the portfolio on her lap. "That very meeting is the reason I'm here today."

"Do tell," said Mr. Brown with a curious smile. He was old enough to be her father, with a neatly trimmed beard of white and a circlet of gray hair that left the top of his head bald. He was well dressed and obviously prosperous, and Maggie hoped his opinion about her pictures had not changed.

"You remarked favorably upon several of my drawings at that time. And now, I find myself in a bit of an embarrassing situation," Maggie said. "Since the death of my husband—"

"My sympathies, my lady. A terrible tragedy."

Maggie swallowed and pressed on. "Yes, thank you. S-since then, I find myself in rather low water. And I th-thought you might consider entering into an . . . arrangement with me."

She opened the portfolio and removed the drawing, then placed it on Mr. Brown's desk.

He studied it carefully and then raised his rather owlish, gray eyebrows. "Randolph Redbush?"

Maggie felt her face heat. "If you were to publish this, I could not very well use my own name."

He returned his gaze to the picture and Maggie clasped her hands at her waist, thinking perhaps this had been an incredibly foolish idea. "It's probably not the best picture of the prince, but I thought—"

"Not at all, Lady Blackmore," he said, chuckling. "This is the best caricature I've seen in many a month. How did you get it? Well, obviously, you drew it, but . . ."

"I can draw more of these."

"For *The Gazette*?"

Maggie nodded and Mr. Brown rubbed his chin. "Pictures like these will sell a lot of newspapers. I would like exclusive rights to your work."

She let out the breath she'd been holding and nodded. "But these must be made available for sale as prints after they appear in *The Gazette*."

"That can be arranged," said Mr. Brown.

Maggie blinked back tears of relief, though she still had to negotiate her terms. "I would appreciate it if you would promise to keep our transactions confidential. Just between us."

"Of course."

Somehow, she managed to contain her excitement. *This venture could actually work!* "I've received quite a number of invitations since returning to Town a few days ago. I am sure the Sabedorian prince has received far more than I."

"You both attended the Waverly ball last night?"

She nodded.

He chuckled. "Hence the picture. I can only imagine the mob of matchmaking mamas that descended upon him. No—not only imagine it." He picked up the drawing and perused it carefully. "I can actually see it."

"Lord Castlereagh was there, too. And Lords Branford and Windham."

Mr. Brown rubbed his hands together. "What are you asking for this drawing?"

"What I'm asking is for a chance to provide you with many more caricatures besides this one."

He raised a brow.

"The season has only just begun, and there will be many events to which I'll be invited. I would like to provide *The Gazette* with many additional illustrations."

They talked of agents and representation and percentages, and Maggie was very careful in her negotiations. She'd kept her head in the sand for too many years, and knew she needed to pay close attention to her instincts. They finally came to an agreement that would net her a good deal of money from the drawings she provided to Mr. Brown, twice every week, and he agreed to send each one to an agent who would have it printed and put up for sale in the fashionable bookshops in the west end.

The arrangement was agreeable to both of them, but Maggie's new venture required that she remain in London indefinitely.

Thomas had accomplished all he needed to do at the Waverly ball. He—the son of a Suffolk horse breeder—had garnered the awe and respect of England's *haut ton*, just as he'd planned. All it had taken was a display of wealth and a few haughty manners, and they'd as much as bowed at his feet.

He could barely wait for the day when he exposed them for the shallow jellyfishes they were. Especially Lord Shefford, whom he had met only briefly. Just enough to take his measure.

Mark Saret had learned a great deal about Shefford's risky investments—the poor marquess was out on a limb and was likely looking for some easy money somewhere. He was going to fall directly into Tom's trap, and they hoped he would use Blackmore funds to cover his risky investments.

Work had already begun on the race course, a final arrow in the quiver he had assembled to use against Shefford. Thomas was pacing back and forth across the plush carpet in the drawing room of Delamere House while Nate Beraza and Mark Saret sat in a pair of expensive chairs near the windows that overlooked a side garden. The place was sumptuous beyond anything Tom had ever seen, in spite of having been invited into a number of prestigious homes in America. Delamere House presented exactly the kind of impression he'd had in mind when they'd gone looking for an appropriate estate to purchase.

"We found Lord Shefford in Garraway's Coffee Shop, just as Lord Ealey told you he would be," Saret said, turning to Nate.

"How did you deal with him?" Thomas asked. "Did it all go as planned?"

Saret nodded. "I sent in a few of my old mates. They were dressed for business and played it out the way you wanted."

Thomas didn't allow himself the smallest hint of a smile of satisfaction, for he knew how much could still go wrong. "So he bought it? Shefford is in?"

"Aye. Five thousand shares in the Manchester canal scheme. Ten thousand pounds altogether. I've got a man who will take the stock certificates to his man of business this afternoon."

"He will pay for them then?"

"Aye," Saret replied with a grin. "I think your old friend Lord Maynwaring will go for the canal scheme, too. He's reputed to be a risky investor."

"Good. Do whatever is necessary."

Saret nodded. "In the meantime, I've managed to locate another old mate of mine, Roddy Roarke. He's the one to lure Shefford into the tobacco plot. As this will be, er, an . . . illegal transaction, I think we'll keep Maynwaring out of this part."

Nate laughed, but Tom took it dead seriously. "You obviously trust Roarke."

Saret took no offense at Tom's question, for they all knew the consequences of failure. "He's the best in the business. Taught me more than I'll ever remember."

"What's the plan, then?"

"Roddy and his mates will follow the pigeon— Shefford—when he leaves his club tomorrow," said Saret. "They'll set up wherever Shefford goes and lure him into the conversation. When the time is right, they'll hook him."

"Roarke is well versed in the smuggling trade?"

Saret smiled, his fair skin going pink with satisfaction. "Roddy's middle name is 'Free Trade.'"

Tom considered the plan. He'd counted on Shefford's greed and the man's belief in his own superiority. They were the two traits that would finish him.

"Has he seen you?" Tom asked.

"No," Saret replied. "Garraway's was full of investors, but I kept out of sight, anyway. And I won't be anywhere near when Roarke plays his part."

"What about Maynwaring? Have we figured out how to get to him?"

"So far, only with the canal scheme. But I've got a man watching his comings and goings. We'll know his inclinations soon enough."

"All right," Tom said. "Almost as good as planting a footman in his house. Perhaps Mr. Ochoa can be useful with the judge."

"Perfect idea. Both versed in the law . . . Ochoa is a natural."

Now all Tom had to do was lure Shefford to Delamere House and interest him in the horse races. As much as he wanted to bring Maggie to the estate and spend the day making love to her, he could not. Their affair would have to proceed on a new timetable, and with a new purpose.

"Can we see about borrowing a riding pony from somewhere, gentlemen?" Tom asked.

Changing his plan for the afternoon, it was just a few minutes past noon when he arrived in Hanover Square. The butler admitted him to the house and Tom had barely stepped inside when he encountered Maggie coming down the stairs. She stopped halfway down, her expression stunned at the sight of him.

The instant wrench of arousal shouldn't have taken him off guard, for this woman seemed always to have that effect upon him. Knowing how responsive she was to his touch had made it sheer torture to sit beside her at the Waverly supper. Even then he'd known that he needed to stay in complete control of their affair, and use it to his advantage. Yet, watching her descend the stairs set off a fierce need in him.

Her gown wasn't particularly alluring, but her pale green skirts hugged her legs as she descended each step. Her bodice was made of some kind of delicate ivory cloth that framed the pretty breasts he'd touched and kissed far too long ago.

Christ, he wanted her now. He shoved his fingers through his hair before he could manage to paste a pleasant smile on his face.

She seemed discomfited as well, and Tom accepted the blame for it, for he was sure she had not expected him to step into her house openly, for anyone to see.

"My lady . . ." said the butler.

Tom gave Maggie a regal nod, quite aware of the butler's puzzled gaze. "Lady Margaret. I am pleased to find you at home."

She recovered and descended the rest of the way down the stairs, offering him her hand with a dubious smile.

"What brings you to Hanover Square today, Your Highness?" she asked. Though she kept her voice level, her expression belied her calm manner.

"At the duke's ball, we spoke of an outing to visit my estate," he said. "I'd hoped it would be convenient for you and your children to accompany me there this afternoon."

"The children? And me?" She flushed deep red and placed a hand on her breast, but did not dispute his words, not with the butler present and other servants presumably nearby.

"Aye." It was not what he'd led her to expect, nor was it what he'd originally planned. But he realized his purpose would be better served by engaging her entire family. He'd planted enough seeds with Shefford during last night's ball to pique his curiosity about Sabedorian horses. When Shefford learned that his sister was visiting Delamere House with her children, he would surely make his way there. It was the best scheme for getting the marquess out there without a direct invitation.

Maggie's indecision lasted only a moment. She glanced at the butler. "Mathers, would you please have Nurse Hawkins prepare the children for an outing?"

"Of course, my lady."

There was a row of buttons spanning from her high waist to her throat. Tom felt a keen urge to unfasten them, to touch the smooth skin he knew lay beneath. Rich, soft curls framed her face and he clasped his hands behind his back to keep from reaching for her when Mathers started up the staircase.

"This is a surprise, Your Highness," she said. "I didn't think you meant for the children to come out today."

"I believe it would be best."

He thought there was confusion in her eyes, but she turned away so quickly he could not be sure. She led him into a drawing room and Thomas closed the door behind him. Then he took her into his arms. "Do not think it's because I do not care to have you alone."

He tipped his head down and grazed her mouth with his lips. "I do. Very much."

He felt her swallow just before she stepped away. Standing several feet from him, she folded her hands tightly at her waist, and bit her lower lip, taking a moment to compose herself.

Tom knew she had no idea what a pleasing picture she made, hesitant and uncertain, and completely unaware of her own appeal. He had to remind himself that the situation was completely changed from the day before. She was the apex in his triangle of revenge.

Later. He would think of it later.

He started to close the distance between them, but before he could take her into his arms again, Lady Beatrice Shefford opened the door and pushed into the sitting room. "Maggie, there you are. I've decided you must pay a visit to—"

"Mother—"

"Have you nothing better to wear, Margaret? You are in Town now and there are certain stan—"

"*Mother.*"

Tom intervened, and made his presence known to Maggie's mother. "Good afternoon, Lady Shefford."

"Oh!" she cried, whirling to the sound of his voice. Her face altered dramatically, her harsh, authoritarian mask changing into a vision of soft femininity. "Your Highness! What a surprise to see you here!"

The older woman made a polite bow, then started removing her gloves and coat. "It's chilly today, is it not? I hope you do not find our climate too damp, Your Highness." Like a strange dervish, she turned quickly away from him and spoke sharply once again to her daughter. "Maggie, where is Mathers? Why hasn't he brought the—"

"He is doing what I asked him, Mother," Maggie said as the butler hurried into the room to serve his mistress's demanding mother.

"Bring tea, Mathers," Lady Shefford said firmly. "And have someone see to this fire. Maggie," she added, softening her tone to one that seemed deceptively sweet, "you must give more specific instructions to your staff. You cannot expect them to know how you want your rooms kept."

"Mother, I—"

"What is the occasion of your visit, Your Highness?" Lady Shefford asked, smiling up at Tom.

"Mother, will you please be seated?"

Tom felt more than a small degree of sympathy for Maggie, whose mother seemed to have no respect for her daughter's position in her own house. He wondered if the woman had always been so overbearing.

"Only if Prince Thomas sits beside me," Lady Shefford said with a coquettish smile that might have been appropriate for a woman half her age. She took a seat on a worn leather sofa and patted the cushion next to her.

"I'm afraid I will have to decline," he said, perversely enjoying thwarting the woman for Maggie's sake. "You must excuse Lady Blackmore and I . . . We were just about to leave."

Margaret could have kissed Thomas for that. She'd never seen her mother so politely rebuked by such a handsome, high-ranking gentleman, especially after turning her most potent charm upon him.

But his request to take the children with them that afternoon confused her. It certainly did not suggest the possibility of an intimate assignation, and Maggie could not help but think he must have changed his mind about their affair. About her.

And yet he'd taken her in his arms only moments ago.

She went to the door to catch Mathers and tell him to cancel the tea her mother requested, but as the children descended the stairs with Nurse Hawkins, she took Lily from the nurse's arms and smoothed Zachary's dark auburn hair.

"Are we going to the park, Mama?" Zachary asked.

"No, darling."

"Hello, young man," said Thomas, coming up behind her.

"You're the captain!" Zachary cried, and Maggie cringed inside. It would be beyond awkward if Zachary told Thomas about the drawings and the tale she'd woven about him for the children.

"No, sweetheart. You remember—this is the man who rescued you in the street. And it would be a very nice gesture if you thanked him for it."

Zachary was prevented from saying anything more by the entrance of his grandmother. She went directly to Lily and pulled her hand away from her face, glaring at Maggie. "You should not allow her to suck her thumb, Maggie. It's a terrible habit."

Maggie set Lily on her feet and took a deep breath, afraid that it would be her mother who embarrassed her, and not her children. "Shall we go?" she asked Thomas. "Mother, may we drop you at home?"

"No," Beatrice replied sourly. "I have my carriage."

"Well then, Mathers will see you out," Maggie said, allowing the butler to assist her with her pelisse. "Hawkins, I do hope you will enjoy your afternoon's holiday."

As she started for the front door with Thomas right behind her, she basked in the warmth of his presence, which overrode her mother's cold, irritating conduct.

Maggie knew she shouldn't allow Beatrice to bother her, but she'd hoped her mother's resentment might have relented. After all, it had been years . . .

She sighed. With her new, secret employment with Mr. Brown, she was going to have to accustom herself to living in Town. And, if the past few days were any indication, seeing her family on occasion.

"Margaret, you must take the nurse with you," Beatrice called out.

"Not this time, Mother," she said with the utmost civility.

"Why, see here. It's entirely improper—"

"The children and I will be just fine," she interjected before her mother's diatribe could really begin. "Would you mind going ahead?" she asked Thomas. "I need a quick word with my children before we go."

Thomas escorted Beatrice out of the house and Maggie turned to the children, admonishing Zachary especially, not to mention the story about the captain. She would be mortified if Thomas ever learned she'd drawn his likeness and made up a heroic tale about him.

"Because he is a true hero, you see," she explained. "And heroes never like to speak of their brave deeds."

Zachary seemed to understand, and promised not to mention either the tales or the drawings Maggie had made. Lily just jabbed her thumb into her mouth again and nodded.

Satisfied that they would not humiliate her, she trundled the two into Thomas's carriage and followed them inside. A minute later, they were on their way.

Maggie's mother was a shrew, and that description was kind. Tom did not understand how such a woman could have borne a sweet, unassuming daughter like Maggie.

"My mama said I should thank you for saving me in the square."

"You are quite welcome," Thomas replied. The boy was just like any other English child, energetic and curious. It was hard not to like him. "I trust you will not be running into the street again any time soon."

"No, my lord."

Maggie placed her hand upon the boy's knee. " 'Your Highness,' " she corrected.

"No," said Tom. "You must call me . . . Thorne. It's an old family name."

"Oh, but—"

"I insist," he said, countering Maggie's objection. The kind of formality followed by high society seemed out of place here. And Thomas felt like a perfect buffoon with a five-year-old calling him Your Highness.

"Nurse Hawkins said you are a prince."

Tom did not respond, finding it difficult to lie outright to the boy. It should not matter. The brat was Julian's offspring, even though he looked nothing like his pale-skinned, blond sire. Zachary favored Maggie with his robust coloring and intelligent eyes.

"Are you like Prince George?" the boy asked.

Thomas laughed, enjoying his direct, ingenuous gaze. *God, he hoped not.* "No, nothing at all like Prince George. Will you introduce me to your sister?"

He could not help but admit that the little girl was charming, clinging to her mother shyly, with large gray eyes like her mother's and the same dark, auburn curls. Thomas didn't think she could be much older than two, and realized she must have been an infant when her father died. She'd put her thumb into her mouth immediately after leaving her grandmother's company, and Maggie had not corrected her.

Tom admired her for that.

Zachary was lively without being unruly, and Maggie was quite clearly attached to both children. She wasn't a mother who would willingly send her daughter off to Sabedoria to wed a prince, no matter how wealthy he might be.

"Where are we going?" Zachary asked, after he'd made the requested introduction. Lily had looked away pointedly, clutching her mother even more tightly at the mention of her name, and Maggie mouthed the word, "shy."

"We are going to visit the house I just bought," Tom said.

The boy's face fell and Thomas knew it was exactly the way he'd have reacted at that age to such news.

"I have several horses there," Thomas said.

"You do? How many?"

"Twelve."

"Are they . . . Thoro-Thoro-"

"Thoroughbreds, Zachary," Maggie corrected gently.

"Papa had some of those horses. He used to take

them away from Blackmore Manor and race them, didn't he, Mama?"

The boy's words brought Thomas back to reality. He had only one purpose here, and that was to discover what he could about Shefford and his habits, and to lure the man out to Delamere's. He could not dwell upon the captivating sight of Maggie cuddling her daughter on her lap, or her bright young son's engaging questions.

"Yes, he did, Zachary," Maggie replied. "And your Uncle Shefford races horses, too."

"Perhaps I should have invited Lord Shefford to join us?"

"No," Maggie said abruptly. "I mean, I believe he has another engagement."

Thanks to Andrew Harland, Tom knew otherwise. He also knew that Harland was going to find a way to inform Shefford that Maggie was visiting Delamere House that afternoon. Tom hoped it would be enough to draw the marquess there. "Well, then. I'll just have to invite him out some other time."

"Do you race your horses, too, Thorne?" the small boy asked.

"Aye."

Maggie held her daughter close as the little girl's eyes began to drift closed. The movement of the carriage as well as the gentle caress of Maggie's hand in her hair lulled the child to sleep.

"Will there be any other children there?" asked Zachary, but Tom hardly heard his question. His eyes were locked upon Maggie's softly moving fingers, and thinking about how they were going to feel on him.

"Thorne?"

"Children? No. I haven't any children."

"Only horses, then?" the boy asked, and Tom tore his attention from Maggie's hands.

"Yes." She could not possibly understand the effect she had on him. She might have experience of the marriage bed, but he'd found her curiously innocent of the pleasures to be shared between a man and a woman. But for the climax she'd experienced the previous morning, Lady Margaret was as maidenly as a virgin—chaste and essentially untouched.

As stirring as that thought was, it was unproductive. Thomas looked away and watched the changing scenery outside the window as he answered Zachary's plethora of questions.

Victoria's husband had not exaggerated in comparing Delamere House to Wynard Park. The estate Thomas had bought was palatial. A row of still-bare, mature oak trees lined the gravel drive, and it was obvious that the grounds were meticulously cultivated and waiting for spring plantings.

Lily was sound asleep when the carriage pulled up to the house. It was terribly impressive, with a massive stone staircase that led to a portico with numerous Greek columns supporting the crown. Thomas stepped out of the carriage first, and helped Zachary down the steps. Then he turned to Maggie. "I'll take her for you."

She relinquished Lily to Thomas's capable hands, and felt more than a slight shiver of pleasure as she watched his gentle handling of her daughter. She knew of few men who had the slightest idea how to deal with a child as young and as shy as Lily. Thomas was neither impatient with the situation nor awkward with Lily, and Maggie watched him with admiration and a tinge of sorrow that her husband had not bothered to take such care with his own children.

Zachary ran up the steps ahead of them, but Lily did not awaken as Thomas carried her effortlessly up the staircase to the portico. The front door opened at Thomas's arrival and a butler appeared, asking quietly if he needed any assistance.

Thomas declined, carrying Lily through an echoing marble entryway, past a number of classically decorated rooms, to a small sitting room at the back of the house. Maggie took Zachary's hand as they followed him, watching as he placed Lily on a cozy settee while Zachary chattered quietly about horses, continuing his interrogation of Thomas about the horses and stable.

Maggie felt as though she was shimmering inside, the blood in her veins pulsing to the cadence of Thomas's discourse with Zachary. He was amazingly tolerant of her son, a boy who had more questions, and more energy than any other that Maggie had ever encountered.

If only Julian had been so attentive. . . .

Maggie supposed she should be grateful that he had not. For she had no intention of allowing her son to grow up in the image of his sire, the wasteful gamester who'd neglected his responsibilities. She intended to see that Zachary became a man who understood duty, who learned to use the power and privilege of his position conscientiously.

A man like Thomas.

Maggie knew she should not think of him in such terms. When he was gone, she would still have to cope with her own difficulties here, including her overexuberant son. But she could not imagine how exposure to the sensible prince could hurt Zachary. They led an isolated existence at Blackmore Manor. Her son needed to interact with gentlemen more often, and not the self-absorbed type like Shefford, or the pompous peers her sisters had wed.

"Do you ride?" Thomas asked Zachary.

"I had a pony once, but . . ." He turned to Maggie, frowning. "What happened to my pony, Mama?"

"Papa took him to Town," she replied, hoping that would be enough explanation, but it was not.

"Why?" Zac asked.

"There was a . . . a family that needed a pony, and Papa thought they should have ours."

It was a quick, insufficient answer, but Maggie had no intention of telling Zachary that his father had callously sold his beloved pony along with most of the other horses. He'd kept only one for himself to ride, and another two for Maggie's carriage.

She felt Thomas's questioning eyes on her, but did not look up at him. Her embarrassment over

Julian's lack of regard for her and the children cut deep.

"I think there might be a pony in my stable, waiting for a young fellow to ride him," Thomas said to Zachary.

Zachary grabbed Maggie's arm. "Mama! Is it all right if I ride?"

She looked at Thomas then, and his expression reassured her. He would never allow Zachary to mount a dangerous horse. "I suppose so, but shall we wait until Lily awakens?"

"Perhaps that won't be necessary," Thomas said as the two gentlemen who'd accompanied him the previous night came into the room.

"Ah, Your Highness," the tall one said, "you're back."

Edward Ochoa came into the sitting room with Nathaniel Beraza, and Thomas introduced the two men to Maggie. "Did you meet my good friend, Ambassador Beraza, last night, Lady Margaret?" Thomas asked.

Nate smiled without cynicism as he bowed over her hand. "I did not have the pleasure."

Thomas felt a twinge of alarm as Maggie smiled innocently at Nate. He frowned and reminded himself that nothing untoward was going to happen to Maggie today. In any event, there was no room in his grand scheme for any proprietary feelings . . . or whatever they were.

"And here is my foreign minister, Edward Ochoa," Tom said, collecting himself.

"How do you do?" Maggie said to the short, balding American.

"Are these your children?" Nate asked, shooting Tom a quick glance of pure malice.

"I'm Zachary Danvers," said the boy, stepping in front of his mother. He put on no airs, but gave a perfectly correct bow. Then he turned to his mother. "Can we wake Lily now? I would like to ride."

"Ambassador Beraza, perhaps you would send for Oliver Garay." He turned to Maggie. "He is my driver. Ollie will walk out to the stables with Zachary while his sister finishes her nap."

"Of course," said Nate. "If the lad's mother agrees."

Maggie seemed taken aback by the quick proposal, but Thomas reassured her. "Mr. Garay is an expert horseman. He will make certain nothing goes awry."

"Well then, y-yes—I suppose it's all right. See that you behave yourself, Zachary. We'll come out soon."

Zachary jumped up with delight. "I will, Mama!"

The boy left with Ochoa and Beraza, and Thomas contained the slight uneasiness he felt. No matter how bitter Nate was, he knew better than to act without Tom's authorization. Zachary would be safe with him.

Tom looked back at Maggie and knew he should not allow himself to feel so damned pleased to have her alone. Well, essentially alone, for Lily was sleeping nearby. His plan for seduction was clear, and there was no room for hurry, or sentimentality. He wanted her, but there was a new dimension in play now, one that Nate wasn't going to allow him to forget.

He took Maggie's hand and stole her away from the settee and her daughter. He led her to a far corner, then drew her into his arms and skimmed one finger along the side of her face. "How long have we?"

"How long?"

"Before Lily wakes up."

She looked up at him uncertainly. "A few minutes, perhaps ten."

"I've thought of naught but kissing you in the hours since we parted."

"I don't understand. You . . . you brought the children with us."

"We will have ample time to be alone," he replied. He slipped his hands down her back and to her hips, then pulled her close enough to feel his erection. Her eyes fluttered closed and her breath caught.

"Aye, feel how I want you, Maggie." She filled his senses, far more than any thoughts of luring Shefford out to Delamere House. Shifting against her, he leaned down and took her mouth with his, and when she opened for him, he sucked her tongue into his mouth.

Her body quivered in his arms, and when she tipped back slightly, he deepened their kiss. He did not open her bodice, but brought one hand up to her breast. Cupping it, he flicked his thumb over the turgid peak and felt her knees buckle. The intensity of her reaction took his breath away, and though he knew they could not finish anything he started, naught could induce him to stop now.

He caught the scent of her arousal and felt the silk of her hair against his cheek. Longing to taste more of her, he pressed his lips to her jaw, then her throat. His arousal became more acute, and he nearly jumped out of his skin when she touched it, sliding her hand over his rigid member.

"Maggie," he said, his voice a raw gasp.

"I . . . Oh . . ." She sounded breathless, and Tom knew then that it had been a mistake to touch her. To kiss her. His desire had grown out of control. He had to bed her. Soon.

Her eyes were glassy with a desire that mirrored his own, but when he took her hand to take her from the room, she halted. "We cannot . . ."

"Lily," he said, suddenly remembering.

"She'll awaken all alone."

"I'll find someone to stay."

She licked her lips and Thomas groaned. "No. She'll be frightened if I'm not there."

"God."

Maggie extricated her hand from his and walked unsteadily to the settee. She pressed a hand to her breast and composed herself while Thomas did the same. He should know better than to kiss her or touch her intimately when there was no possibility of making love to her. He wanted her far too desperately for that.

The child stirred. "Mama?"

"Right here, darling," said Maggie. She circled around the settee and crouched before her daughter. "Did you have a nice rest?"

The little girl sat up and nodded, rubbing her eyes. "Where Zac go?"

"He is outdoors. Shall we go and find him?"

Tom didn't know how she managed to sound so normal, so unscathed, when he felt as though he'd been dragged behind a horse without a carriage. He thrust his fingers through his hair and thought of Norfolk Island and the Marquess of Shefford, both sure ways to kill an arousal as fierce as the one that spoiled the line of his trews.

Chapter 6

Tom was counting on Shefford arriving soon, so he'd had the horses turned out into the paddock for him to see, to evaluate. It was all part of the plan to entice the marquess into the final, most devastating stage of the scheme.

He had barely noticed the gardens before, but as they walked toward the stable, he saw that Maggie was impressed with the grounds as well as the house. He'd wanted a palace, and that was what he had. It gave him the credibility he needed.

Maggie took Tom's arm and he tamped down yet another rush of desire and slowed his pace to match hers. He had to focus.

"You have a magnificent garden," she said.

Thomas nodded. He'd had nothing to do with planning it or maintaining it, so he took no credit. "Delamere kept up his property satisfactorily."

"I admit I am surprised that he sold you this house so easily," she remarked.

He laughed. "I assure you it was hardly easy."

"I should have said 'quickly.'"

"Aye. I knew what you meant," he said. She smelled

of roses again, far better than any garden Tom had ever visited. He breathed deeply as they walked to the door of the stable. Workmen were inside, making the improvements Tom had specified.

"Would you like to see the horses, Lily?"

Maggie's daughter looked up at him with those big, softly lashed eyes, and nodded. He reached down and picked her up, holding her in one arm as he walked to the paddock with her mother.

Maggie seemed surprised that Lily allowed it, but she gave a small, incredulous smile and walked on. "You brought horses from Sabedoria?"

He nodded. "My best racers. I don't like to be away from them too long."

"Then," she said hesitantly, "you're planning to stay in England for some time?"

He shrugged, glad that she hadn't asked about the logistics of travel from Sabedoria to England. Six or more months aboard ship with twelve restless horses? Tom couldn't imagine a worse voyage. Luckily, they'd only had a three-week trip from New York. "I haven't decided."

"I see," she said quietly, and he realized his mistake. She must have known he would not remain in England permanently, but would likely reconsider their affair if she thought he was staying only a few weeks.

"No, I don't think you do, pretty Maggie."

She looked up at him in surprise and he had the distinct impression that no one had ever called her pretty.

"We'll be here through the summer, at least,"

he said, suddenly realizing he wanted it to be the truth.

She was quiet for a moment, then changed the subject entirely. "Someone told me last night that you learned to speak English from pirates."

He smiled, genuinely amused at the way his lie had been altered in the telling. "Indirectly, perhaps. Several years ago, some Sabedorians were captured by English pirates. When they escaped and returned home, they taught us your language."

"You learned it very well."

"Thank you," he said, even though the lie did not settle well with him.

They arrived at the paddock, where all but one of his horses grazed or trotted restlessly. His ringer, Arrendo, remained hidden in the barn on the other side of a thick stand of trees, tended by his trainer, Dickie Falardo. Tom had yet to pay a visit to the huntsman's cottage not far from it, but as he stood close to Maggie, he decided to make his exploration very soon.

"Would you like to ride?" he asked, his tone low and suggestive.

Her expressive eyes darkened at his evocative words, and she bit her lip, clearly understanding his meaning.

"I would very much like to ride," she said, her tone soft and provocative. "But I have not practiced in some time."

Her words made Thomas feel as though someone had punched him. Christ, she made him burn.

She swallowed, and he watched the delicate muscles of her throat. "I was thrown from a horse when I was very young."

Tom barely heard her. He wanted to take her somewhere and lay her bare.

" . . . and when my fractures finally healed, my mother did not allow me to ride again."

"What? I beg your pardon?" he said. "Your fractures?"

"Such a clumsy rider . . . I broke my leg and my arm in the fall." She rubbed her thigh unconsciously, and Tom realized that was the cause of her slight limp. "At least my arm healed well."

"But your leg?"

"Not exactly. It was a very bad break and didn't mend quite properly. The doctor said that kind of fracture seldom does."

This time, he felt like gathering her into his arms and telling her that it did not matter. That some conventional notion of perfection was entirely too dull for his taste.

Nate came out of the second stable and started toward them, reminding Tom of their purpose out there. Grounding him. "Ah," said Nate, smiling. "What do you think of our horses, Lady Blackmore?"

She gave them a cursory glance. "Very nice, I'm sure. Where is Zachary?"

"He is under the expert care of Oliver Garay," Nate replied. "They're taking a turn around our little meadow, but I'm sure it won't be much longer before they return. You have a spirited lad there."

"Yes. He is a very active child."

Tom sensed Maggie's tension. She didn't like having her son out of her sight. In spite of Nate's presence, and Lily in his arms, Tom drew Maggie close, merely to reassure her. "Don't worry, Lady Blackmore. Ollie will be careful with Zachary."

"It's just that Zac isn't very familiar with horses," she said, trying to mask her nervousness.

Ollie came into the clearing just then, leading the pony Saret had borrowed early that morning from a neighboring farm, for just this purpose. Maggie relaxed and Tom released her as she returned her son's happy wave.

Lily took her thumb from her mouth. "Look, Mama! Zac!"

Lily squirmed to get down, but Thomas managed to hold her, his touch gentle, careful with her. "Come with me," he said, starting toward Zachary as Mr. Beraza left them and returned to the house. "The ground is uneven—Can you manage it?"

He was solicitous, but gave no indication that he thought her incapable. Maggie rarely spoke of the fall she'd taken all those years ago, and had not planned to speak of the accident to Thomas or her disappointment in being forbidden to ride again. He hardly seemed to notice her limp.

Every cell and pore of her body still pulsed with awareness of his suggestive words, of his potent masculinity. Her nipples tingled and her womb clenched, anticipating a repetition of the pleasures they'd already shared.

She wanted more. Much more.

She forced her attention from her sizzling reaction to Thomas's nearness and watched Zachary. Her heart warmed at the sight of her son's happy face and she realized how much Zac missed the open spaces at home. Unlike the situation in London, there was little danger for the children at Blackmore Manor, and Zachary was able to run free there. He climbed trees, waded in the pond, and chased for hours with the other little boys on the estate under Nurse Hawkins's watchful eye. London was difficult for him, but Maggie had no choice now but to keep her family there.

She had done some computations, and knew it was going to take several months of attending social functions in order to acquire enough material for Mr. Brown's caricatures. They'd agreed on two drawings a week for *The Gazette*, but even if she managed to sell one or two prints made from each drawing, it would be a long time before she had enough money to pay Julian's debts and could return to Cambridgeshire.

"Thank you for this," she said to Thomas. "Zachary will be talking about his pony ride for days."

He took one of her hands in his and would have lifted it to his lips, but for Zachary's happy shout.

"Mama! Do you see me?"

"Yes, I do!" she called out happily. "You are riding!"

"Mr. Garay said I am a very good rider," he proclaimed proudly. Maggie smiled at the man who led the pony, and he grinned back. He was a small man, several inches shorter than Maggie, but many years older, the skin on his face as weathered as an old sailor's. He handled the pony as well as any of the expert grooms her stepfather had employed.

"Look at all the horses," Zac said, pointing to the herd in the paddock.

"Yes, I saw them."

"Do you race them, Thorne?" Zachary asked.

"Yes, I do."

"Are they very fast?"

"Of course. They're the best in Sabedoria."

"Which one is the best?"

Thomas came up alongside Zachary and pointed toward the paddock. "See the chestnut with the white stocking?"

"Stocking?"

"Yes," Thomas replied, smiling as he carefully placed Lily on the pony in front of Zachary. He kept his hold on her as they continued to walk with Maggie alongside him.

Lily's eyes grew huge, but she pulled her thumb from her mouth and grabbed hold of the edges of the saddle as she rode.

"In Sabedoria, we call it a stocking when a horse's leg is covered in white."

Zachary frowned. "But there is only one."

"True. Arrendo has only one, on his left rear leg."

"That's funny. I always wear two stockings!"

"So you do," Thomas said with a laugh, and Maggie's heart clutched in her chest. She could not recall ever having such a pleasant exchange with Julian and their children, and felt deeply offended that he'd avoided them to pursue his more stimulating pursuits in Town.

"Hello!" called Ambassador Beraza, coming out once again from the house. Maggie was surprised to see Shefford striding alongside him, rushing to match the pace of the longer-legged Beraza. He would not like that—feeling as though he had to hurry to catch up to another man.

She shielded her eyes against the bright, spring sunlight and watched her brother's dark eyes take in every bit of their surroundings, from the barns and other outbuildings, to the horses in the paddock and the empty fields beyond. It was the same calculating look that Maggie had seen in him many times before. Her brother could be a very shrewd man, and Maggie knew he intended to orchestrate a race against Thomas's horses. Somehow he would figure a way to ensure his own horse's victory.

"Margaret," he said when he reached her, "I had no idea you planned on visiting here today." She heard an edge of admonishment in his voice. As though he had anything to say about her activities.

"Nor did I, Shefford," she said, lying just a little bit. She hadn't planned on coming out and visiting Thomas with the children, nor had she thought she would see her stepbrother there.

Shefford nodded toward a distant field. "You're excavating?" he asked Thomas.

Only now did Maggie take notice of the men in

the distance, working far afield with shovels. But it hardly mattered. The mood was ruined.

Tom nodded, then spoke sharply to Mr. Garay. "Take the horses inside, Ollie." He seemed to be bothered by Shefford's presence near the paddock.

"Yes, Your Highness," Mr. Garay said.

Thomas took Lily down from the pony and Mr. Garay lifted Zachary down. He took the horse's lead and trotted toward the paddock, as though it was imperative that he get the horses into the stable, and out of sight.

Thomas turned to Shefford. "We're merely smoothing out a patch of turf out there."

"For racing?" Shefford asked.

"Aye. I do not travel without my horses, and they need their exercise."

"Did you know that we have a racing tradition here in England?" Shefford asked.

"Do you." Thomas's words came out like a statement, rather than a question, and Maggie felt a distinct change in his mood. He became cold and distant, and seemed displeased by Shefford's arrival. It was clear that he had not wanted her brother to see the horses.

"Our racers are Thoroughbreds and are registered with a very stringent organization that oversees races. The Jockey Club." Maggie cringed at Shefford's superior tone.

She felt an underlying sense of rivalry at play, a kind of competition that seemed to occur often among men, though she'd known a fair number of women who engaged in the same kind of foolishness. Yet Shefford was the guest here, of a man whose wealth and station was far above her brother's. He should not be spouting off like a boastful schoolboy.

"It sounds very official, indeed," Ambassador Beraza remarked. "We would not care to break any English laws while we're here, would we, Your Highness."

"No," Thomas said, frowning. "We will not be doing any racing. We just wanted the horses to have a reasonably clear course to avoid suffering any injuries when they exercise."

"Seems a shame," said Shefford. "You have some fine-looking horseflesh."

Thomas looked pensively toward the paddock, where Mr. Garay was herding the horses back to the stable.

"Your big chestnut looks promising," said Shefford.

A muscle in Thomas's jaw flexed. "Why don't we go back to the house?"

"I was thinking," said Shefford, standing still, "that you might be interested in running a few races—unsanctioned, of course—English style. You can try your beasts against some fine English runners. See how they match up."

Thomas could not have asked for a more willing subject than Shefford. The man's arrogance prevented him from entertaining even the vaguest possibility that he had been manipulated and was about to be duped.

He'd picked up Lily again, and found the weight of her small body against his chest strangely calming. She melded into his hard angles, the shy little girl who had become surprisingly accustomed to him, trusting him completely to hold her safe.

If things had been different, Tom might have had his own little daughter by now, or maybe a few sons. He restrained the urge to slip an arm around Maggie's waist and pull her close, as though the three of them were family. It would be a huge mistake to allow his emotions to become involved here.

Maggie was just a means to an end, and her presence that afternoon had served exactly the purpose he'd hoped for. Shefford had come running, just as Tom and Nate had anticipated.

"You've got a few that would give my Thoroughbreds a run for the money," said Shefford, watching carefully as the horses returned to the stable, one by one.

"No doubt." He set Lily on her feet next to her mother and Maggie took the little girl's hand in her own. She appeared perplexed, as well she should be. Tom's attitude had shifted completely, his attention entirely focused on the marquess and the horses. All was going as planned, and he could almost hear the machinations going on in Shefford's mind.

Bringing Maggie and her children out here had succeeded in getting Shefford to come, without directly inviting him. Racing against Tom's horses had to be his own idea, and the way Tom planned it, Shefford was going to have to talk him into racing.

Zachary pulled on Tom's coat. "Have you any dogs?" he asked, distracting Tom from the cunning light in Shefford's eyes.

"No, Zachary. Sorry. No dogs." He noticed that Shefford kept his eye on the paddock until the last horse was inside.

"Why not?" Zachary asked.

"That's enough questions, Zachary. It's rude to pry."

"But I like dogs," the boy said. "I miss Bloom."

Maggie sighed and glanced apologetically at Tom. "Most of our neighbors in Cambridgeshire have dogs."

"But not you? Who—*what*—is Bloom?" he asked. Anything to demonstrate a disinterest in racing.

Maggie licked her lips before she replied, and Tom's breath quickened. "Our old sheepdog died last winter." She patted Zachary's shoulder. "She was big and furry, but the most well-behaved canine in all of Cambridgeshire. Zac and Bloom were inseparable."

The boy's expression darkened, but he scampered away and climbed up a few of the rungs on the paddock fence to look at the pony that Garay had left outside. Tom refused to be touched by the boy's loss. It was nothing compared to the harm the boy's father had cost Tom.

"It's been diffic—" Maggie began, but Shefford interrupted her.

"I believe I could get a few good English Thoroughbreds out here for a friendly race or two."

Thomas clenched his teeth at the man's rudeness toward his sister, disliking the marquess more than before, if that could even be possible. In spite of his disgust, he acknowledged that things were progressing exactly as he'd planned.

Slowly and deliberately, he turned his attention from Zachary and looked at Shefford dubiously, playing his part in the farce. He shrugged with feigned indifference. "Even if I agree to race them, they won't be ready for at least six weeks. What do you think, Beraza?"

Nate rubbed the back of his neck, as though mulling it over, although they'd already discussed the way they would handle this question. "No. It will be two full months. The horses have been inactive onboard ship for months—except for a few breaks at our ports of call. And we'll have no easy time finding qualified riders."

"I don't mind waiting until you're ready. Shall we arrange for a meet?" Shefford asked.

"Perhaps," Thomas said, appearing reluctant. He'd brought some of his best American racers, but to an untrained eye, they did not appear as refined as the horses his father bred up in Suffolk, not even his champion, Arrendo. It seemed that the difference was going to be enough to fool Shefford and his friends into thinking they could be bested on the track.

Ted Careaga had already told Tom he would have the horses ready in three weeks. They'd been in top racing form when they departed New York and he believed it wouldn't take long to get them back in shape. Since Careaga had trained horses before his conviction and transportation, he knew horses well.

For further insurance, Tom had his ringer.

Arrendo was the fastest race horse Tom had ever seen, and his look-alike, Sarria, was the big chestnut with the white stocking that Zachary had noted before Shefford's arrival. The two horses were identical, down to the marking on their left rear legs. They had the same ginger mane and tail, both lacking any cornets or heel markings, although Sarria had a small nick behind his left ear. It was the only way to tell them apart, but only the closest inspection would reveal the difference. Shefford would never know he'd been duped when they put Arrendo in Sarria's place and raced him instead.

All of Tom's American horses were great competitors, but Arrendo had never lost a race. As fast as Sarria was, his "twin" could beat him.

There were a great many variables in Tom's plan for Shefford's destruction, but he'd tried to anticipate every possibility, down to keeping Arrendo in his own barn. But it was almost laughable, how easy it was to deceive such an arrogant man. Shefford never guessed that he was about to be swindled out of his last pound and pressed to desperation to win a horse race.

"How do you feel about a wager?" Shefford asked.

Thomas looked away. "Lord Shefford, I'm not certain I care to race my horses. It's nothing personal, I assure you."

"You're going to run them on that new track, are you not?" Shefford coaxed. "Why not make some sport of 'em?"

Beraza spoke up. "I don't think you want to race your horses against our Sabedorians."

"I wouldn't be too sure of that," Shefford said, hiding a confident smile under his thick mustache. "In fact, I would wager money against the sweet bloods you've got here. As fine as they look, I know of a pair of stallions that can outrun anything."

Tom believed he was talking about his own Palmer's Gold and Paragon.

"All right, you're on," said Beraza, appearing to be answering impulsively, although Thomas knew that was not the case. They'd gone over several possible ways that this conversation might go. "Ten thousand pounds on Arrendo against any British horse you name."

Shefford's complexion paled, but there was no other indication of a loss of composure. Tom guessed he was considering when the best time would be to sell the shares he'd just bought in the Manchester Canal, and what his net profit might be, based on the lies he'd been told by Saret's men. "Arrendo?"

"Aye, our best racer," said Beraza. "He's the big chestnut with the left rear stocking."

Shefford narrowed his eyes as he looked at Beraza, likely calculating the time factor, and making a mental evaluation of the horses he'd just seen before they were hustled away into the stable. "I know of— In fact, I own a stallion that will give him a good run. Shall we double your ten thousand?"

Tom heard Maggie's gasp, but could not acknowledge it. All was going according to plan. "Hold, Beraza. I have not given you leave."

"What harm will it do, Your Highness?" Nate asked. "Arrendo thrives on a good contest."

Tom shook his head. "I have no interest in having to shoot my favorite horse when he breaks a leg in a foolish race."

"He won't fall, I'm sure!" Nate entreated. "I think you should give him a go."

Thomas paused, obviously considering Beraza's words. He finally shrugged. "Very well. But I hold you responsible for the good health of that horse."

"Of course!" Beraza gave Tom a quick bow, then turned back to Shefford. "Twenty thousand pounds? How paltry. Shall we say forty?"

Shefford cleared his throat. "Only if we can move the race up to . . . shall we say, four weeks?"

Tom swallowed his satisfaction. It was exactly what they'd hoped Shefford would say.

Especially since they knew the marquess did not have nearly enough ready cash to cover the bet. He was going to have to buy into Roarke's tobacco smuggling scheme and turn a quick profit in order to back up his foolish, foolish wager.

Chapter 7

"**F**orty thousand pounds!" Maggie hissed after they'd climbed into Shefford's carriage. "What can you possibly be thinking?"

Shefford lowered his eyelids to slits and allowed the hint of a smile to brush his lips. "That I will soon be a very rich man, indeed."

Maggie was taken aback. If he had such enormous wealth, he should have offered to resolve Julian's debts. Or at least, helped Maggie deal with them. "You have that kind of money?"

"Of course not. But my estates are worth far more than forty thousand."

"Are you saying you would mortgage them?" she asked, appalled. Good heavens, he was as bad as Julian.

"I won't need to."

Maggie didn't know anything about racing. She'd had very little contact with horses after her accident, only riding in her small gig at home, or in her carriage in London. But she knew that Shefford bought and sold horses as though they were corn.

"You have a horse that can win, then?"

His smile broadened. "I can beat any one of those cows with Palmer's Gold. Or Paragon."

Maggie gave him a questioning glance.

He shuttered his gaze as he spoke. "Bought them both last year. Either one can outrun any of those Sabedorian horses."

"You hope."

He made a disparaging noise, and Maggie felt her brows crease. This was the worst side of Shefford, one he usually managed to hide. But she had witnessed enough of his underhanded exploits in years past, when he'd gotten the better of some poor prey, through means both underhanded and dishonest. She wondered what he was thinking now.

"As I mentioned last night, the Sabedorian prince is obviously your *particular* friend," he remarked with an ugly sneer. "I don't see why we cannot profit by it."

"How absurd. There is nothing I can do to help you win this preposterous race."

Shefford looked at her thoughtfully. "I've noticed the way he looks at you, Margaret. As though he cannot wait to toss your skirts up around your ears."

"Hush, Shefford!" Maggie felt her face color, and turned away, refusing to give him the satisfaction of seeing that he'd flustered her. Glancing at Zachary, she saw that her son was occupied with counting light posts as they drove through the streets toward Hanover Square. He did not appear to have heard his uncle's crass remark. "Anyway, don't be ridiculous."

"It's hardly ridiculous, Margaret. Any number of women would—"

"I thought you wanted me to marry some wealthy friend of yours."

He smiled and his expression called to mind a sly dog, slinking away with a stolen treat. "This is so much better. There is no need to shackle yourself to this foreign prince, but he seems to have no end of blunt. Even that demned ambassador of his is rolling in it. You can get all the information I need about his stables while you . . . *earn* a few valuable gifts. If you play it right, you'll be able to pay off Julian's debts by the time the upstart sails back to Sabedoria."

"I cannot believe you would suggest such a thing." Or that he would consider somehow trying to bilk Thomas, who was clearly a man of consequence.

"Don't be so picksome, Margaret. None of the ladies at the Waverly's ball seemed to find the man distasteful. I don't know why you should."

"This discussion is over, Shefford. Do not count upon my cooperation."

Maggie busied herself with the ribbons on Lily's bonnet and tried to understand what had just happened with Thomas. The afternoon had made no sense. She'd been in a state of constant awareness, and the brush of his hand, even his slightest glance, had set her heart palpitating in her breast. He'd kissed her senseless while Lily napped, as though he had no intention of delaying their tryst. He'd been so caught up in their kiss that he'd even forgotten Lily's presence in the room.

Even now, Maggie's skin tingled with frustration, her womb tight with desire.

But after Shefford's arrival, Thomas could not have spared her the time of day. Maggie was no petulant girl, but neither was she a fool. Thomas had taken her to the heights of arousal, then let her fall back to earth in a state of extreme frustration.

He was toying with her, amusing himself with the poor widow whose husband had not respected her, either. Not that he could know anything about Julian's duplicity, but Maggie wasn't going to allow herself to become vulnerable again.

The prince of Sabedoria could find some other likely woman to tease with the promise in his eyes and in his kiss. Clearly, she was not meant to engage in an affair, for it was much too complicated for her inexperienced heart.

Besides, her decision to engage in an illicit romance had been a hasty one. It had been the direct result of her anger and hurt over Julian's disloyalty. And Thomas had come along just then, and muddled her senses with his incredible kisses and his intimate touch.

She pressed her hand to her breast and forced herself to erase the memory of all that he'd done to her while riding in his carriage, and the passionate kiss they'd shared while Lily slept in his sitting room. Such sensations were much too intense to sustain, and besides, Maggie had much more urgent matters to think of. With her life in chaos, she needed to deal with it without complicating it. She could not allow a foolish flirtation to make matters worse.

There was no room for the frustration she felt. She had lived without a man for the past two years—no, it had been the entire duration of her marriage. For Julian had hardly been a husband to her. And the prince of Sabedoria was only a distraction, who wouldn't even tell her how long he planned to remain in England.

She had to get another picture to Mr. Brown by week's end, and it would require that she attend another social event in order to acquire some subject matter. Maggie realized she couldn't possibly draw a satirical tableau from every affair she attended, or someone would surely figure out the identity of Randolph Redbush.

Which meant she would have to attend more than two social occasions every week. Just the thought of so much socializing tired her, or perhaps it was the afternoon's letdown that had worn her out. She'd been so very keen to be with Thomas again . . .

No. It was because she was accustomed to country hours and country activities in Cambridgeshire. Now it would be necessary to miss the children's bedtime while she stayed up until the wee hours, far too often. With the schedule she'd need to keep, her morning jaunts to the park with Nurse Hawkins and the children would be out of the question. She would have to dress in stylish—

Her heart sank. She had no gowns appropriate for what she must do, and it was going to be a long time before she could afford any new clothes. It was certain she could not go out repeatedly into society wearing the one gown her sister had already loaned her.

Though she had no desire to ask her family for any favors, she resigned herself to what she must do.

"Shefford, would you please take me to Stella's house?" Maggie did not imagine that her sister would be pleased at her request.

"But Mama," Zachary protested, "I want to go home and tell Nurse Hawkins about my pony ride."

"I'll take him back to Hanover Square," Shefford said.

Maggie felt a frisson of unease at his devious glance. She didn't want Zac or Lily to spend any more time with their unscrupulous uncle than was absolutely necessary. "No, the children will come with me. Thank you kindly for the offer, though."

"You and I will talk again, Margaret. I am quite serious about what I said."

"And I am serious about the answer I already gave you. I don't know what you can possibly be thinking, Shefford."

A few minutes later, Maggie and the children entered Stella's house and discovered her mother having tea with her three other daughters in the drawing room. As Beatrice looked up at her, she resisted the urge to smooth back her hair, and check to be sure that her buttons were fastened correctly.

She wished it was not necessary to come here for help. If there was any other option, she would have taken it. But she was capable of swallowing her pride for her children's security.

She took Zac's hand, raised her chin and held Lily against her breast as they walked into the drawing room.

"Good heavens," Charlotte drawled. "Must you dress like a governess or an upstairs maid when you go out, Margaret?"

This time, she did glance down at her plain attire, which was all she had. "I—"

"Well!" said Beatrice, ignoring her eldest daughter's blatant insult. "I'm surprised you deign to visit us."

"What do you mean, Mother? I've only been in Town a few days." She crouched down to unfasten Lily's coat and decided they would not bother her today. No matter what they said—

"Never mind, Margaret," said Stella. "Tell us what happened."

"What do you mean?"

"You know perfectly well."

"Don't be coy, Margaret," said Charlotte, whose husband, the wealthy baron of Aughton, seemed to absent himself from most family gatherings that Maggie could recall. He was significantly older than Charlotte, and a widower with children when she married him. Any number of Beatrice's tirades included the complaint that it had been difficult to secure good marriages for the girls after the Chatterton scandal.

Lord Aughton was no duke, but he was a well-heeled and well-respected gentleman. Charlotte could have done worse, but it was quite clear she did not see it that way.

"We heard you went out to Delamere House with the Sabedorian!" Elizabeth said. "Do not tell us nothing happened."

It was beyond annoying that it was only Thomas's notice that had piqued their interest.

"Is Delamere's house as grand as they say?" Elizabeth asked as a maid came in and took Maggie's pelisse and gloves from her.

Maggie sent Lily and Zac along with the maid to the kitchen for a cup of milk and something to eat, aware that she would have to satisfy her sisters' curiosity. She needed their cooperation. "Yes, it's beyond grand."

"And so is the prince," said Elizabeth. "I never got a chance to dance with him at the Waverly's."

"I heard that he only danced with the girls on the marriage mart," said Charlotte, and Maggie wondered if that was true. She felt a twinge of jealousy toward all those fresh young ladies. Clearly, their mothers hoped Thomas would favor one of them, judging by the way they'd flocked around him at the ball.

"I wouldn't know," Maggie said.

"But he went to your house this morning," said Elizabeth, who did not bother to hide her astonishment.

Maggie took a seat and tried not to clench her teeth. "He only wanted to see if Zachary was truly unhurt after—"

"Oh, Margaret, don't be simple!" Stella said. "He took a specific interest in you."

"You're mistaken," Maggie said quietly but firmly. "And I would appreciate it if you would not mention such nonsense again."

She did not miss the continued calculating expressions in her sisters' eyes, but she ignored them. "I've decided to go to Lady Sawbrooke's musicale tonight."

"Well, that's a piece of good news," said Beatrice. "I am pleased to see that you've finally come to your senses."

Maggie gave her mother a puzzled look.

"Clearly, the prince isn't thinking about making you his wife," said Stella, and Maggie swallowed her shock—and hurt—at her sister's blunt statement. It might be true that a man as attractive and desirable as the prince of Sabedoria wouldn't want to marry her, but he'd found her appealing enough to make love to her.

It was a piece of information she had no intention of sharing with her sisters.

Beatrice nodded, agreeing with Stella. "A suitable, English husband will not just appear out of thin air."

Unless his name happened to be Kimbridge, Maggie thought. She blinked back the sudden sting of tears at the back of her eyes, and wished her family did not have such power to wound her.

She did not bother to correct Beatrice's misconception that she'd decided to seek another husband. She was through with men and their confusing ways, and needed to get out into society for another reason altogether. "I wonder if I might borrow another gown, Stella. For the musicale."

"Did you not bring any decent clothes to Town?" Stella asked petulantly.

"I had not really planned on staying more than a few days," Maggie replied, even-toned. "And in any case, I haven't been to a party in years. I have nothing suitable."

"You will have to order some new gowns, Margaret, if you intend to go out into society," Beatrice said. She turned to Stella. "Clearly, she cannot wear your blue crepe again so soon."

The silence in the room was palpable, but Stella finally spoke. "I suppose I can find something for you to wear."

"Well, you needn't sound so keen on it," Maggie retorted. "I'll just go and see if Victoria Ranfield can spare something."

"Don't you dare," Beatrice hissed, aghast.

"She's much taller than you, in any case," said Elizabeth.

"You don't know how much wheedling I must do in order to get Horton to put up funds for a new gown," said Stella, her whine grating on Maggie's nerves. At least she had a reputable husband who could give her the funds she needed.

"I'm sorry," said Maggie, curbing her frustration. "If I cannot borrow from Victoria, I suppose

I'll just have to ask Shefford if he will pay for—"

"Oh twaddle," said Beatrice, standing abruptly. "Margaret needs clothes if she's to catch another husband. She cannot wait to have new ones made." She turned to Elizabeth then. "You're all of a size now. Elizabeth, you must have a few suitable gowns to contribute."

Elizabeth kept her eyes down and sipped her tea, while Maggie thanked God that her mother hadn't yet learned of the dismal state of her finances. Nor would she.

Maggie had no interest in speaking to her family of Julian's betrayals. There was a very good chance they knew of his affairs, but Maggie didn't care to share his financial failings with them, too.

"It's not as though I'm asking for your dowries," said Maggie, restraining her frustration. She hoped her own children would not grow up to be such selfish, petty adults. "If it's any comfort, I'm sure I'll tire of society very quickly." Which was true, except that it didn't mean Maggie would be free of it. But at least she could set aside some money to have a few of her own gowns made.

Without the least bit of enthusiasm, Stella put down her teacup and pushed up from her chair. "I have the apricot satin that I wore last season to Lady Dartwood's party."

"I should think that would do nicely," said Beatrice.

"Thank you, Stella," Maggie said tightly. She could hardly wait until the moment she had the funds and the wherewithal to return to Blackmore

Manor. Perhaps she should bet on Shefford's horse, too.

"He took the bait nicely, did he not?" Nate Beraza said with a grin.

Tom washed his face and hands, wishing he could cleanse away his sense of having been sullied by the marquess. And he had not enjoyed handing Maggie into the carriage with him. He would have preferred to keep her with him at Delamere House. Or at least to have been the one to drive her home.

Yet she had been dealing with Shefford a great deal longer than Tom had, and nothing untoward had happened to her. He gave himself a mental shake and recollected that Maggie's well-being was not his concern. He needed to keep everything in perspective.

"Aye, he took it," Tom said. "But forty thousand pounds? I can't believe he's so reckless."

"It was too great a temptation for the grasping toad," Nate said.

"You're right." Shefford hadn't changed in all the years since Tom's youthful encounter with him.

When he met him at the Waverly ball, Tom had sensed the same old edge of malice in the marquess, the meanness that had prompted him to toy with Tom's life and probably others. The bullish bastard liked playing some twisted games of fate, but only with the odds tilted in his favor.

"Roarke will have no trouble luring the bloody

bugger into his smuggling scheme." Nate laughed. "I wish I could be there to watch."

"No. As satisfying it would be, he knows you. And he'll see the rest of us here and there. I even want Saret to stay out of sight."

Nate's satisfied expression was contagious and Tom finally gave some credit to his years of planning. His scheme might actually work.

"It's all going according to plan," said Nate. "When Saret returns from Town, he'll have Shefford's first ten thousand pounds in his possession. We know the marquess only has about twenty thousand total—besides his lands—and you've figured a means to relieve him of every shilling he possesses."

True. And he would have to sell off all of his unentailed properties and possessions, and borrow Blackmore funds, before Thomas was finished with him.

Yet it wasn't about the money for Tom or any of the others. They cared only about exacting vengeance against the miserable scoundrel. Tom wished he could put Shefford aboard the prison hulk where he'd had first been incarcerated. And then personally shackle him to the pillory for his first flogging.

"Lady Blackmore does not resemble her brother in the least," said Nate. "Are you certain they are siblings?"

"Saret learned that he is her stepbrother," Thomas said. It should not have made any difference, but he was mightily pleased she was not related by blood to the bastard who'd put him in shackles. It was bad enough that she'd been married to his accomplice.

"I saw how you looked at her. You aren't by chance forgetting our purpose here?"

Tom skirted the question altogether. What happened with Maggie was none of Nate's concern. "We still need to see if we can draw Maynwaring into some scheme or other." He didn't want to think about the actual purpose of his affair with Maggie. Sending her back to Cambridgeshire in shame with her fortunes ruined did not sit well.

He wished the thought of it did not rankle. He forced aside his unproductive ruminations and went out to the stable and mounted Marcaida, his riding mare. He rode the short distance to the land that was being cleared for the racing course and checked on the workmen's progress, then headed to Arrendo's isolated barn.

Dickie Falardo was inside, brushing him down. He tipped his hat as Tom came inside and dismounted.

"How is he?"

"Restless," Falardo replied.

Tom had been considering his stallion's need for activity and exercise, and thought he might have a solution. "Can we paint his stocking? Turn it as brown as the rest of him?"

"Paint him?"

Tom nodded. "There's got to be some compound that can cover his white leg—disguise him—until race day."

"Aye. I'll look into it," Falardo said. "It would be best if we could run him against the others, especially Sarria. He needs to keep his competitive edge."

"I agree. See what you can find."

Tom left the barn and led his horse to the nearby cottage. It was a thatch-roofed house in excellent repair, with a garden in back, and a cobblestone walk all around it.

He tied the horse and let himself inside, finding it fully furnished with comfortable furniture. He walked through the sitting room in front, found a kitchen in back, and a workroom on the west side, with a wall of windows facing a dense woods. It must have been cleaned recently, for Tom detected no musty odor or dust. He climbed the wooden stairs to the second floor, and looked into the two bedchambers.

The first was small, and contained two soft pallets. A room for the huntsman's children, perhaps. The second bedchamber was only slightly bigger, and held a large bed, piled with soft blankets and quilts. It also faced the woods to the west, above the workroom. It was perfect for what he intended with Maggie.

He left the cottage and mounted Marcaida, then took the long route back to the road. It was possible to reach the cottage from the road, without going past Delamere House. None of his men ever need know she was there.

He returned to the main house and prepared for an evening of diplomacy with Nate and Edward at a well-known club in town, and then a social event at the home of a prominent earl. He chuckled to himself as he pulled on his cloak.

"What?" Nate asked.

Tom gave a shake of his head. "Here go the son of a Suffolk horse breeder, a rookery brat and an American felon to meet with the prime minister of England and his chief foreign officials."

Nate grinned at the audacity of their actions. "Aye. Ain't life grand?"

They took three separate carriages in order to keep up their opulent façade, and because opportunities might present for each of them to pursue their end goals separately.

They rode into St. James's street, down to Brook's Club where each carriage was greeted with utmost courtesy by a doorman. Their drivers took their coaches away, and the three men were ushered into the building.

Lord Ealey—Shefford's very good friend— welcomed them to the club, introduced them to Lord Liverpool and several other ministers of government. The gentlemen drank fine whiskey and spoke casually of relations between England and Sabedoria. Edward Ochoa performed brilliantly, especially when Sir William Maynwaring joined them. Ochoa singled out the judge for his particular attention, flattering him and discussing points of law as only another lawyer could do.

It was clear that Ochoa had given a great deal of thought to a Sabedorian judicial code, for he spoke eloquently of the Sabedorian concepts of justice and mercy, of fairness and benevolence. Maynwaring disagreed with a good number of Ochoa's points, but Tom's man was unwavering, even as he praised the judge's clear thinking.

Tom contained his hatred for the man who had sent him to hell, and trusted Ochoa to figure a way to draw him into a well-deserved trap. He observed as Ochoa manipulated Maynwaring into a discussion of finances and investments, leading the judge to believe that the Sabedorians had discovered some promising projects in which to invest.

Ochoa spoke to Maynwaring of the Manchester Canal sham, garnering his rapt attention with talk of huge profits to be made. And if he had any interest in racing, he might enjoy a visit to the Delamere stables to see the Sabedorian Thoroughbreds.

The crystal chandelier and wall sconces in Lady Sawbrooke's music room gave off a soft, glowing light. The conversation sounded like a quiet hum all around Maggie.

It was no surprise that none of her sisters had offered to accompany her to the musicale. Elizabeth didn't generally attend musical recitals unless she was the one performing, and the others rarely took an interest in events that were not premier social occasions of the season.

Maggie had come with Victoria and her husband so she wasn't truly alone. But the press of so many warm bodies all around her, and the noise of all their voices was as daunting as the Waverly ball.

"Your gown suits your complexion beautifully, Maggie," Victoria said.

"Thank you."

"But the style . . . it's so unlike you."

Maggie glanced down at her décolletage and resisted the urge to cover the expanse of bare skin with her hands. She was unaccustomed to showing quite so much.

"I cannot believe I said that." Victoria sighed. "It's something your mother or one of your sisters would say. You look wonderful."

But Maggie did not feel wonderful. Her years at Blackmore Manor had not prepared her for a return to social life.

"Don't look just yet, but who is that thin, blond man speaking with Lord Randall? At the refreshment table."

"Why?"

"He keeps trying to catch your eye. Go ahead. Look now."

"Oh no. Robert Kimbridge." She took Victoria's arm and led her to the opposite side of the room, away from Shefford's overweening, perfectly dressed friend.

"Isn't he Viscount Bowgreave's son?"

Maggie shrugged. The less she knew about Mr. Kimbridge, the better.

Victoria thought a moment. "Bowgreave is exceptionally flush in his pockets, if I remember correctly. And Robert is the youngest. Right?"

If Maggie could believe all she'd overheard, that was true. But she had learned that wealth and titles did not count for everything. Her late husband was the perfect example. He'd had an impeccable lineage, and yet his shortcomings were numerous.

Julian had not cared much for reading, and Maggie knew that was because he had difficulty with the skill. She had never seen him review their steward's records, nor had he taken more than a superficial interest in his estates.

He had not been particularly clever, but he'd been far from unattractive and Maggie realized now that he had traded on his good looks and his title to make his way in society. It seemed so odd now that she'd never had more than a few trifling conversations with him—with her own husband, the father of her children. And it was embarrassing to recall the times she'd tried to engage him, only to be bluntly rebuffed.

His mind must have been too occupied with his many mistresses and all his exciting wagers to spend time thinking of a dull wife and the boring pursuits to be found at Blackmore.

"Shefford thinks I should marry him."

"Mr. Kimbridge?"

Maggie nodded. "But I have no reason to think he'd be any better than Julian. He even resembles him. Vaguely. All that blond hair and those deceptively angelic looks."

"You're not going to do it. Are you?"

Maggie clenched her teeth and gave a shake of her head.

As much as it had hurt to learn of Julian's true

nature, she was glad she knew the depth of his betrayal. It would help to keep her from making another disastrous marriage, not that she had any intention of binding herself to one more hand-some slacker. Kimbridge actually did look a bit like Julian, and as Maggie glanced at him, she saw he possessed the same vacuous smile that she had mistaken for sophistication in Julian. It was merely a mask, and Maggie knew better than to believe there was anything of substance behind it.

"Look, there's Lady Teversal. Shall we join her?"

Maggie was glad for a legitimate reason to dis-tance herself even further from Mr. Kimbridge, as she and Victoria approached Nettie and her husband. They were exchanging pleasantries with an older couple that Maggie did not know.

Nettie greeted them and introduced them to their companions. "Lady Victoria Ranfield, and Lady Margaret Blackmore, may I introduce to you Major General Joseph Foveaux and Mrs. Foveaux?"

"I understand we'll be enjoying an evening of Mr. Haydn's work," said Mrs. Foveaux while her husband, a large man with a florid complexion and small, dark eyes, gave a cursory bow at the intro-duction. He looked over Maggie's head, observ-ing the guests as though evaluating each one by some personal standard. Maggie took comfort in the knowledge that she wasn't under the general's command.

"Yes, I'm sure it will be most enjoyable," Maggie remarked as a new rumble of energy suddenly passed through the gathering. She looked toward the door to see what had caused it.

"Look, it's Lord Castlereagh and Lord Bathurst with the Sabedorian ambassador," said Nettie's husband, Lord Teversal.

Maggie felt a shivery wave of anticipation, a desperate hope that Thomas would be with these important personages, but she managed to squelch it. He'd had his opportunity with her, and he'd wasted it. She looked away from the door.

"I wonder if the prince is with them," Teversal added, putting words to Maggie's thoughts.

"Oh my," said Nettie, opening her fan and beating it rapidly in front of her face. "Here he is. The prince himself. I believe you know him, Lady Blackmore. We didn't have the opportunity to meet him at the Waverly ball. Will you introduce us? I-I'm sure we would *all* dearly love to meet him."

Maggie bit back a refusal, her thoughts a tangle of confusion. First Kimbridge, now Thomas. Two men with differing agendas for her, but both intending to use her for their own purposes.

She drew up short, realizing she had to be honest—with herself, at least. She'd intended to use Thomas for the very same purpose from which she'd been spurned that very afternoon.

She wasn't ready to face him. And yet she said, "Of course."

But the opportunity did not present itself right away, for Thomas and Mr. Beraza split up, each one drawing his own following. The women fawned over Thomas, flapping their fans and fluttering their lashes, while the men bowed and gave him their utmost attention.

Maggie tried to squash her immediate reaction to seeing him, but her heart thudded in her chest and her pulse pounded in her ears. The thought of his intimate touch brought a blush to her cheeks, and she tried to dismiss it, even as she anticipated the moment when his gaze would light upon her.

Would she see the longing that she felt to the core of her being? Would his eyes show some regret for the lost opportunity that afternoon?

He gave his attention to his companions, looking over the crowd only sporadically. No doubt there were matters of great importance for a prince to discuss with the ministers of government, and Maggie had experienced the power of his undivided attention. He held them rapt, even as his gaze met hers, but suddenly stopped speaking. He looked at her with his mouth agape, and absolute shock in his eyes.

Tom recovered himself quickly, in spite of the sour burn that rose to his throat. *Maggie Danvers could not possibly be speaking to Major Foveaux.* His immediate pleasure at seeing her was ruffed by the sight of the vile commandant of Norfolk Island. The man had personally overseen three of Tom's most brutal floggings, and had quite obviously taken intense pleasure in the fatal beating of Duncan Meriwether. The man was the devil incarnate, and it would be all Thomas could do to refrain from dragging the bastard out to the mews behind the Sawbrooke house and shoving his fist down his throat.

"If you'll excuse us a moment." It was Nate's voice, and Tom felt his friend's hand on his arm as he drew him aside.

"It's him," said Nate. "Foveaux."

Tom sucked in a deep breath, hardly able to believe his eyes. "We heard he was dead."

"The rumors were obviously wrong. What are we going to do?"

"He won't know us," Tom replied, tamping down his shock and his fury. He felt as though he'd used up all his patience in dealing with Shefford during their encounter at Delamere House, and seeing Foveaux now was beyond the limits of his tolerance.

"How can you be sure?" Nate was always the calm one, coolly adding his insights to Tom's plans. But Nate's worry now was palpable.

Foveaux was directly responsible for far too many deaths. He'd had absolute control over the prisoners on the island, and every one of them had suffered because of him. Not just the men, but the women prisoners and children, old and young. The commandant had had no conscience whatsoever.

"It's been years," said Tom, forcing a calm he did not feel. "We were half starved lads when he last saw us. We neither look nor speak anything like the poor young rips who were under his control all those years ago."

He watched Nate compose himself. "Aye. You're right. He couldn't possibly remember us."

Thomas's mind raced. He had never considered the possibility of encountering Foveaux again, not when they'd heard he'd died in some sort of uprising. Tom would be perfectly justified in killing the bastard with his bare hands if it were possible . . . But Tom was a civilized man. As satisfying as such brutal violence would feel, he was not the animal Foveaux was.

"What do you think about causing the bastard some financial difficulties?" Tom asked.

"I'll ask Saret to look into it right away."

"It shouldn't be too difficult to find out where he keeps his money. And what his vices are."

"You mean something besides the sight of a back laid bare and bloody from the lash?" Nate said bitterly.

"What do you think? Should we approach him now?" Tom asked, more calmly than he felt. The tracks of his own scars burned as he looked at the man.

"Christ, no."

Tom ignored Nate and faced his old nemesis. It was nothing short of bizarre to see Foveaux now, when Tom had significant status and power. It felt so very different from those years on Norfolk Island, when he was subject to the whims of every prison official and guard.

Foveaux was an old man now. And he was a good deal smaller than Tom remembered him. He had no authority here, and even if he suspected he knew Tom and Nate from the penal island, he would never trust his memory on it. Not when he was looking at Tom in his princely garb.

"He's talking to Lady Blackmore," said Tom, bolstering his nerves. "I think I'll join them." He walked away from Nate and started toward Maggie's group as Nate composed himself and rejoined Lord Castlereagh and some of the other men they'd accompanied from Brook's.

Maggie regarded him pensively, her eyes darkening as he came near, and he understood her reticence. He had not lived up to his promise of an afternoon of shared pleasure, and he regretted it as much as she appeared to.

If she was having second thoughts about their affair, she was fully justified, though Tom believed—hoped—he could convince her otherwise. But for now, he could not afford to focus his attention on Maggie while Major Foveaux stood so close, glowering at him.

Tom locked eyes with the old commandant as he approached, wondering if perhaps he had not changed as much as he thought he had. His credibility as the Sabedorian prince could be lost with one word from Foveaux, but Tom decided it would not happen. As he'd said to Nate, it had been a long time ago since they'd stood before Foveaux while he dispensed his vicious punishments. Tom had been little more than a boy at the time, and powerless against the old tyrant.

"Your Highness, what a surprise," said Maggie, her voice tight, her manner polite in the extreme. He could see that his work was cut out for him.

"Lady Blackmore, it's a pleasure to see you."
He took her hand and bowed over it, then moved
to her side, her presence surprisingly calming. She
wore an elegant gown of a color that reminded him
of a ripe peach, and made him hunger for the sensation of her peach-soft skin against his. The gown
had short sleeves and a daringly low neckline that
clung enchantingly to all her curves. Tom blew out
a surreptitious breath of appreciation and tried
to dismiss his burning hatred for Foveaux for the
moment, while he gazed into her vexed eyes.

He shared her frustration. Their afternoon had
not gone as Thomas would have wished, either,
and he despised that the desire that surged through
him had to mingle with the loathing he felt for Foveaux. He did not think there was anything in the
world that could make him forget the horrors of
Norfolk Island, and Foveaux had been largely responsible for the brutal conditions there.

And yet Maggie's presence took the raw edge
from his intense hatred. He found that he could
speak normally and look Foveaux in the eye with
confidence, divulging nothing of his secrets. Somehow, he even managed to refrain from ripping
Foveaux's sword from his side and running him
through, all at once.

Tom realized he needed to manage Maggie
carefully throughout the evening so that she
would not reject him altogether. She was justified
in doubting the seriousness of his advances, and
it was up to him to reassure her. Which he would
do. Later.

Now, he had to make the most of this chance meeting with Foveaux.

He greeted Lady Ranfield, whom he had met on the previous evening at the Waverly ball. Maggie's posture remained stiff as she turned partially toward him, without looking into his eyes. "May I introduce you to my friends, Lord Teversal and his wife, Lady Nettie Teversal."

Thomas made the appropriate gestures of greeting, and when Maggie introduced him to now-General Foveaux and his wife, he did the same.

"Have we met, Your Highness?" Foveaux asked, and Tom could almost see the wheels of his brain turning. Tom's face was familiar to him, but it had been thirteen years since he was an inmate at Norfolk. Tom reassured himself that the old commandant couldn't possibly remember him.

At the same time, Tom could not help but enjoy the words "Your Highness" on Foveaux's lips. He almost wished he'd established a more demeaning form of obeisance for those who greeted him, if only for this moment. Tom would have dearly loved to see Foveaux on his knees before him.

"Have you ever been to Sabedoria, General?" he asked.

"I am forced to admit I had never even heard of it before I read about you in the newspaper," Foveaux replied with doubt in his tone.

"And you Englishmen are said to be such explorers." Tom tried for a blend of curiosity with facetiousness.

Foveaux reddened with the direct hit to his English pride. "I *have* done some extensive traveling."

Tom grinned. "It's strange that no British ships discovered our isle on any of their travels in the South Seas," he said, glad for the opportunity to berate the British marines who'd manned the prison ships and "kept order" on the isle under Foveaux's command, the bloodthirsty scoundrels.

"I would say so, yes," Foveaux said, and Thomas greatly enjoyed the helpless scowl on the man's face. "I say, your English is remarkably good for a . . . a foreign-born gentleman"

Tom resisted the urge to look away. "Aye. We learned from some well-versed teachers." He changed the subject. "I understand you tried growing flax on one of your prison islands south of my country."

Foveaux's flush deepened. Flax production had essentially failed on Norfolk Island, and Tom knew the commandant would not enjoy being reminded of it, in addition to Britain's failure to discover Sabedoria.

"No. No, you are correct. The endeavor on the island did not yield what we'd hoped."

"We Sabedorians might have saved you a great deal of time and trouble," Tom said, enjoying his ability to rankle Foveaux. "But of course your ships still have not reached our shores."

Foveaux cleared his throat and was saved from having to respond by the appearance of another guest. He was a bland-featured, fair-complexioned man about Tom's age. He bowed to Maggie, whose eyes darted from her friend, Lady Victoria, up to

Tom, then back again, clearly unnerved by the man.

If Tom's hackles rose any higher, they would lift him off the floor.

"Lady Blackmore! What a delight to see you here!" the man said.

"Mr. Kimbridge, how do you do?" Maggie replied, returning his bow. Her jaw was set tight, and Tom bristled at the notion that Kimbridge might have done her some harm in the past.

"Lord Shefford never mentioned that you would be attending the musicale," he said.

"It is not my habit to inform Lord Shefford of my comings and goings," she said curtly, and Tom touched his mouth briefly to cover his smile.

She introduced Kimbridge to their small group, but the man took little note of Tom, of his prodigious title or the impressively royal costume he'd donned for his meeting at the fashionable men's club. Kimbridge was entirely focused on Maggie, taking her arm in an attempt to draw her away.

"The music is about to start," Kimbridge said. "Please do me the honor of sitting with me, Lady Blackmore."

"You are too late, Kimbridge," Tom said, having gone far past amusement with the bloody rascal and on to frank irritation. "I've already asked the lady to join me."

Maggie slipped her hand through the crook of Kimbridge's elbow and stared straight into the other man's eyes. "I would be most pleased to have you accompany us, Mr. Kimbridge."

Chapter 8

Maggie avoided Victoria's questioning eyes. How could she explain the situation with Thomas to her very proper friend? Victoria would be scandalized.

And Maggie hardly understood it herself.

"Thank you, Lady Blackmore," said Mr. Kimbridge, taking her hand again and kissing it dramatically. "I've been hoping to see you ever since I heard you were in Town."

"Oh?" Maggie doubted that very much. Kimbridge hadn't shown the slightest interest in her until Shefford had told him how easily she could be duped. If her brother had his way, she would become a doormat all over again.

She did not care to be anywhere near Mr. Kimbridge and his dreadful fawning. She'd heard enough of his conversation with Shefford to know she wanted naught to do with him. Under any circumstances. And yet Thomas's presence and his proprietary assumptions had jarred the ill-advised invitation from her lips.

She hoped Mr. Kimbridge's presence would discourage Thomas from thinking he had any further chance with her. Perhaps if he was aware of another admirer, he would withdraw his attentions. She could not go through another night feeling as though she might crawl out of her skin for lack of his kiss, of his intimate touch.

General Foveaux and his wife went away to take their seats, and Lord Ranfield came back to join Victoria, who seemed to have stopped trying to figure out what was going on between Maggie and Thomas. Still, she stayed close, claiming the available pair of seats that were directly behind the one Maggie had chosen for herself.

"My lady, may I say you are looking particularly lovely this evening," Mr. Kimbridge said.

"Thank you," she replied, though she took no pleasure in his words or his whiskey-laden scent. She added his tendency to over-imbibe to the list of his faults.

"I trust you are finding London to your liking."

"Not particularly, Mr. Kimbridge," she replied. Thomas stood so close that she could smell his subtle, appealing scent, and Maggie fought the urge to close her eyes and inhale deeply of him. "I am most anxious to return to Cambridgeshire."

"Ah, yes. Blackmore Manor." Kimbridge frowned as though he just realized exactly what she'd said. "But you must find it terribly dull in the country."

"Not at all, Mr. Kimbridge. It's peaceful and quiet there. I very much prefer it to Town."

"I believe I visited there once," said Kimbridge.

Maggie recalled the visit, and the fact that she had not cared for him much. He'd drunk too much even then, had laughed too loudly with an oddly forced conviviality, and had played a vile game of tossing her little son into the air and catching him. Julian had not put a stop to the dangerous sport in spite of Maggie's entreaties.

She always wished that Julian remain at home with their family in Cambridgeshire, but since he seldom came home alone, Maggie never did mind his leaving when it meant that he took his dreadful friends away with him.

"I hope you enjoyed your visit out to Delamere House today," said Thomas.

"Yes, of course," Maggie replied tersely. "You have a very fine estate."

"I believe the children were entertained."

Maggie tipped her head slightly, but could not bring herself to look at him. She feared she might very well be lost if she did. "They enjoyed the pony ride. Even Lily, who is not very daring at all."

She wished she had not used that word—daring—and tried to ignore the frisson of awareness in her lower back and the tightness in her chest. She was no more daring than her little daughter.

And yet, even Lily had climbed readily into Thomas's arms.

"I hope they'll come back one day soon."

Her eyes flew up to his face then, and his expression confused her. Nothing about this affair was clear, and she feared her emotions would not settle down until she put some distance between them.

But it would not be possible yet, not while Kimbridge flanked her on the left and Thomas on her right. She sat down between them, refusing to allow Thomas's proximity to reduce her to a raging puddle of need. He had made it abundantly clear that he'd reconsidered his proposition. And yet—

"If you enjoy the country," Thomas said quietly, "you would enjoy Sabedoria."

His voice sent shivers of longing through her, even though his words were not an invitation for her to go away with him. It was just another sensual trap, one she was unwilling to fall into again. She managed a courteous, distant reply. "It is pastoral, then?"

"Very. Plenty of open land, and our cities are not as crowded or as noisy as London."

Kimbridge leaned forward and spoke to Thomas. "But your country is upside down, is it not?"

"I beg your pardon?" Thomas said.

"As I understand it, Sabedoria is at the bottom of the world."

"Some would say *this* part of the world is the bottom," Thomas replied in a wry tone. "But yes, Sabedoria is very far south."

"I'm not much given to travel," said Kimbridge. "Don't like ships."

"Weak stomach?"

"Of course not!"

Maggie suppressed a smile at Mr. Kimbridge's indignation. Perhaps his stomach tolerated rough seas, but the wind might disturb his thickly pomaded hair, and the itinerary would certainly interfere with his schedule of foolish entertainments. Gambling and womanizing, no doubt, just like Julian.

Lord Ranfield leaned forward and spoke to Thomas. "How long a journey is it to sail to England from your country?"

"Six months."

"Oh my," said Victoria. "I cannot imagine such a long time on shipboard!"

"You would be surprised what a person can withstand, my lady," Thomas said solemnly.

"How is your climate?" Ranfield asked.

"Warm all year," he replied. "But we have a rainy season in spring—which would be your autumn."

"Really," Victoria said, thoroughly engaged. "So everything is reversed?"

Thomas nodded, adding nothing more.

"How long will you be staying in England?" she asked.

Thomas gave an engaging shrug. "We haven't yet decided."

Victoria nudged her husband. "Charles, you should invite the prince to our house party this summer."

"Oh yes, of course," Ranfield said. "We always have a party at the end of the season at Ranfield Court. If your schedule will allow it, we'd be honored to count you among our guests."

"I will see what Mr. Ochoa has put on my schedule," said Thomas. "Thank you."

Maggie had a sudden, vague inkling that Thomas

had some reason, other than trading Sabedorian flax, for coming to England. He clearly had more wealth than any nobleman she could name, and she wondered if all of Sabedoria was so prosperous. If so, they would have no need to sell their flax to England.

He was not hostile, and the English ministers seemed to have welcomed him gladly. So his purpose was not war, thank heavens. England had had enough of that during most of Maggie's adult years.

She wondered about the Sabedorian language and culture, and how Thomas had come by his name. It sounded altogether English, and yet his country was on the other side of the world. Perhaps it was an English version of a Sabedorian name.

"Lady Blackmore," Kimbridge said, shifting in his seat so that Maggie was forced to turn from Thomas, thereby shutting him out of the conversation. Facing him so closely, she saw that his eyes were bloodshot, reinforcing her unflattering opinion of him. "Would you do me the honor of accompanying me on a drive in the park tomorrow?"

"A drive?" Maggie said, dubiously. She wanted nothing to do with him.

Kimbridge smiled forcefully. "Yes. In the park."

She felt Thomas at her back, could almost see his arms crossing his chest as though he had any right to dictate her activities.

"A drive would be lovely," she said to Kimbridge, and wished she could bite her tongue the instant the words came out of her mouth. She had no desire to go on an outing with such an odious companion, but some contrary part of her had insisted upon demonstrating her disinterest in Thomas.

The quartet took up their instruments and started tuning. "Cancel it, Maggie," Thomas whispered near her ear, and Maggie shivered. "Meet me tomorrow. Alone."

The voices quieted as the music started, and Maggie could not recall ever feeling more uncomfortable than she did at that moment.

"I apologize for this afternoon," he said, as quietly as before, the instruments masking his voice.

Maggie's breath caught.

She knew better than to credit his words. There had been no reason for him to include her children on their trip to his estate. If he had truly wanted to spend time alone with her, he could have done so that afternoon. He had chosen not to.

He spoke quietly again. "I neglected to consider how many people would be present at my estate today and would take note your arrival."

She swallowed at the implication of his words. Turning to him then, she was sure there must be unspoken questions in her eyes.

"I did not care to have any of my men speculating about you."

Maggie made no reply, feeling flattered at first, that he had considered her reputation. But then she became wary, and perhaps a little bit cynical. She'd swallowed many a tale told by her husband, and never received any serious answers to her questions about the estate, or the tenants and livestock. And she knew where that had gotten her.

No man was ever going to make such a fool of her again.

She turned to face forward, and focused on the quartet that was midway through Haydn's lovely concerto, admonishing herself to pay closer attention to it. To relax and try to enjoy it, in spite of Thomas's provocative words.

The soft candlelight reflected all the glittering jewels in the room, and the starched white of the gentlemen's collars. Maggie felt overly warm in Lady Sawbrooke's music room, even with her arms and half her chest exposed in Stella's satin evening gown.

She found it difficult to relax, feeling entirely out of her element beside the most fascinating man in the room. A man who had acted to protect her reputation, if she could believe him.

She ached for his touch, certain it was the only thing that could end the torture of the heavy physical awareness she felt. Her body drifted toward his, as though tugged by some unseen magnet. She felt his heat beyond their small point of contact at the shoulders, and it seared through her entire body. When he shifted slightly in order to touch her hand, she felt as though she were on fire.

She dreaded another night of denying needs she hadn't known she possessed.

The concerto ended and the room erupted in applause. "I believe I've done us both a great disservice," Thomas said, his words drifting softly to her ear. "I want you."

They were exactly the words that could incite her, and dear God, she did not even care if anyone heard him. As she clapped her hands in applause for the performance, she tried to temper her thoughts and the urgings of her body, for it was all impossible. She was a respectable woman, certainly not meant to be paramour to any man, but especially not the prince of Sabedoria.

Maggie's rose fragrance had not left Tom since he kissed her that afternoon at Delamere House. Her scent reminded him of the sunshine and abundant fresh air at his estate in New York. Tom had no doubt she would enjoy Thorne's Gate far more than she cared for Julian's holdings in Cambridgeshire.

Significantly more than any absurd drive in the park with Kimbridge.

The Englishman's attentions should not matter, but Tom could not help being annoyed by the way the man gaped at her. As though she were a pastry he could not wait to taste.

He forced himself to retreat, releasing his tight grip from his knees. Easing back slightly, he listened as the next piece of music began. It was Maggie's decision whether or not to accompany Kimbridge, but there was no reason why Tom couldn't ride through the park at the same time she would be there. He could ride the entire bloody day if he wished.

He turned slightly and caught Foveaux's glance,

and the commandant made no attempt to disguise his direct stare. Tom managed not to recoil from those piercing eyes, meeting the man's stare head-on. He allowed himself the slightest hint of a smile, remembering that he was the one with the power now, not Foveaux. Tom had a feeling the man would eventually remember why he and Nate looked familiar, in spite of their assumed names. In their days on Norfolk Island, the old commandant had never forgotten anything.

It was only a matter of time before he figured out Tom's true identity.

He hoped the old commandant wouldn't do or say anything foolish. Tom's incredible wealth should protect him from any rash statements Foveaux might make, for who would ever believe a convict could amass the riches Tom possessed? And which of the English foreign ministers would care to admit they'd been duped?

Even the fiction of Sabedoria was impossible to disprove. There was a tangled maze of islands northwest of Botany Bay. It was entirely possible that no European ships had ever encountered the location that Thomas had given for his island home. He was safe for the time being.

Foveaux was not, however. Mark Saret had the connections to investigate the state of the general's finances and from there, they could figure a way to do him a vast amount of damage. It was an opportunity Tom could not let alone, for the bastard deserved nothing less for his treatment of the convicts on Norfolk Island.

Tom looked away from Foveaux and turned to the far more pleasant occupation of observing Maggie. Her lips were full and pink, her skin as smooth as alabaster except for the light smattering of freckles across her nose and cheeks. He knew how sweet her skin tasted and remembered how those alluring freckles blanketed her shoulders.

He meant to taste them again.

She kept her hands properly folded in her lap, her ivory gloves shielding every inch of her skin from her fingertips to a few inches above her elbows. Tom would never have believed the sight of a woman's bare hands could be erotic, but when he remembered Maggie placing one of hers on his full erection, he reacted with an immediate tightness in his groin. He suppressed a groan at his reaction and turned his thoughts to something—*anything*—that was less arousing.

She did not seem to be enjoying the music, and Tom hoped it was Kimbridge's presence that caused her unease. She'd been rash in agreeing to accompany the man to the park, obviously piqued by her afternoon at Delamere. He received her message quite clearly.

He did not think she meant anything by it, beyond the frustration they'd both experienced earlier in the day. He'd wanted her badly. But he'd accomplished what he'd needed—getting Shefford to the estate without a direct invitation. Of his own accord, Shefford had traveled to Delamere House, and had posed his astounding wager.

Tom and Nate hadn't had to do anything but

appear reluctant and slightly naïve. It was all part of the plan.

As Foveaux was not. But causing the commandant some pain was an opportunity Tom could not ignore.

He still felt the man's scrutiny again, and was aware that Foveaux was not the only one observing him. Tom and his men were a puzzle to many, which was exactly the way Thomas wanted to keep it. It was the reason they'd devised foreign-sounding surnames for themselves, and concocted their absurd explanation for the way they'd learned English. They wanted nothing to cue anyone to their true backgrounds.

The farce had to go on as planned, though Tom found himself putting Maggie's part in all of it to the back of his mind. He didn't know exactly how every one of his machinations would unwind, only that he had more than enough threads in play to succeed.

Or fail, spectacularly.

If all went as planned, Tom would eventually pull those threads, each one separately, or all together, and destroy the marquess. The horse race was only the final thread, the one that would drag down Shefford and all his friends, for Tom wouldn't be satisfied until the bastard's good name and all his friendships were destroyed.

In the meantime, they had to keep the charade going. Edward Ochoa was scheduled to meet with the British foreign ministry office the following day, ostensibly negotiating trade treaties. Nate was

meeting with Lords Liverpool and Tenterden to
establish governmental ties, while Saret had insti-
tuted negotiations to buy the bank in which Shefford owned shares. Thatcham's Bank was going
to fail at a crucial moment. It did not matter how
much money Tom lost in the process. There was
always more. Substantially more.

So far, Tom could not have asked for better
results. Even his encounter with Commandant
Foveaux had provided some degree of satisfaction. The man had been required to bow and pay
homage to Thomas Thorne, one of his former convicts. Nothing could have been more fitting.

Tom would have Mark Saret do some digging
into Foveaux's finances, just as he'd done with
Shefford. Taking away his home and his personal
fortune was the only strategy Tom could think of
to destroy the old bastard. He was not aware of
anything he could do that would result in the man
being stripped of his rank or his attachment to the
New South Wales Corps.

But Tom intended to give it his full consideration, right after he made sure Maggie understood
that Kimbridge was not even vaguely suitable.

She moved slightly, and Thomas saw that Kimbridge had shifted, spreading his legs wide to allow
his thigh to press against hers. She did not seem to
enjoy that slight contact, in spite of her agreement
to ride with him on the morrow. She was trapped
between them, and Tom was pleased to note that,
while she tried to remain perfectly neutral, she
tilted slightly in his direction.

* * *

The musicale could not end soon enough. Mr. Kimbridge might be dressed as a well-heeled gentleman, and he might be flush in his pockets. But he smelled like Old Rudy Mitchner, a Blackmore villager who spent far too much time in the public house. They both reeked of alcohol. And he had no sense of decorum, sprawling so that his legs splayed out unattractively and encroached upon her space.

It was all she could do to keep from turning to Thomas and pressing her nose into his clean-smelling chest. Kimbridge was unbearable, and Maggie knew she could not possibly accompany him on his afternoon ride. She intended to inform him of a "forgotten" previous engagement before leaving the Sawbrooke House that evening.

Thomas's thigh also pressed against hers, but Maggie's reaction to it was the complete opposite of her response to Kimbridge. And yet she was quite clear on how foolish it would be to pursue it. She recognized that she was not the kind of woman to engage in an affair, even if it was with the most striking, most mysterious man she had ever encountered.

Whatever his reason for foregoing their planned assignation, their separation had given her a chance to breathe, to reconsider what she was about.

Nor would she be used by Shefford. Whatever his wagers might be, they had nothing to do with her. She was going to take care of her own concerns and make two drawings a week, for as long as it took to get her family out of debt.

She noticed General Foveaux's direct gaze, and saw that it was leveled at Thomas. The man seemed to be just as puzzled by Thomas as she was, and it occurred to Maggie that it might be interesting to make a drawing with the general and Thomas as subjects together. It was clear that Foveaux believed he'd met Thomas before. But it couldn't have been in Sabedoria, for no Englishman had ever visited there. Perhaps he and Thomas had had contact somewhere near Botany Bay, where General Foveaux mentioned he'd been stationed for several years.

Or perhaps not. Thomas had denied knowing the general, and Maggie could think of no reason why he would lie.

When the concert was finally done, Victoria leaned forward and spoke quietly to Maggie, and the two of them excused themselves. As everyone else in the room rose from their seats, she and Victoria headed to the ladies' retiring room. Victoria said nothing as they walked, but Maggie could practically feel her bursting with questions.

And Maggie had no idea how to answer them. At least Victoria was willing to wait for a private moment before asking what she wanted to know— about Thomas, of course.

"You'll come to Ranfield Court at the end of the season, too, Maggie," she said as they left the music room.

"What are you plotting, Victoria?"

"Plotting?" she asked innocently.

"The man won't—he can't possibly—stay in England."

"Who says a paramour must be permanent?"

And Maggie had worried about shocking Victoria. "I cannot believe you are suggesting such a thing."

Vic locked arms with her and took a conspiratorial tone. "He's clearly interested in you."

Maggie looked at her with surprise. "Vic—"

"And you're a widow . . ."

They entered the retiring room, and since there were several other ladies present, Victoria had no chance to pursue the subject that had clearly taken her fancy. They went about their business, chatting about their children, and were ready to leave when the elderly dowager Countess of Dinsmore detained Maggie. Since she was grandmother to the earl whose estates bordered Blackmore Manor, Maggie had no choice but to exchange niceties with the old harridan.

Lady Dinsmore tottered unsteadily, barely able to stand, and Maggie looked around for whoever had accompanied her. Seeing no one, she took it upon herself to look after the dowager until someone could be found.

"Please take a seat, Lady Dinsmore," she said, then turned to her friend. "Go on, Victoria. Ranfield will be waiting for you, and perhaps you can locate Lady Dinsmore's family for her." The last thing she wanted was to remain sequestered there with the countess, but she saw no alternative.

Victoria was reluctant to leave, but she also saw that there was no choice.

"I always liked you, Lady Blackmore," said the wrinkled old dowager when Victoria was gone. The rest of the ladies cleared out right behind her, as if they were afraid they might get stuck having to talk to the old crone. "Couldn't abide that milk-sop husband of yours, though, from the time he was in short pants."

A surge of surprise shot through Maggie at such an outrageous remark and she felt more than a twinge of indignation, in spite of what she knew of Julian's character. It was not for anyone else to say what her husband's shortcomings might have been.

"Such a little cheat, even as a child," the woman added brazenly. "Why, I forbade my late son from inviting him to my grandson's birthday."

Maggie stood abruptly. "Lady Dinsmore, it's not fitting to speak in such a way of the dead."

"Rubbish. You can't have been happy with him. Sit down."

"No, thank you, my lady," Maggie countered, horrified. "I—"

"You'll want the genuine article next time," the woman said, smacking Maggie's wrist lightly with her fan for emphasis. "A man with some back-bone about him. Some fortitude and no dearth of bolloc—"

A young woman bustled into the room, inter-rupting Lady Dinsmore just in time. "There you are, Aunt Philomena!"

Maggie felt as though she'd been slapped. Learn-ing about Julian's recklessness from Victoria was bad enough, but this . . . It was the scene Victoria had feared—the reason she'd forewarned Maggie about Julian's failings.

"I'm not finished, Florence," Lady Dinsmore protested as her niece tried to get her to stand.

"Oh yes. Yes, you are." Quite obviously chagrined, Florence turned to Maggie as she helped her aunt up. "I am dreadfully sorry for whatever my aunt might have—"

"Nonsense!" Lady Dinsmore's voice rose, attracting the attention of the ladies who had just entered the room. "I am forthright and honest, that's all."

"I would say there's quite a bit more to it than that. Come along now," said Florence. "My most abject apologies, Lady Blackmore."

Feeling more than a little distressed, Maggie exited ahead of them and slipped down a quiet corridor in the opposite direction of the soiree, where she could regain her poise before returning to the music room.

She let herself into a deeply shadowed room with a wall of mullioned windows. Taking a deep breath, she pressed one hand to the bare skin of her chest, right where the hollowness felt the worst. Julian's betrayals were bad enough. The fact that Shefford and Beatrice had probably known of his failings at the time of their marriage galled her. They'd encouraged the match in spite of Julian's poor character.

Lady Dinsmore hadn't liked Julian even as a child. She'd called him a cheat.

The woman had been right. And Maggie was angry, so very angry now. Julian had cheated his wife and children of everything that mattered—his love and affection, his fidelity and reliability. She was furious, not just with Julian, but with Shefford, who'd foisted him on her. With Beatrice, who'd accepted everything Shefford had said about Julian, and with her sisters, all of whom were older and far more experienced, but none of whom had cared enough to raise any objections.

Maggie had been a naïve little wife, trying to please her family, yet Julian had never attempted to be more than just an adequate husband. He'd shown no particular interest in her, even on the occasions when he bedded her. And though he'd said he wanted another child after Lily was born, Maggie suspected he'd only cared about siring a second son. The Spare, as was expected of him.

She let out a shuddering breath as she recognized the broader scope of her disastrous marriage. Not only had Julian been an idler of the worst kind, her mother had encouraged her to wed him, merely because he'd been in possession of a title. Worse, neither her mother or sisters had cared about the kind of life she would be sentenced to, married to a fraud like Julian Danvers.

She took a moment to calm herself, then swallowed hard, smoothed down her skirts and started for the door. She pulled it open and collided with Robert Kimbridge, who stepped into the room and shut the door behind him.

"Lady Blackmore. I wondered where you'd gone. Been looking for you." He had the same lanky build and narrow shoulders as Julian. His brows were as pale as his hair, making them almost invisible. His nose was long and somewhat hooked at the end, though at least his chin was passable. But as she did not care to see it any closer, she sidestepped as he approached.

"I would have a word with you, my lady."

"This isn't quite proper, Mr. Kimbridge," she admonished, "and you must know it."

"Propriety is not strictly necessary for what I am about to say to you."

Maggie moved to the other side of a chair. "Then you can have nothing to say, because I do not intend to listen."

"You are the one who invited me to sit with you, my dear lady." He stalked her, circling around the chair, and forcing Maggie to move to yet another piece of furniture to use as a barrier between them.

"Sitting is one thing . . ."

Kimbridge stayed between her and the door, and she began to feel a bit worried, afraid that she may have led him on. They were far from the rest of the party, and it was unlikely anyone would come looking for her. Perhaps—

"Lady Ranfield will be right back," Maggie tried.

"No, she won't. I saw the two of you leave the music room, but only she returned." He moved suddenly then, and grabbed Maggie's arm at the elbow, pulling her off balance.

"Unhand me, sir," she said, pushing away from him.

"My dear Lady Blackmore, you should know that even widows—*especially* widows—are not allowed to tease and tempt a man, and then refuse him."

She tried to wrench her arm away. "Sitting beside you was certainly neither, Mr. Kimbridge. You had to sit somewhere," she said harshly. "Now, let go."

Instead of releasing her, he sidled closer, holding tightly. "I never really noticed your lovely eyes before, Margaret."

She felt her pulse pounding in her throat as he lifted his free hand and feathered the backs of his fingers over her cheek.

He allowed his gaze to drift down below her neck. "And I never saw you in anything that displayed your . . . attributes . . . quite so well."

His hand glided lower, and when he stroked the upper curve of her breast, Maggie slapped him. "Do not touch me again, sir!"

She was shaking so badly, it was difficult to keep her balance and march away from him with any semblance of dignity.

If only she had not been so foolish as to try to hide in this remote room to recover from Lady Dinsmore's offensive words, the confrontation with Mr. Kimbridge would never have taken place.

She gave a quick glance toward her exit and stopped short when she saw Thomas step into the room, his face a mask of fury. He seemed to be

considering his choices when Maggie stepped in
front of him. She stopped him from acting rashly,
placing her hand against his chest. She hoped Sabedorians did not feel honor-bound to duel in such
situations.

Chapter 9

"**T**ake me away from here, please," Maggie said, her voice sounding shaky.

Tom weighed his options and decided he could not afford to thrash Kimbridge, at least, not here at Lady Sawbrooke's house with so many ministers of state present. At the same time, it was obvious that Maggie could not return to the music room in her troubled state, or there would be talk. He drew her away to an empty room that was even farther from the party, away from Kimbridge.

"In here," he said. He took her inside and closed the door behind them, quickly gathering her into his arms. She was shaking. "Are you all right? He did not hurt you?"

The room was dark but for a stream of faint moonlight. When she tipped her head back, Tom could barely see her. Only her glittering eyes, bright with barely contained tears. He ignored the tug in his chest, and allowed himself to take satisfaction in Kimbridge's incensed expression.

"No. It was only . . ." She took a shuddering breath. "O-only an inconvenience. I was thoughtless . . ."

Tom held her until her shaking ceased. For all her bravado, it was obvious that she'd been distressed. Afraid.

"We should get you back to the festivities before someone notices your absence."

"Only my friend, Victoria. Lady Ranfield," Maggie said. "She will be concerned."

But she made no attempt to move from the circle of his arms. She pressed her face against his chest, and Tom reacted as he always did when she was near.

This slow seduction was hell.

He skimmed his hands across her back, wishing he could lie with her on the nearby sofa and do what he'd been thinking of for days. "I will come to you tonight."

"*What?*" she cried breathlessly. "What do you mean?"

"Unlock your doors after your servants retire," he whispered. He grazed her cheek with his lips and felt her sigh in response.

"Thomas, I cannot—"

"I want you, Maggie." He let his hands drift to her sides, his thumbs caressing the sides of her breasts. He wanted them free of her gown and chemise so he could hold them in his bare hands. "Tell me you don't feel the same."

She gave a frantic shake of her head.

"Shall I climb up to your bedroom window?"

"No! Of course not!"

"No one will know I'm in the house," he said quietly. "Send the servants to bed as soon as you get home."

His mouth touched her lips and she surrendered to his kiss. As difficult as it was, he broke away. "God, I want to taste you, Maggie," he said. "But your lips will be swollen if we keep on."

She caught her breath and put one hand to her mouth. "I must be losing my mind."

"As am I. I would lay you down here in this room if it were possible."

"Oh God." Her words were hardly audible, but Tom felt their vibration from her chest to his.

"I'll watch for a candle in a front window."

"I must be insane."

"Aye, Maggie. So must I."

The children were asleep when Maggie arrived home, and Nurse Hawkins said they'd behaved, even though they'd only had a book story to settle them down at bedtime. Maggie somehow managed to control her nerves, thanking the nurse and dismissing her, giving her leave to take to her own bed. She gave her son and daughter a kiss without waking them, then went downstairs to her own bedchamber. Tessa was waiting for her, and Maggie tapped her foot nervously while the maid unfastened her borrowed gown.

"That will be all Tessa," Maggie said, her head spinning with the complications of carrying out a secret tryst with a lover. She would prefer to meet him in the drawing room, fully dressed, and allow things to progress gradually.

But she couldn't very well send Tessa away without having the girl unfasten her gown and corset. Tessa would think Maggie intended to sleep in it, which would be lunacy.

As if what she had planned was not lunacy.

"Don't you want me to take down your hair, my lady, and brush it?" Tessa asked.

"No, thank you, I can do it," Maggie replied far more calmly than she felt. Her hair was much too wild to leave it down . . . it might frighten him off. Perhaps she *ought* to frighten him off! "It's late and you look sleepy. Go to your bed. And tell Mathers I won't be needing anything more."

"Are you all right, my lady?" Tessa asked, frowning, and Maggie realized she must be acting strangely. Tense. Unsettled. Flustered.

Because that's how she felt.

She softened her tone and tried to relax. "Yes, just fine. Tired, I suppose. Go, Tessa. Have a good night's sleep. I'll see you in the morning."

Only the three servants lived in, for the cook came in daily. Once Nurse Hawkins and the other two retired, it would be all clear for Thomas.

Maggie's heart pounded at the prospect of her clandestine meeting. She knew she shouldn't put the candle that Thomas expected in the window, but some other being seemed to possess her as she pulled a dressing gown over her plain, decidedly *un*alluring chemise. She clasped her hands together at her waist and tried to calm her nerves while pondering whether she was making the worst mistake of her life.

The answer was no. Her marriage to Julian had been the mistake.

Her train of thought was interrupted by the sound of wheels in the square, and she knew it must be Thomas's carriage. She gulped nervously. Obviously, he would have his driver bring him here. Drop him off. Which meant that Mr. Garay would know the reason for his employer's late visit.

She looked up at the ceiling and pictured the dimensions of her children's room. They were directly above her, with Nurse Hawkins at the back. Hawkins would not hear them if they happened to—

"Oh God," Maggie whispered to herself, hardly able to believe what she was contemplating.

She started to leave her bedchamber, but saw her drawing tablets in plain sight. She grabbed them and quickly hid them under some clothing in her trunk. She had to keep them hidden, or Thomas would see his face on her pages. He might very well figure out who Randolph Redbush was, but beyond that he would realize how much his magnificent face occupied her mind.

Taking a deep breath, she went down to the main floor to make sure Tessa and Mathers had retired. She told herself that she hadn't yet decided whether to go through with it or not, but she moved through the house with a distinct purpose.

The whole house was dark and still. Her body vibrated with arousal, with the need for one man's touch. The arguments she tried to make against an affair with Thomas sounded feeble to her own heart.

It was now or never.

With the kind of friends Tom kept, he had learned early on how to pick a lock, so it would be no problem to get into Maggie's house. He knew how to move undetected through a dark house, too, but tonight was Maggie's choice.

He kept watch on Julian Danvers's house as he leaned against his carriage across the square, telling himself that the seduction of Blackmore's widow was all part of the plan. It was just one of the threads he was going to pull when the time was right. That she was entirely delectable made it so much the easier.

He tossed away his cheroot when he saw the light appear in the window, and spoke quietly to Oliver. "Drive around to the mews and wait for me there. Take a nap, Ollie." He had no idea how long he would be, though he was hoping for several hours.

The door to number eight was unlocked, and Tom entered the house, picking up the lamp Maggie had left for him on a table near the staircase. He climbed quietly while his heart thudded loudly in his ears. He could not recall another time when he was so eager to sink into a lover. Knowing that it was Maggie who waited for him was almost more than he could bear.

Suddenly she was there, standing in the doorway

of her bedchamber. Her hair was still pinned up as it had been earlier, but she'd changed out of her evening dress. Now she wore some loosely flowing gown of white with tiny sleeves that left most of her shoulders and arms bare. Lit by the fireplace behind her, Tom hardened at the sight she made.

He closed the distance between them. All at once, he took her into his arms and kissed her hungrily, starved for the taste of her. Ravishing her mouth, he moved abruptly and pressed her back against the wall, spearing his tongue into her mouth. He slid his hands down her spine and cupped her bottom, feeling the smooth skin beneath her thin chemise.

"Ah, Maggie," he said, breaking the kiss, surprised at the harsh rasp of his own voice. "You are so sweet."

He pulled her tight against his erection and groaned at the staggering sensation of her feminine cleft cradling him.

She pushed his coat from his shoulders, and Tom was grateful for the foresight that had caused him to unfasten his waistcoat, and leave his cravat in the carriage. She opened the buttons of his shirt, and pulled it from his trews. But before she could pull it over his head, he started on the combs in her hair.

He turned her around so that her back was to him as he loosened her hair, letting it fall in exquisitely feminine waves to her shoulders, the scent of roses floating all around them. "So soft," he said, slipping one small sleeve down, giving him space to kiss her bare shoulder. Whispering light kisses up to the crook of her neck, he moved one hand to her abdomen and pulled her back against him. He felt the fullness of her breast above his hand, but he had no intention of going too fast.

He eased her hips back against his hard thickness and shuddered with her exquisite femininity. Maggie reached back and bracketed his hips with her hands, and Tom felt as though he would come out of his skin.

He swept her into his arms and sat down on a chair near the bed, keeping her on his lap. The firelight glowed softly on her face and he cupped her cheek as he leaned forward and kissed her mouth. She responded with the same incredible ardor he'd experienced every other time he'd kissed her, though this time he felt her tugging his shirt up over his back.

Tom broke the kiss and helped her, more than anxious to yank it over his head and have it gone. She put her hands on his bare chest near his collarbones and inched them down. "Aye. That's it—touch me."

Her touch was delicate, seeking, examining him tentatively, as though she had never touched a man's chest before. Her fingers slid through the dark, wiry hair, and when she brushed his nipples with her fingertips, the awesome sensation shot directly to his groin and he groaned.

"Oh!" she whispered, drawing her hand away.

He captured it and put it back. "More," he growled, aroused beyond belief by her naïve explorations.

She resumed her gentle torture, then made it worse by leaning forward to kiss one of his nipples. She swirled her tongue over it while caressing the other with her fingertips. When she sucked it into her mouth, Tom's cock grew, aching to be inside her.

He lifted her chin and caught her lips with his own as he pulled the ribbon at the front of her chemise, loosening it so that the skimpy garment slipped down her arms. The fragile fabric caught on the tips of her breasts, and Tom nudged it down, baring her breasts. He brushed his fingertips across one pebbling nipple, then palmed her breast in his hand.

The sensual touch startled her, and Tom wondered if it was possible that she had never felt the kind of sensations he was creating now. It made him feel far more powerful than it should, but he was grateful to her negligent husband. Being the first to show her carnal pleasure was far beyond erotic. Tom could not imagine being harder or more impatient to make love to a woman.

Maggie grabbed hold of his shoulders and sighed, letting her head drop slightly back while he toyed with her breasts. He dipped his head down and pressed an openmouthed kiss to the rapid pulse in her throat, then progressed upward, finally taking her lips with his in a light kiss that quickly deepened.

As their tongues tangled, Tom felt Maggie's hands on him, sliding down, exploring again. When she reached the waist of his trews and touched him through the heavy cloth, Tom took control and unfastened the placket. He drew out his hard flesh and took her hand, wrapping her fingers around him.

Her intimate touch was breathtaking. She ran her fingers lightly over the tip, then down the shaft, holding him loosely and stroking gently at first, then with a tighter grip. She progressed to a faster stroke that made Tom feel as though he might explode.

When he could take no more, he stood, setting Maggie on her feet before him. She watched with avid interest as he pulled off his boots and stepped out of his trews. He started on her chemise, but it caught on her hips, and Tom slid his finger between the cloth and her skin. Maggie grabbed his hand, seeming reluctant to bare herself before him.

"Naked, Maggie," he whispered. "Let me see you."

"But I'm not— My pregnancies . . ."

"Made you the most enticing woman I've ever known."

He dropped down to one knee and pressed his face to her abdomen, easing the chemise down, slowly exposing her feminine mound. He skated his fingers across the hair at the crux of her legs, then down her thighs as the gown fell to the floor. He pressed a kiss to the soft skin of her belly, then lower. He skimmed his hands back up her legs, compelling her to open for him.

"Christ, you are beautiful."

"What are you— Oh, God."

He slid one finger across the sweet feminine notch between her legs and touched the center of her pleasure. Then he leaned forward and pressed a kiss to the spot, and licked it with his tongue.

"Thomas!"

She grabbed his head, but did not push him away. He cupped her buttocks and sucked her, then stroked her with his lips and tongue. He looked up at her as he pleasured her, past her smooth torso and her full, enticing breasts, all the way up to her eyes, watching him with wonder.

His cockstand became almost painful, and when she suddenly stiffened and gave out a soft cry, Tom nearly climaxed himself. He managed to keep up his sensual assault until her trembling slowed, and he kissed his way up to her breasts, then fondled her nipples until she came again.

As he rose to his full height, Maggie pressed herself against him, as if to shield her body from any further caresses. "Aye, it's nearly too much," he said quietly. "But there is more."

Tom felt her trembling, so he wrapped her in his arms and kissed her. "Don't be nervous."

"I-I'm not."

No, she wasn't nervous. She was in a full panic. No one had ever touched or kissed her so intimately. The pleasure he gave had been entirely absent throughout her marriage. And she feared she would never be able to please him in return.

Maggie felt as though she was floating in a sea of absolute sensation, and she couldn't even tell which way was north. She should have known Thomas's lovemaking would not resemble Julian's in the least. Yet she hadn't known the two experiences would be worlds apart, that with Thomas, it would not include any part of lying flat on her back and waiting for him to do what he'd come for.

Once again, she felt like that other woman who'd put the candle in the window. Someone bold and confident, who could ask her lover for instruction.

"I don't know what to do," she whispered.

"There's no recipe, Maggie. Do whatever comes to you."

"But I—I—"

He kissed the corner of her jaw and she sighed, her eyes drifting closed. "There are no mistakes in the bedchamber, sweetheart."

She slipped her fingers up his chest and around to the back of his neck. Rising onto the tips of her toes, she drew him down for her kiss. He swept his hands down to her bottom, pulling her flush against the hard ridge of his erection.

"Touch me," he said.

"You cannot imagine how much I want to."

His breath caught at her words, and she realized she'd said them aloud. And yet she was not embarrassed. She was glad he knew how she felt.

She created a fraction of space between them and lowered her hands down to his waist where his erection strained against her, hard and hot, impatient for her touch. There was a small bead of moisture at the tip, and Maggie covered it with her palm, then spread her fingers down its length, encircling him firmly.

"That's it, love. Aye, I've lived for your touch these past few days."

She stroked him, discovering which caresses made him groan with pleasure, learning every inch of him.

"Lower, Maggie. Cup me."

He kissed her madly as she felt the sacs beneath his shaft, and used both hands on him, one to fondle him, the other to stroke his erection.

He suddenly broke their kiss and lifted her into his arms. Taking her to the bed, he set her down on the soft mattress and stretched out over her. Maggie felt an instant of panic, and fought against the reticence she'd felt with Julian. She opened for Thomas.

"Open your eyes, sweetheart."

She wasn't aware that she'd squeezed them shut.

"Look at me when I come into you."

He held himself up with one thickly muscled arm, and eased her legs apart. Maggie slipped her hands around his neck and held on as he entered her all at once.

It was not uncomfortable at all. In fact, it felt nothing like the act she'd suffered through with Julian.

He started to move, the rhythm of his body slow and languid at first. Pleasure built inside her as he increased the pace, starting in her womb and extending outward. She wrapped her legs around his waist and angled her bottom to maximize contact with his body with every stroke.

"Christ, yes!" he rasped.

The sensations in her womb suddenly flashed in a tight surge that was beyond anything she'd felt before. Her muscles tightened and her womb quivered with a fierce intensity that took her well past simple pleasure. It was sheer ecstasy, but in the midst of her contractions, Thomas withdrew abruptly, spilling his seed on her stomach.

Her body quaked for want of his. She felt bereft when he pulled away, even though he still lay between her legs. He reached across her and found a cloth to wipe his seed from her belly, then rolled to his side, pulling her with him.

His heart beat rapidly against her chest, and Maggie took a tremulous breath while her own heart slowed. He smoothed her hair from her forehead and gathered the uncontrolled mass of hair at the back of her head while he kissed her so gently Maggie could scarcely believe the tumult they had experienced only moments before.

She closed her eyes and took a long breath as reality struck her. She'd taken a lover, one who hadn't seemed to notice, or care about, the thick scarring on her thigh. He'd passed his hands over every inch of her legs and hardly even paused at the site of her old fracture. He hadn't noticed the silvery marks that remained after the birth of her children, and when he'd taken down her hair, he'd touched it as though it were made of coppery silk. He'd kissed her so intimately it had taken all the strength from her legs.

He thought she was enticing.

She hugged him close. "What's this?" she asked, feeling a smooth ridge of skin on his back.

"Nothing. An accident when I was a child," he said quietly. "Do you think Kimbridge is aware that you will not be taking a ride with him tomorrow?"

"Please don't remind me."

He pulled her even closer. "Come out to my estate tomorrow."

"With the children?"

"Not this time," he replied. "I want you all to myself."

Her heart warmed, and she was afraid it would soon be in danger of breaking. As Victoria had said, paramours were meant to be temporary.

Maggie could not allow herself to think of that now, not when he slid his leg up between hers, pressing against the spot that ached for his touch. "What about all the people you mentioned before? Your staff at Delamere House."

"I have a much better plan now." He gathered her close, tucking her head under his chin. "I will come for you at three."

Chapter 10

Tom returned to Delamere House before dawn, aware that he could not spend his entire day awaiting the moment he could collect Maggie and take her out to the huntsman's cottage. Much as he wanted to.

The memory of her touch was burned into his brain. She'd started as a trusting pupil, and quickly become an avid student who mastered every technique to drive him wild. She'd responded to his caresses as though she'd never been touched before, and her arousal had fired his own.

He wanted her still.

It was a perfect morning for a ride, cool, but sunny, and it reminded him of his days as a boy at Lockhaven Stables. Life had seemed so simple then, his future assured and comfortable. And then he'd encountered Shefford and Blackmore.

It was still early. Tom changed clothes, then left the house and went alone to the stable where he saddled his mare. He missed the freedom of his vast acres in New York, where there were no expectations of him and no pretense to maintain. If all went well, he'd return there with his parents and sister. It was only a matter of weeks.

He mounted Marcaida and headed east at a slow trot, watching as the sun's rays inched up through the trees. He hoped the ride would help him to set aside his thoughts of Maggie so he could consider the previous night's encounter with Foveaux. The commandant had never before figured into Tom's plans for revenge, but his presence in London presented a challenge and an opportunity Tom could not ignore.

The man had done well, having been promoted to the rank of general. Tom knew Foveaux had owned property in New South Wales, and it seemed he had some fair amount of money at this stage of his life. He and his wife looked prosperous, if not seriously wealthy.

Tom didn't know if it would be possible to discredit him and take his commission from him, but he could take his wealth. That would give Tom only a fraction of the satisfaction he wanted, and it would be worthwhile only if Foveaux knew that it was the ex-convict Thomas Thorne who had done the damage to him.

He considered what to do as he kept riding, finding himself heading more south than east, toward Town.

And yet he could not arrive in Hanover Square just yet. Nor could he haul Maggie onto the back of his horse and ride away with her. Instead, he went to Limmer's Hotel, where he broke his fast while reading the sporting journals, and listening to gossip about horses. He paid close attention, learning all that he could about Arrendo's competition.

"Throw it to me again, Mama!" Zachary called as he backed away from Maggie, across the lawn. The horse riders were out in force in the park, as were a number of fashionable ladies, casually strolling with their parasols up, holding the arms of their escorts. Maggie tried not to miss her own escort, the man whose touch had caused rivers of pure heaven to flow through her veins. She could wait the few hours before she would see him again without splintering into mad bits of anticipation.

Only because she had to.

Besides, her children needed her attention, and their jaunt to the park helped to calm her nerves.

Maggie tossed the ball and her son almost caught it. She laughed as he lunged and missed, then ran to recover it.

"That boy has an overabundance of energy," said Nurse Hawkins.

Maggie just smiled, her body still sparkling with a deep satisfaction that was unlike anything she'd ever known, coupled with a contradictory eagerness to repeat everything she'd shared with Thomas. Even now, she could feel his lips upon her shoulder, her breast, and even down *there*, where he'd known exactly how to touch her, how to bring her to climax, again and again.

Maggie understood now that Julian's lovemaking had been cursory. He had hurried through it as nothing more than a perfunctory duty.

Perhaps it was her own fault that she hadn't figured out how to bring forth the same kind of passion with her husband as she had with Thomas. Yet she had not known what to do.

And Julian had never bothered to show her. Why would he, when he could experience passion with women of his own choosing, and merely take care of his obligation with the plain, naïve wife he'd married.

She would not brood over it now, nor could she dwell on the questions that had arisen the moment she'd awakened alone. She was entirely unaware of the conventions of her new situation, and found herself unable to stop thinking about the love affair that still caused tingles of desire to resonate through her. The quiet, predictable life she'd enjoyed in the country had changed, irrevocably.

She didn't believe she could ever go back to the existence she'd known before Thomas. She was very different from the woman who'd come away from Cambridgeshire with her children only a few days before, and she needed to acquire some sophistication. Obviously, a widow in her position could have no expectations of the man in her bed—nothing beyond the night's pleasure. Thomas had made her no promises, nor had Maggie asked for any. And she knew he would leave her behind one day.

The thought of it made her feel more than a little melancholic, but she gave herself a firm reminder that she had no claims on him. He was her paramour. She could not think the way she'd done as a young wife with a husband, with prospects for the future. This was entirely different. She and Thomas had followed no customary courtship, and he could not have made his desires more plain. Maggie needed to reconcile herself to the knowledge that there was no future for them, nothing beyond the next few weeks.

If that.

Desultorily, she tossed the ball to Zachary again. Her situation was so very different now than when she'd married Julian. And now that her husband was gone, she did not trust Shefford to take care of her family, not when he'd made such a mess of Blackmore Manor and all of Julian's holdings. Which left it to Maggie to manage things. She had much to do in order to salvage and hold on to whatever she could of Zachary's birthright.

It was perfectly clear that Shefford intended to manipulate her into doing his wishes, whether that be marrying Mr. Kimbridge, or wheedling information—and funds—from Thomas. Maggie intended to do neither. She was going deal with her troubles herself, and keep the caricatures for Mr. Brown and her resulting income a secret. No one would ever need know of her employment or her liaison with Thomas.

It was no one's concern but her own, and she could not bear to think of what would happen to her reputation if either secret was discovered.

At least Thomas planned to stay in London long enough to race Shefford's horses, which gave them at least four weeks, but she did not know what he intended to do after that. Perhaps his business with the government would be completed by then and he would return to his home.

Maggie pressed a hand to her chest. She had children to raise, an estate to manage, and debts to pay. When Thomas left, their affair would be over and she would be left alone, just as she'd been for the past eight years.

Even so, she'd been little more than a green girl up until a week ago, when she'd opened her eyes and realized that all was not well. Never again would she fool herself into believing what she hoped was true.

"Zachary, let me tuck in your shirt," she called, aware of the way he must appear to the fashionable couples who strolled by—an ill-bred boy from the country.

"Catch me, Mama!" He ran to the low branch of a tree where he jumped up and hung by his hands. He quickly swung his legs up, giving the impression of a wild animal on a spit. He could not be more indecorous.

Luckily, Nurse Hawkins hurried over to retrieve him, but not before two supremely fashionable ladies walked past, looking down their noses at their small, unruly party. They said nothing as they passed, but the flame-haired one glared at Maggie before moving away.

"Er, my lady . . ." Hawkins said quietly. "Isn't that . . . ?"

Maggie swallowed back the hurt she felt at her sister's obvious snub. No matter how often it happened, it still stung. "Yes, it is. My sister Charlotte." The one who believed she'd been most injured by Maggie's supposed recklessness. If not for Maggie's loud and horrified revelation of Chatterton's perversion, Charlotte would be a duchess today.

A vastly unhappy one, no doubt, considering where her husband's interests would lie—but she would be a duchess, nonetheless.

Maggie could not meet Nurse Hawkins's gaze just then, but turned away from the walk to pick up Lily, who was perfectly behaved, as always. She hurried toward Zachary, taking his grubby hand in hers. She would speak to him later about proper park behavior. "Come on, let's go to the pond. I'm sure there will be some ducks to chase."

After twenty years, her family still held her responsible for Chatterton's assault, as though *she* had been the one who'd instigated his horrible behavior. She'd been unfairly punished for exposing him for what he was, and blamed for his subsequent despair and suicide.

She'd felt responsible for years, and it was only after her experience in the marital bed that she understood how truly monstrous Chatterton had been. And what he'd intended to do to her that afternoon in the deserted nursery. Something had been dreadfully wrong with the man to behave in

such a manner, cousin or not. Charlotte's fiancé
. . . or not.

Her sisters' rejection no longer mattered. They'd
all managed to acquire decent husbands, in spite of
the Chatterton affair. Maggie took a deep breath
and allowed herself to feel cleansed of their vitriol.
She would observe the proprieties with her mother
and siblings, but nothing more.

Maggie and Hawkins followed Zachary as he
ran in the direction of the duck pond, and Maggie
called to him to wait before crossing the bridle path.
He turned and looked at her as impatiently as only
a five-year-old could do, but then his expression
changed, and he broke into a broad smile.

"Thorne!" he shouted.

At that, Zachary came running toward Maggie,
veering past her to greet the horseman who was
approaching from the direction of Town.

Her heart fluttered at the sight of her prince,
dismounting to capture a speeding Zachary in his
arms. "Hello, young man."

The sound of his voice sent waves of anticipation through Maggie, and she forced a composure
she did not feel. Her sisters might think little of
her, but that was not true of Thomas. He made her
feel precious and unique.

He came toward her, carrying Zachary and
leading his horse.

"Mama, it's Thorne!" Zac turned to the man
who held him. "Did you come to see us?"

"Of course," Thomas said, though Maggie was
sure that was not true. He was a man of many

responsibilities and she was only a diversion, no matter how precious he made her feel. "Who else would I want to see?" He'd given no indication that he'd intended to return before three o'clock, and he couldn't have known they were coming to the park. Maggie had not even known it until an hour ago.

She reminded herself that she had no right to wonder whether he'd returned to Delamere House after leaving her bed, or if he'd had appointments in Town. Who he met and what he did were not her business. A mistress would never ask.

Zachary ran ahead. "We're going to see the ducks!"

"I'll just make sure he doesn't get into trouble, shall I?" Nurse Hawkins scooped up Lily into her arms and hurried to catch up to Zac.

Maggie's skin prickled with awareness and her chest filled with excitement at the sight of him. His gaze was warm, and held the secret knowledge of the intimate hours they'd spent together. Maggie shivered with the memory of the wanton and altogether magnificent kisses they'd shared, and felt slightly breathless with expectations of the afternoon they would spend together.

Thomas fell into step beside her as though he belonged there, keeping a proper distance between them. And yet his eyes held hers as they walked.

She looked away, afraid her own eyes showed too much. She *really* needed to cultivate some sophistication. Surely a mistress would know how to mask her emotions.

"Zachary is very happy to see you," Maggie said in an attempt to lighten the moment.

"Maggie," Thomas said, his voice low and seductive. "I can still taste you."

Her breath caught.

"I want more."

Arousal coursed through her, making her feel warm all over, and not a little shaky. Her stays pinched, and the cloth of her chemise felt rough against her skin. She forced herself to contain what she felt, for they were in a public place, and there was nowhere they could go to assuage their desires.

"You should not say such things."

"That doesn't change the truth of it."

Maggie swallowed and kept walking, unsure how she could keep going without touching him, without feeling his lips on hers. She looked for a secluded area—a copse of trees, or a hidden pavilion—any place where she could quench the fire he flamed inside her. And yet such recklessness was impossible. Purely ridiculous. She could no more make love with him in the park than she could fly.

They arrived at the pond where Nurse Hawkins held Lily safely in her arms and Zachary tossed bits of grass into the water toward the ducks. They quacked and swam closer, much to her son's delight.

But Maggie could hardly appreciate his glee while Thomas stood within reach, and she was unable to touch him. "What time is it?" she whispered.

A muscle in his jaw jumped. "Still morning," he rasped. He cleared his throat and took pity on them both, putting some distance between them as he strode toward Zac. "Have you ever made a paper boat?"

Zachary looked up at Thomas with curiosity. "A *paper* boat? How would it ever float?"

"Shall we see?" Thomas reached up to his saddle and brought down a newspaper.

Maggie sensed no interruption in the intensity of Thomas's attention, even though he was engaging her son. His voice held the promise of pleasures to come, and as his big, capable hands started to make folds in the newspaper, Maggie quaked at the knowledge of what those hands would soon be doing, with her.

"Hello there!" called a woman's voice, shattering the spellbinding moment.

Maggie turned to see Charlotte and her friend hurrying toward them, both of them breathing heavily, as though they'd had to run to catch up. The two women came abreast with Maggie. Charlotte put her hand on Maggie's sleeve, smiling at her as she'd never done before.

Charlotte turned her back to her friend and confronted Maggie, and her smile fell from her face.

"What?" Maggie asked. Obviously something was amiss, or Charlotte would not have returned. "What is it?"

"Don't play the green girl with me, Margaret," she whispered.

"What do you mean? W-we just came out for a bit of exercise."

"I can see that, of course," Charlotte retorted loud enough for her companion to hear. Her tone was superficially polite, yet her words were not quite civil.

Maggie glanced at Charlotte's friend, and took note of the sparkle in her eyes and her excited demeanor. Her stomach dropped as she comprehended Charlotte's unexpected return.

She said nothing to Charlotte, but walked toward Thomas, certain that her sister would be right behind her. "Prince Thomas, may I present my sister Charlotte, Baroness of Aughton. I'm afraid I don't know your companion, Charlotte."

Charlotte curtseyed deeply, smiling as attractively as possible, then introduced her friend. When the formalities were completed, Charlotte deftly slipped her hand through the crook of Thomas's elbow and started to maneuver him away from Maggie. "It's such a pleasure to make your acquaintance, Your Highness. I cannot believe this is the first we've met!"

"I have not been in Town long, my lady."

"My husband has many connections in the foreign office and is anxious to meet you."

Maggie stood motionless—and powerless—as her sister drew Thomas away.

"I am sure we will encounter each other one of these days, then," Thomas said to Charlotte.

"Lord Aughton is at home at the moment and I'm sure you would enjoy a visit to—"

Thomas extricated himself from Charlotte's grasp and returned to Maggie's side. When he placed his hand at the small of her back and steered her toward the children, she felt as though her soul had swelled and was burning a little hotter.

He turned back to give a quick glance in Charlotte's direction. "I don't believe so, my lady. It was a pleasure to meet both of you, but I've made a promise here . . ."

"But Aughton House is so close, and my husband—"

Thomas crouched down at the water's edge, ignoring Charlotte's entreaty as he picked up the newspaper and started making Zac's boat. "Go and find a long stick, Zachary."

While Charlotte stood looking stunned by Thomas's rebuff, he finished making a series of complicated folds in the newspaper. Maggie glanced up at her sister and was taken aback by her wrathful glower. It was obvious that she intended to use Thomas to some personal end, perhaps not quite as Shefford did, but the thought of it made Maggie queasy anyway.

But at least her sister could have no doubt that her conversation with the prince was over.

Zachary returned, and Thomas set the boat into the water, showing her son how to push it with the stick while he stayed far enough away from the water's edge to remain safe. As Charlotte and her friend made a show of taking their leave of the prince, Maggie felt grateful for her children, for the two uncomplicated young souls who wanted nothing but her love and affection.

Lily clamored for Nurse Hawkins to let her down, and when she ran to Thomas, he clasped her against him to keep her from getting too close to the water. He spoke softly to her and she giggled, then squealed happily when the ducks surrounded the boat. He sat down in the grass near the pond and Lilly hugged his neck happily.

And, as Maggie watched her lover charm her children, the earth shifted under Maggie's feet.

Thomas hadn't expected to see Maggie in the park, but the sound of her voice and the sight of her sweetly smiling face had been more than captivating. His hands had itched to pull her into his arms, but social convention prohibited it, just as it forbade him from insulting Lady Charlotte to her face.

But he had come close. He had disliked her instantly, mentally categorizing her alongside her officious mother and unscrupulous stepbrother.

He had not missed the way Lady Aughton slighted her sister, and he felt a particular satisfaction in declining her invitation. It was a retaliation of sorts on Maggie's behalf for her sister's direct callousness. Charlotte could not have been more obvious in her desire to draw him away from Maggie, as though her sister was of no consequence.

Tom stood near Maggie and resisted touching the wisps of hair that curled so prettily near her ear. Somehow, he managed to restrain himself from taking her hand in his and pressing a kiss to its palm, from pulling her into his arms and feeling every one of her soft curves against him. He heard her shaky breath and knew she felt the same lust that tore at him now.

"Well," she said, her voice low and a little bit breathless. "You'd already made a fair impression on Zachary and Lily. But I believe it's sealed now."

"And what of you, Lady Margaret?"

"I believe you already know what I think of you."

His throat thickened and he clenched his teeth with frustration. With impatience. "Did I say three o'clock?"

She nodded.

"I could not have been so foolish. It's far too long to wait."

Maggie laughed. "Let's catch up to the children."

It was a reprieve they both needed. They walked to the far side of the pond, keeping their eyes on Zachary and Lily. The children laughed as they chased after the newspaper boat, squealing with pure delight.

Lily came to Tom to be lifted into his arms, and Zachary called to him, asking if they could have one more boat. This time, for his sister.

And Tom suddenly realized he had not enjoyed such a simple pleasure in years. The children's utter glee felt like a breath of fresh air gusting through his lungs, and lifted the burden of vengeance from his shoulders, if only for the moment.

Chapter 11

Tom had been loath to leave Maggie and the children, but Nate Beraza and Mark Saret would be waiting to report on their investigations.

He returned to Delamere House and joined Saret for lunch at the richly carved Italian mahogany table in the dining room, counting the hours until it was time to fetch the woman who occupied the majority of his thoughts.

"Where is Nate?"

"I haven't seen him yet this morning," Saret replied. "I'm sure he has a great deal to do."

Nate entered just then, and placed a folded newspaper on the table, turning it so that Tom could see the drawing in it. "Take a look at this."

"It's a very good likeness, isn't it?" Saret asked with a grin.

"Look at all those women around you," Nate said with a laugh. "This Redbush fellow has drawn their eyes to look like deer. Fawns. They're fawning."

Saret laughed aloud, and Tom could not suppress

a small smile. The artist had caught his likeness very well, and his satire possessed a clever bite.

He set the newspaper aside. "Have you learned anything about Foveaux?" he asked Nate.

"*Foveaux?* What?" Saret exclaimed.

"Aye. Our old commandant, right there last night in Lord Sawbrooke's music room with us," Nate explained. "Tom spoke with him and the bastard never recognized him."

Saret's expression remained incredulous. "Is it true, Tom?"

Tom nodded. The meeting seemed like ages ago. He hadn't given Foveaux more than a fleeting thought since the night he'd spent with Maggie.

A prickle of pure desire crept up his back at the thought of her lying naked and sound asleep under her thick, woolen blanket. He'd left reluctantly after touching his lips to that sweet spot where her neck met her shoulder. She'd stirred, but not awoken, for it had been exceedingly late when they'd fallen asleep, after their thirst for each other had finally been slaked.

But not completely. Their chance encounter in the park made it clear he'd come nowhere near to having his fill of her.

"Tom?"

He looked up and gathered his thoughts. "I don't think I was entirely unrecognized," he said to Saret. "But it seemed that Foveaux just couldn't reconcile his memory of the young, scrawny boy he'd known on Norfolk Island with the wealthy prince who stood before him last night."

And he hoped Foveaux's mind would never allow him to make the connection. At least, not until Tom had settled the score between them. Then, he wanted Foveaux to understand the full ramifications of his brutality in the penal colony.

Tom didn't understand how anyone could possibly believe his far-fetched story of Sabedoria, but he had counted on his vast wealth—along with the allure of cheap, high quality flax and an alliance with a rich nation in the South Seas—excusing a multitude of sins. He'd counted on the *haute ton* overlooking any shortcoming or discrepancy, as long as the perpetrator was rich enough. And he'd been right. No one had challenged the existence of Sabedoria, not even Foveaux, who'd spent many years in the vicinity where it was supposedly located. The ruse was successful purely because of the enormous wealth he and his men had flaunted since their arrival.

And yet one solid challenge could bring down their house of cards. Someone who'd known Tom or one of his men in years past could expose the charade. A word from Foveaux would not be taken lightly.

"*Foveaux*. I can't believe it," said Saret, who hadn't been with Tom and Nate on the island, but had experienced the commandant's cruel hospitality at Port Jackson. "After all these years! I thought he was killed in some mutiny."

Nate made a disparaging sound.

"The rumors were inflated," Tom said. "The

man was very much alive in Lord Sawbrooke's
house last night. And he's a general now."

Saret let out a long breath. "Will he say anything? What does this do to our plans?"

Tom suddenly wished he had not told Zachary to
call him Thorne, after the care they'd taken never
to use any of their real names. If anyone made the
connection with Tom's true surname, it would take
some explaining.

"We sting him along with the others," he said.
"See if we can relieve him of his commission. And
find out about his finances."

Saret's face brightened. "Aye. Brilliant!"

Tom gave a shake of his head. "This is a good
reminder that we need to be very careful. No slips
in our names or our story. We must use the utmost
care in searching out information, and when dealing
with the authorities. They are not complete fools."

"Right," Saret said gravely.

"Not to worry, Saret. Who would believe
Foveaux if he said he knew us, anyway?" Nate
laughed. "Even if he suspected, he didn't even
believe it himself."

"I hope you're right," Saret replied.

Nate turned to Tom. "I met up with Andrew
Harland last night," he said. "He had a few hours
off, and managed to get away from Shefford's
house without being noticed."

"Has he learned anything?"

"Shefford belongs to some club—they call it
the S.C.H. club, and Harland says the members
frequently meet in an abandoned building some-

where on the east end and get on with whatever they do."

"Which is . . . ?" Tom asked.

"Unknown. But Harland is going to make sure he is the footman who accompanies Shefford on S.C.H.'s next outing."

Tom's butler, an American ex-convict named Mickles, came into the dining room. He was a tall, dignified-looking fellow with white hair and a thin white mustache who had once actually served as a butler. He knew his duties and what needed to be done by the other servants—all sailors from Tom's ships—to keep the household running. And to keep it safe.

"A messenger just brought this, Your Highness," Mickles said, his words and manner in keeping with the role he played. He carried a salver with a sealed scroll on it, which he placed on the table beside Tom.

"Well, well, well, what have we here?" Nate asked, though they all had a fair idea that it must be a royal pronouncement. They'd seen nothing like it to date.

Tom broke the seal and removed the encircling golden ribbon, then unrolled it. He read it quickly, then passed it to Nate as he spoke to Saret. "It seems the prince regent wishes to host a state dinner in our honor."

Nate laughed as he read. "It will be in two weeks, when he returns from Bristol."

"Good Christ, could you ever have imagined?" Saret said.

Tom smiled, gratified that his plans were falling directly into place. Recognition by Prince George would give him the final touch of credibility. Once the regent recognized Tom as a fellow monarch, it would be difficult for any Englishman to rebuff his Sabedorian claims. Neither Foveaux nor anyone else would want to embarrass Prince George in such a way.

"We're to reply as soon as possible, and send a list with the names of our entourage on it."

"Add Lady Blackmore's name," Nate said to Thomas. "Then it will be clear that she is your—"

"I'll consider it," he said, cutting Nate off. It was exactly what he should do, take Maggie to Carlton House and expose her as his paramour. His whore. And yet the thought of it turned his stomach.

"Maybe we should get the regent to bet on the horse race," said Saret.

"No!" Nate exclaimed. "We'll get Shefford to bring him in. Can you just imagine the kind of disfavor Shefford would—"

"Too dangerous." Tom's tone brooked no argument. "Duping the regent is not part of the equation, no matter how well a huge royal loss would work to discredit Shefford. We do it the way we planned." It was that kind of overconfidence that could get them all hanged.

Nate accepted Tom's decision and turned to Saret. "What about the tobacco plot?"

"Shefford is in," Saret replied. "He fell for Roarke's scheme without hesitation."

"Excellent," Nate said. "His wager against Arrendo pushed him past his ready resources. What about his bank?"

Saret nodded. "I'm meeting Mr. Thatcham—of Thatcham's Bank—this afternoon. I'm hoping I'll find Blackmore funds there, because I haven't been able to learn much about them."

The thought of taking Blackmore funds gave Tom a distinctly raw sensation in the pit of his stomach, but it was part of the plan. He could not bring himself to change it, even though . . .

"We've still heard nothing from Salim and your family," said Saret. Tom had sent Sebastian Salim to Suffolk immediately on their arrival in England.

"He's only been gone five days," Nate said. "It will take some time to locate your people, especially if they've left Suffolk."

Tom knew that, of course. But he was anxious for his reunion with his parents and sister, though he steeled his heart against disappointment. Anything could have happened in seventeen years. His parents were much older now, and Jennie might have married and would no longer be a Thorne.

Tom had been raised to be an honest man, which made him more than a little uncomfortable with all his schemes and charades. But it was all necessary. The Sabedoria fiction was absolutely essential in order to take vengeance on the men who had wronged him and his family so grievously. He didn't think he would ever find peace without dealing with the fiends who'd come so close to destroying him.

He realized his emotions were raw. His night

with Maggie should have quelled his passions, and yet he felt even more restless than he had before bedding her. All his machinations had finally been put into motion, and he should feel a great deal more satisfaction than he did. But he found he could not concentrate on horse races, bank shares or tobacco smuggling.

He was preoccupied by thoughts of Maggie's tender expression as she watched Zachary and Lily at play, and even more by the innocent trust her children had shown him. He reminded himself on the ride back to Delamere House that he was allowing himself to be distracted by the woman who was a key component in his schemes. He could not allow himself to become sidetracked or to lose focus.

Tom left to go in search of Edward Ochoa, who'd had more contact than anyone with Judge Maynwaring. He found the American in the library, sitting beside a tall window, reading. Ochoa was generally a quiet man who kept to himself, but he was not aloof. Tom knew little of the man's history, only that he'd been a lawyer in Virginia, and convicted of some felony. But he fit the description of a dignified government minister, and was a valuable asset to the Sabedorian tale.

Tom could not fathom what Ochoa's offense might have been, for he seemed a fine and decent man. In need of funds, of course, or else he wouldn't have signed on for Tom's risky venture— one which would see them all hanged if they were exposed.

Ochoa looked up from his book when Tom entered the room.

"Thomas." He started to rise from his chair.

"Don't get up," Tom said. He joined the older man at the window and sat down in a nearby chair.

"You're wondering what I learned about Maynwaring," said Ochoa.

Tom gave him a slow nod. "Anything?"

"He is unmarried and owns a large house in Kensington, not far from here. He is the younger brother of the Earl of Gosdale, and inherited a substantial fortune from his father, the previous earl. He does not frequent gambling houses, or play the horses."

"No vices?"

"I didn't say that," Ochoa replied. "Only that we haven't found them yet."

"What were your impressions when you met him?"

"He's a righteous prig who believes he's the final word on jurisprudence," said Edward. "He is courteous to me only because of my position as a Sabedorian minister, and he cannot quite understand the Sabedorian social strata. He is a snob, and had he met me as a mere lawyer, he would not have given me the time of day."

"I don't remember him much. From my trial."

Ochoa shook his head. "It was a long time ago."

Tom looked out at the front drive and the sculpted lawns and shrubs. Meaningless accoutrements to his performance. He very much preferred the open lands of Thorne's Gate, and yet he had the oddest feeling that his estate was not quite complete. Perhaps when he took his parents there . . . "My father petitioned the court for mercy. Repeatedly. Maynwaring had no interest."

"He believed your accusers."

"Aye. The sons of peers. They wouldn't lie, would they?"

"What did you do to offend them?" Ochoa asked.

"It all happened so quickly," Tom said, frowning. "I'm not sure."

"They might have taken a dislike to your looks, but I would venture to guess they took exception to something you said or did."

Tom shrugged, thinking back to that monstrous day. "We'd gone to the house in Hanover Square to deliver the horses the previous Lord Shefford bought in Suffolk," he said. "I was a groom . . . of no significance whatsoever."

He'd been quiet and polite, just as his father had instructed, looking after Shefford's horses. He could not imagine how that would have offended the two boys.

"I never even saw Leighton's father, the marquess," he said, remembering the day. "But Leighton and Julian were in their riding gear, getting ready to go out."

"You were all of an age, I'd guess?"

Tom nodded. "I think Julian might have been a year younger. But yes. All about sixteen or seventeen."

It had been raining, and the courtyard and gardens were a soggy mess, with deep tracks and puddles. The two boys had shouted for grooms to clean the mud from their boots, and Tom remembered thinking they were a pair of inept clods if they couldn't take care of their own gear. But he remembered someone else . . .

"There was a crippled young girl." Tom struggled to recall what she looked like. "She came into the courtyard and stumbled. I happened to be close by and I caught her arm. Kept her from falling into the muddy carriage tracks."

Oh Christ. He could see her now, hardly more than a child in an ill-fitting gown, moving awkwardly toward the boys on a crutch when she tripped. *Maggie.*

"You touched her." Ochoa said it without any inflection, but as a statement of fact. "They couldn't allow that."

Tom stood and jabbed his fingers through his hair. He remembered her clearly now, her glorious hair falling out of its braids, her face slightly sunburned, her freckles dancing across her nose and cheeks. He'd thought she was sweet even then, and how exceedingly unfair it was that she was lame.

She had said little about her accident, and Tom hadn't realized how bad it must have been. He'd noticed the scar on her thigh, and he understood how amazing it was that she was able to walk as well as she did.

If Ochoa was right, then it was Tom's quick

reflexive action that had caused her brother and his friend to decide to take him down a notch. Considering the way her siblings treated her, Tom wondered if Shefford would have preferred to see her fall into the mud rather than allow a bumpkin from a horse farm to touch her.

"Well," said Ochoa, "it's no matter now. You'll do what needs to be done."

"Aye," Tom said, reeling from his sudden insight. Maggie had triggered everything. Norfolk Island, Port Jackson, the pirate slave ship. He swore under his breath.

"Maynwaring invited me to lunch with him today," said Ochoa. "We meet at one."

Somehow, Tom managed to reply. "Keep me apprised."

Mr. Brown laughed out loud when he saw the caricature of Lord Castlereagh. Maggie had put him at a desk with the Sabedorian prince, alongside a pair of dueling pistols and a bolt of flax.

"How clever," Mr. Brown had said, laughing, "to play on Castlereagh's propensity for dueling with important dignitaries. This will tickle our subscribers and—if I'm not mistaken—make you a very rich woman!"

Maggie sat back in her chair, more than pleased.

"Your first picture caused quite a stir," he said.

"That's very good for me, then."

The editor picked up Maggie's drawing and chuckled again. "The public has an insatiable curiosity about that Sabedorian," he said. "And this caricature with Castlereagh—ha!—absolutely priceless!"

"I hope it's not too—"

"Hel— Heavens, no! This is better than anything I'd hoped for, Lady Blackmore. Your drawings have an edge that go beyond mere satire. The public enjoys a good farce, and you are racking up *Gazette* sales with yours."

"Well, thank you, I think." She hadn't intended to make Thomas a farcical character, and now she wondered what he thought of the Redbush drawings. If he even saw them.

"Yes, yes, it's a compliment. Definitely. I understand they've had to go back and reprint that first caricature because sales were so brisk."

"Really?"

"This one will sell like hot muffins from a hawker's barrow on a cold day. Now that we know how popular these pictures are . . . well, we'll have a much larger number made up as prints for sale."

Perhaps Thomas did not look at the London papers. There was a good chance he did not know of the caricatures. Maggie felt slightly queasy at the thought of his reaction to her drawings.

"You've earned quite a tidy sum already, my lady," Mr. Brown said. He removed a folded, wrapped sheet of vellum from his desk, and when he handed it to Maggie, she realized it was her first payment for her work. "Keep the Sabedorian as your primary subject, and your . . .

ahem . . . financial difficulties will be a thing of the past."

Maggie put the all-important payment into her empty portfolio and stood, giving Mr. Brown a curt nod. She hoped she hadn't made Thomas an object of ridicule, for that had not been her intention. And she hoped that by placing Lord Castlereagh in the picture with him, she had not soured Castlereagh's, or any other important minister's willingness to deal with Thomas. She had not meant to thwart his mission in England.

"Can we expect another caricature from you next week, Lady Blackmore?"

"Yes. Yes, of course." Because there wasn't any other way to escape her debt, and the heft of the packet in her reticule was a sure enticement to do more.

She returned home and went into Julian's small study. Not that her husband had ever studied anything there, but a writing desk was there, and some paper and ink. She quickly penned a letter to Mr. Clements, asking him for a list of Julian's debts. And as long as she was writing, she asked what the procedure would be for naming a new trustee for Zachary's estate. Clearly, Shefford was not suited to the task.

She had just put her seal on the letter to the solicitor when Mathers came in with a note from her mother. Maggie's stomach clenched as she unsealed Beatrice's note and read the scathing message within.

"Is everything all right, my lady?" Mathers asked.

Maggie swallowed. "Yes, Mathers. Thank you."

"Is there any reply, ma'am?"

"No, that will be all. Thank you."

No doubt Charlotte had given their mother some perverse version of the encounter in the park, leaving out Charlotte's rude treatment of her youngest sister. But Maggie had no interest in correcting her sister's version of events, in spite of the repercussions she was sure to face from her family.

She was determined not to become embroiled in some petty family altercation and allow them to spoil her expectations of the afternoon she was going to spend with Thomas. Maggie had never felt such a breathless anticipation for anything before, and she suffered a tiny twinge of guilt that she had never been so anxious to see Julian.

Her attraction to Thomas had proved to be irresistible, and his reciprocation was beyond anything Maggie had ever experienced. His kiss was compelling, a simple touch of his hand made her yearn for more. It was amazing that she had not dissolved the first time he'd taken her in his arms. *Or perhaps she had*, she thought, her skin tingling at the memory of the intense interlude they'd shared in the carriage.

She felt a sudden chill and rubbed her arms, aware that any respectable woman would be appalled by her behavior. *She had taken a lover,* and did not think it was entirely due to her shock at Victoria's and Mr. Clement's revelations about Julian's affairs and what he'd done to their finances.

She stood abruptly, and went upstairs to her bedchamber. Standing in the doorway as she looked in, she could hardly believe all that had transpired the night before. She stepped into the room and skimmed one hand over the coverlet of the bed, aware that she would never lie in that bed again without remembering the hours she'd spent there with Thomas. She could not press her face to the pillows without recalling his scent, the rough texture of his hands, or the crisp rasp of his hair against her breasts.

She closed her eyes and shivered again, even though there was a fire in the grate and the room was comfortably warm.

The candle she'd put in her window was still there, and Maggie quickly removed it. Anyone might have noticed it, might have drawn some unsavory—but true—conclusions about its purpose.

Nurse Hawkins tapped at the open door, and Maggie dropped the candle on her dressing table.

"The children are in the nursery, having lunch," the nurse said. "And I decided to take this opportunity . . . Even though I understand I may be speaking out of turn—"

"What is it, Hawkins?" Maggie interjected.

"Well." She was at least ten years older than Maggie, and had been a solid, reassuring presence at Blackmore Manor ever since Zachary's birth. She'd always known what to do when someone was hurt or ill, and was completely dedicated to Maggie's children. Hawkins smoothed her skirts.

"I think you should know that Zachary is a perfectly normal little boy. And Lily might be a bit shy, but she will outgrow it."

"I had hoped so," Maggie said.

"Lady Aughton's attitude this afternoon . . ." Hawkins wrung her hands and her face colored with emotion. "My lady, I swear, it was all I could do to keep from slapping her right in her righteous—! Oh, I beg your pardon, ma'am."

Maggie laughed, for she could do so now. There would be no mirth later, when her mother confronted her, as she was sure Beatrice would do. "Why, Hawkins, I do believe you are showing somewhat more temper than usual."

"I am sorry I must admit to such base and violent feelings, my lady. But there is a reason that prince of yours turned his back on your sister and stayed with you and the children."

"Oh?" *That prince of hers?* Good lord, did everyone know?

"It's obvious he understands true character. And I'm glad he does. You deserve . . . well, pardon my saying, but you deserve a decent man who cares for you."

Maggie bit her lip. "Nurse Hawkins . . ."

The woman took a step back, holding up one hand. "I do apologize for putting my nose where it clearly does not belong. But my lady, it's very pleasing to see you smile again."

Hawkins left the room and Maggie sat down in the chair where Thomas had made love to her. The nurse was mistaken if she thought he cared for her. Maggie was his paramour, and their arrangement was nothing more than a temporary liaison that would last only as long as Thomas remained in London.

Or it burned itself out.

Maggie knew her reputation would suffer badly if anyone learned either of her secrets. But she wanted to touch Thomas, wanted to feel his hands and lips on her body, and return the shuddering pleasure he'd given her. She longed for him to hold her in his arms, to feel the heat and security of his embrace.

And it was surprising how much she enjoyed the potency of earning her own funds. Of using her small talent to get her family out of debt. It was almost as exhilarating as the feelings that came over her when Thomas held her.

Maggie realized she had to think of the consequences of her actions. There could be repercussions for Lily and Zachary. If anyone learned what she was doing—on either front—it would be her children who suffered. She knew better than to count on her family to rally around her. If her activities were somehow exposed, she would have to retreat to Cambridgeshire and try to live down her shame.

She closed her eyes and wished she knew what to do. She was afraid she'd already fallen partway in love with Thomas. No one had ever stood with her against her sisters, and she feared she was hopeless when he'd taken over with her children, even winning over her shy little daughter.

Maggie was so new to all this, to the shivery sensations in all the hidden parts of her body that made it impossible to think. She glanced toward the mirror and saw the same awkward girl she'd been at the time of her marriage to Julian. And yet so very much had changed. She'd lived a great deal of her life in the previous eight years, bearing two children and learning a lady's duties to her husband's tenants. And yet she felt she'd lived more in the past few days than during her entire marriage to Julian.

It wasn't just Thomas. Maggie wished she'd become wiser over the years, but she knew she'd been a naïve fool. Since her return to London, she'd had to grow up quickly and had to set aside a number of her prior beliefs. Her husband had betrayed her in every possible way.

Her family did not even signify.

And now she was embarking upon a sensuous adventure that could have serious consequences for herself and her children. She knew that a prudent woman would send a message to Thomas at Delamere House and decline their rendezvous.

But it wasn't until his carriage arrived that she made her decision.

Chapter 12

Tom was glad to see that his champion horse was limber and moving well, in spite of their weeks at sea. But he had stayed longer than he intended in the paddock with Arrendo and the horse trainer. He realized it was nearly time for Maggie to arrive, and he had not yet washed off the smell of the stable. He summoned one of his men to have a bath prepared for him at the huntsman's cottage and left the paddock soon thereafter.

He was just coming off the path in the woods toward the cottage when he saw Maggie stepping out of his carriage with a hand from Oliver Garay. The driver walked to the door of the cottage with her, pushed open the door, tipped his hat to her, then left her there. Garay drove away, and Maggie remained standing under the lintel, looking uncertain.

She hadn't seen the cottage before, and probably wondered where Garay had brought her and why Thomas hadn't come to escort her himself. He started walking toward her, thinking his timing ought to have been better. He should have been inside, waiting for her.

Even better, he'd have preferred to go down to London for her himself. And yet his earlier discussion with Nate had made him realize he needed to establish some boundaries. Lady Blackmore had far too easily become a fever in his blood. She was an obsession he could not afford. He needed to put some distance between them.

Enjoy her, but set her aside when it was time.

She turned as he approached and he felt the power of her gaze at the base of his breastbone. The corners of her mouth turned up slightly, and Tom picked up his gait. His coat billowed out behind him as he hurried toward her, and she stepped away from the door.

In spite of Nate's reminders, Tom caught Maggie up in his arms, and she did not seem to mind that he smelled of leather and horse and earth. She took his kiss greedily, as though she'd been waiting for it since the moment they'd parted in the park, and Tom trembled with the need to be inside her.

Her shy eagerness was an aphrodisiac that cut directly to his straining cock.

Tom pulled away and took her hand, leading her into the cottage. There was not much light inside, but he made his way unerringly to the staircase, keeping Maggie in tow. Dropping his coat on the floor, he started up the stairs, unbuttoning his shirt and pulling it over his head as they climbed. He picked her up and carried her to the top of the steps, smiling at the sound of her delighted squeal.

The door of the master bedchamber was ajar, and through it, Tom saw a flickering light. He carried Maggie inside, and eased her down to her feet near the fireplace, beside the tub of steaming water. Pressing a line of kisses to her jaw and neck, he slipped her coat from her shoulders, then cupped her face in his hands and took her mouth with his. He sucked her tongue inside, tasting her, breathing in her roses, pressing his erection against the softness of her body.

He broke away long enough to start on the buttons of her bodice. "I apologize for not coming for you myself," he said, nibbling the sweet spot just below her ear.

She slid her hands up his bare chest and Tom shivered at the exquisite sensation of her touch.

"You are so hard," she said, and then blushed at his quick grin.

"Aye. For you." He took one of her hands and placed it on the hard length that had been aching with need since the moment he'd left her.

He sat down on the bed and pulled her between his legs. A haze of arousal softened her eyes, and he watched her while he lowered her bodice and dispensed with her gown. Then he turned her around and started to work on her laces. He pressed a kiss to the delicate indentation of her spine, then closed his eyes and took a deep breath to keep from rushing this. They had all afternoon and at least part of the evening to spend together. Tom intended to enjoy every hour.

"Tell me what to do," she said, turning to face him.

Tom pulled the corset over her head and absently tossed it to the floor, his attention entirely focused on her. On sweet Maggie in a thin chemise that barely concealed her pretty breasts and the shadow between her legs. Her arms were dappled with freckles and Tom skimmed one finger from her wrist to her shoulder. With his light touch, her nipples pebbled through the cloth of the thin linen, and the air suddenly felt too thick for him to breathe.

"Just touch me," he said. At least, he thought he might have said it aloud, but it was entirely possible that his voice had not functioned.

Maggie scraped her hands down his chest and stopped at his nipples, then slid down to her knees so that her mouth was level with his chest. She circled one hard nipple with her tongue while teasing the other with her fingers.

Then she moved lower.

She looked up at him uncertainly, then bit her lower lip and reached for the placket of his trews. Tom's breath caught when she unfastened it and freed his cock into her cool hands.

"Aye, lass." It was all he could do to keep from exploding right then, yet he should be able to withstand far more of her sensual touch.

"Maggie, wait." His voice scraped across his throat.

He stood, moving past Maggie, pulled off his boots and shoved off his trews. He stepped into the water that was still hot. Turning to face Maggie, he saw that her gaze had caught on his fierce erection.

"I smell of horses," he said taking the soap and spreading it across his chest, under his arms, and down to his erection.

He sat down in the water and Maggie came to him then. She reached into the tub and took over for him, sluicing water over his chest and running her slick hands over his skin, washing him.

His cock surged rigidly when she encircled it, and his heart seemed to stop in his chest when she slid her other hand underneath, gently stroking him.

Tom could not take much more. He rinsed off quickly, then came out of the tub, splashing water down the sides as he took Maggie into his arms. He felt hot all over, in spite of the dampness of his body. He speared his tongue into her mouth and she tilted her head as he deepened their kiss.

He slipped her chemise from her shoulders and when the damp garment fell to the floor, she stepped out of it. Tom lifted her into his arms and took her to the bed. Putting one knee on the mattress, he laid her on the blankets, but she pushed herself onto her knees and reached for him.

Her breasts swayed with her movement, and Tom could not resist cupping them in his hands. He bent to lick one of her nipples, and Maggie put her hands on his shoulders and pushed him onto his back on the bed. "Your turn."

She straddled him, resuming her attentions where she left off before his bath, stroking him gently, then bending to place a light kiss on the tip of his cock. Tom bucked in her hand when she swirled her tongue around the head and sucked him fully into her mouth. He grabbed fistfuls of the blanket beneath him as she became even bolder, licking and sucking, sliding him in and out of her mouth.

He'd never known anything as erotic as the sight of Maggie's full lips gliding over his cock, pleasuring him to the limit of his control. She pushed him to the very brink, but he had no wish to stop her.

She moaned and cupped her own breasts, and Tom almost came, watching her pleasure herself. That she was aroused by what she was doing to him was beyond anything in his experience.

He shifted suddenly, unable to take any more, and drew her upright to lower her onto his erection. Her legs bracketed his hips and her eyes met his as she moved above him, driving him toward the most volatile climax he'd ever known. His muscles quaked, and when she went still, tightening around him in spasms of pleasure, Tom exploded inside her.

He'd forgotten to withdraw from her at the last instant, but couldn't find the energy to care.

Maggie lay against Thomas, her head tucked under his chin, her breasts against his chest and one of his thighs resting between her legs. She wanted to know everything about him, and yet . . . It was not really her place to know.

Maggie felt his breath ruffling her hair, his big hand caressing her back, and wondered if her contentment in Thomas's arms was naïve or out of place. She admitted to being far too unsophisticated to understand men and their motivations.

Yet there'd been no question that Thomas had wanted her, and it seemed that he felt just as satisfied as she.

"You have barely any accent," she said in an attempt to keep it light, keep it simple. She was the man's mistress, and nothing more.

"Hmm . . ."

"What is your country like? Mr. Kimbridge said it's on the bottom of the world. What did he mean?"

His hand resumed its lazy circles across her back. "You've seen a globe—a spherical map of the world?"

Maggie nodded. Her stepfather had had one in his study. She'd been surprised to see how tiny England was, compared to all the other countries.

"If you think of the globe in halves," he said, "split horizontally through the center, Sabedoria lies in the lower half."

"It's a very long way from England, then." A mistress would not feel the same painful twinge in the region of her heart at the thought of the many miles that would soon be between them.

He said nothing for a moment. "It will take several months' travel to return to Sabedoria," he finally replied. He rolled her onto her back and settled himself over her, keeping one of her legs between his. He bent toward her and nuzzled her lips. "You'll be pleased to know your questions are along the same lines as those of your esteemed foreign minister, Lord Castlereagh."

"Perhaps I should be a government minister," she said in an attempt at a jest. The last thing she wanted to think about was Thomas returning to his country.

"Aye," he growled as he moved down her body. "You would dazzle your adversaries with your pretty smile."

He took one of her nipples into his mouth and rolled his tongue around it while he slid his hand down to the crease of her thigh.

Maggie arched her back. "M-my smile?" she squeaked.

He teased her other nipple with his forefinger and thumb, and then started to move downward. He made a hot trail to her navel with his lips, and Maggie took his head in her hands as he moved farther south. She opened for him, whimpering as he played with her, using his tongue.

The earth shifted beneath her as Thomas sucked and licked, then added the touch of his hand to his ministrations. Maggie felt her muscles flex and her womb tighten, and Thomas suddenly raised himself up. Gathering her into his arms, he thrust inside her. He held her close as he moved, his rhythm intense and fast. Maggie's climax came upon her immediately, and every subsequent move that Thomas made took her to greater heights.

He took her mouth in a wild, savage kiss that possessed her while taking a piece of him. She sucked his tongue hard and tightened her legs around his waist, and he suddenly erupted with a harsh groan, his muscles contracting in a tremulous rush of completion.

Maggie felt boneless as she eased her legs down, but Thomas pulled her onto her side and they lay facing each other, their hearts and breaths slowing. She gazed into his eyes as though she could see into his soul, and realized this was no way for a mistress to behave. He was going to be gone before long . . .

Or perhaps one day he would decide to take another mistress.

Maggie closed her eyes and pressed her face to his chest against the sudden pang of distress that filled her. Her breath caught as she fought to compose herself, quelling the foolish emotions that had no place in an affair.

"What is it?" he asked.

"Oh, I . . ." She had to lighten the moment. Even more, she needed to return to reality. "I'm surprised you don't have a social function to attend tonight."

"I do," he said, sliding out of her, but holding her close. "There is a ball somewhere or other. Later."

It had already grown quite late, dusk at least. Their only light came from the flickering of the dying fire. Maggie watched the solid thrum of Thomas's pulse in his throat and tried not to feel superfluous. She'd hardly been able to think of anything but their tryst all day, yet Thomas had been so busy he'd had to fit her in between whatever

activity had kept him from coming to Town for her
. . . and a ball somewhere or other.

What would a mistress do? Surely not lie about,
missing her lover before he'd even gone.

"I should go."

His pressed his hand against her back to hold
her close. "It's still early."

"It's gotten dark, Thomas." Maggie extricated
herself from his embrace and slid to the edge of the
bed. She needed to put some space between them,
and if it required running from him, so be it. "You
probably need to get ready."

"Not yet."

She took a deep shaky breath, turned, and gave
him a smile she did not feel. "Yes, *yet*. And I should
get back to my children."

He came up behind her and started to feather
kisses down her shoulder. Maggie closed her eyes
and fought the urge to slip back into the bed. She
could do this. She could muster the control necessary to leave now, while her heart was still intact.

"You are so anxious to leave?"

She shook her head. "Of course not, but you
have things to do. Important things, I'm sure."

"What if I asked you to stay?"

She forced a quiet laugh and tried not to think
about the months it was going to take him to get
back to Sabedoria. And the life that awaited him
there. "But you won't. You are needed elsewhere."

She slid down to her feet and reached for her chemise, discarded on the floor near the tub. Thomas
came right after her, taking the simple garment

from her hand. They stood still for a moment, and Maggie resisted the urge to cover herself with her hands. It was far too late for modesty, and his expression kept her from moving.

She couldn't allow him to mean more to her than an afternoon's diversion, an hour or two of pleasure. Exquisite though it may be. It was hardly prudent to have become as deeply involved as she was, but Maggie could barely think when he skimmed one finger down the side of her face, sending ripples of pure desire straight to her womb.

His green eyes were dark and guarded, and Maggie followed her impulse to take hold of his arms above the elbows. She raised up onto her toes, leaned in and kissed him hard, then pulled away, taking her chemise from his hand.

She pulled it over her head quickly, before she could change her mind, or Thomas could change it for her. She bent and picked up her corset, and dragged it on. But before she had a chance to begin struggling with the laces, he placed his hands on her shoulders and slid them down her arms. "Let me do it for you."

He moved her hair aside, and Maggie held her breath as he carefully laced her into her stays. She suppressed a shiver at his gentle touch, and fought to maintain the control she knew she needed. When he finished, he put on his trews and Maggie sat down to pull on her stockings.

It felt entirely foreign to dress in the presence of anyone but her maid. Not even Julian had seen her naked—had never wanted to, she supposed.

But there were advantages to sharing a dressing room. Maggie openly admired the exquisite definition of Thomas's shoulders and arms as he pulled on his boots and shirt, then jabbed his fingers through his hair. He did not seem pleased with her decision to take her leave, but neither did he seem inclined to argue.

Maggie wasn't sure whether to be grateful for that or not.

"We'd better hope that the English nobility doesn't shun us because of the newest caricature in *The Gazette*," said Nate as they exited the carriage on their way to the ball. Maggie had not mentioned that she would be attending the event, which made the trip to Town seem a waste of time. Tom's mood was foul and he snapped at Nate.

"What difference does it make?"

"So far, Redbush has poked some very good fun at a few important personages. And you know the English—they love a good joke, but don't like to be the brunt of one."

Tom had seen only one of the pictures, and it hadn't seemed so bad. "Don't worry about it. We've already made the connections we need. I will not be disappointed if I never have another meeting with any of the ministers."

There was only one person he was interested in seeing, but she had not agreed to meet him on the morrow. She'd smiled mysteriously as she dressed, then climbed into the carriage driven by Oliver Garay, and disappeared from sight with barely a word. Tom didn't know what had happened. While he lay with Maggie in his arms, his body simmering with the rarest possible contentment, she'd decided to slip away and take her leave of him. It made no sense at all.

They entered the house and split up after learning that Shefford was not in attendance. Which was fortunate, because if he'd been present, Tom might have decided to chuck all his plans and just shoot the bastard on sight.

"You look ever so serious, Your Highness," said the lively young daughter of some earl he couldn't name. He supposed her features would be considered perfect, and he saw that her gown and hair had been designed and arranged for absolute impact on potential suitors. And yet Tom found her far too angular, her personality much too brittle. She had no freckles, and her smile seemed well practiced and overly contrived.

"I beg your pardon, Miss—"

"*Lady* Rowena," she said with an admonishing smile, tapping his shirt front with her fan. "Your meetings with all those tedious ministers and such must be endlessly dull."

"Not at all," he replied. "There is a great deal to be accomplished between our two countries."

"Do you not dance tonight, Your Highness?" asked another of the young women who'd gathered around him.

Tom wondered where in hell Nate had gone, and why he wasn't rescuing him from all these toadying females.

"Not tonight, no." He offered no explanation, and ignored the dark looks shot in his direction by the mothers of these pampered sycophants.

He resisted the urge to ride into Hanover Square and go up to Maggie's bedchamber and demand to know what had happened between them earlier. There wasn't a woman in her right mind would want to hurry away from such bliss.

"Your Highness, it's a pleasure to see you again."

"Ranfield," he said, glad for the reprieve from the attentions of the tiresome coquettes who batted their lashes and their fans at him. "How do you do?"

He realized Maggie might have accompanied the earl and his wife to the tiresome ball. It was possible that she'd declined to mention it, thinking she would surprise him. He glanced around for some sight of her, but failed. He did not even see Lady Ranfield.

"I am very well," Ranfield said, then nodded toward a distinguished gentleman standing with a group of other men. "Have you met Lord Marsden?"

"I don't believe so."

"You'll want to meet him. He oversees the purchase of cloth for naval—"

"Yes, I would very much like to meet him," said Thomas. "Where is your wife, Ranfield? I don't see her."

"Ah, I am on my own tonight. My wife is preparing to go out to Richmond with our sons for a few days, to our country estate."

"I see."

"She prefers the freedom of the countryside, and since Richmond is so close to London, she is able to escape Town every now and then while Parliament is in session."

"How convenient."

But even as he spoke, he found it impossible to put Maggie from his mind, remembering that he'd heard her say the same thing to Kimbridge. She preferred the country.

Tom wondered what she would think of Thorne's Gate.

Startled by the thought, he had no chance to pursue it when Edward Ochoa approached him and drew him away to a deserted balcony.

"Saret has uncovered something, Tom," he said as they stepped outside. "It's about Maynwaring."

A shard of anticipation shot across Tom's shoulders. "Aye?"

"The judge frequents a particular sort of bawdy house."

"I'm not sure it's relevant, Ochoa. Why—"

"It's a molly house. The place is populated by young men."

"Men? You're saying Maynwaring is a . . . a *sodomite?*" Tom hissed.

"There is no doubt about it," said Ochoa. "Saret himself saw him go into the house this very afternoon."

Tom blew out a breath. It was beginning. He was about to reap the satisfaction he'd craved for so long. "It's illegal, isn't it?"

"Absolutely. The patrons keep it highly secret. Maynwaring will be destroyed when this comes out."

"Does Saret have a plan for that?"

Ochoa nodded. "Tonight. He's ready to bring a magistrate here, along with the witnesses from the house who have agreed to accuse him. With your approval, of course."

A public humiliation, then. It was no less than the man deserved for the cold injustice Tom and countless others had received at his hands. Tom gave him a nod. "Is Saret here?"

"No, but he's ready. I'll send one of our drivers for him."

Tom revised his decision to leave as soon as possible. He would stay and see Maynwaring's downfall. He and Ochoa returned to the ballroom, and no more than half an hour had passed when Ochoa came to him with the despised judge alongside him. "Your Highness," said Ochoa, "you remember His Honor Lord Justice Maynwaring?"

Thomas could not bring himself to smile in greeting. "Yes, of course."

"We had a very enlightening discussion on Sabedorian jurisprudence this noon," said Maynwaring.

"How does it compare with yours?" Tom asked.

The judge gave a superior shrug. "You Sabedorians are far too lenient. How will you ever master the criminal element without incarceration, without restitution?"

Thomas would not have dignified the question with his answer, except he needed to support Ochoa's efforts to keep the old bastard on the line.

"Perhaps you might give Mr. Ochoa a few pointers, sir."

Maynwaring laughed. "Of course! Always willing to use my vast experience to advise."

Tom had a difficult time resisting the urge to go outside and spit to clear away the bad taste in his mouth. The memory of his day in court returned, and Tom saw that Maynwaring hadn't changed much since he'd commuted Tom's death sentence to a mere seven years' transportation.

His Honor, the Lord Justice paled suddenly, and Tom turned to see a tall, somber man coming toward them, with two constables alongside him, and two younger men following. Maynwaring started to retreat, but Tom caught his arm. "Where are you going, Judge?"

Everyone nearby took note of the newcomers, and crowded around Tom and Maynwaring. Tom noticed beads of sweat suddenly dotting Maynwaring's forehead.

"Sir William," said the solemn fellow, clearly the magistrate. "A warrant has been sworn against you."

Tom's host barreled his way through the crowd and protested the interruption. "Preposterous! What is the charge?"

"Sodomy," said the magistrate, clearly and far louder than was strictly necessary. "And these two young gentlemen are the witnesses who've sworn against you."

All was quiet in Hanover Square the morning after Maggie's tryst with Thomas in the little cottage, until Shefford appeared shortly after breakfast to pressure her into seducing Thomas.

If only he knew.

"I have plans for your prince," he said.

"What plans? And he's not *my* prince, Shefford." No one knew that better than she.

"It's none of your concern. You just do your part and we'll have no more financial problems."

"We? You are having difficulties, too?"

"Again, not your concern, Margaret. I want to get out to those stables again, but I can't very well go to Delamere House uninvited. But *you* can."

"What makes you think I can do such a thing?" she asked.

"Because I know he stopped to visit with you in the park yesterday. He has taken a particular interest in you."

"He was only being friendly," Maggie retorted. "And he's a virtual stranger in Town. I'm one of the few people he knows." Clearly, if even Shefford knew about their encounter in the park, Charlotte had been busy. No doubt the entire family had heard her sister's version of what had transpired there. "And I'm sure he is not sitting about at Delamere House, waiting for guests to call."

"Why? What have you heard?" He never looked

more bullish than when an idea had hold of him. She remembered countless times when Shefford had badgered her and her sisters, and worst of all, Julian, into doing his bidding. Even Beatrice succumbed to his bullying more often than she should.

"Nothing. I've heard nothing, Shefford."

"But you could," he said, pacing the length of the drawing room. "He likes you. Which gives you the perfect opportunity to find out all sorts of things. Where he's investing his money. What his favorite horse's weakness is—"

"No." Absolutely not. She was through being manipulated by Shefford, done with caring what her mother and sisters thought of her. It was past time that she developed some backbone and stood up for herself. No one else was going to do so. "What I'd like to know is what you intend to do about Zachary's inheritance," she said. "You're his guardian. You should have been dealing with the mess Julian left us."

"What do you expect me to do?" he asked, obviously taken aback by her remark. "Julian is the one who put the estate into debt. Not—"

Mathers entered the room and handed Maggie a letter, but she did not look at it right away. She was angry, mostly with herself. If only she hadn't been so trusting, so incredibly stupid. "Shefford, you are Zachary's guardian and the trustee of the estate—"

"What, you expect *me* to pay for Julian's mistakes?"

Maggie didn't answer him as she glanced at the short note from Victoria. It was perfect. Just what she needed.

An escape.

"You'll have to go now, Shefford," she said, walking out of the drawing room.

"What do you mean by this, Margaret?" he called after her. "You can't just shove me out of your house."

"No thanks to you."

"What's *that* supposed to mean?"

"It means—it's my house for now, *no thanks to you!* Now see yourself out. The children and I are leaving Town for a few days."

Chapter 13

Ranfield Court, Richmond

"Y ou haven't been able to sit still all week," Victoria said to Maggie. "Something is bothering you."

They sat in the richly appointed breakfast room at Victoria's country estate, only an hour's ride from London. Maggie wore a two-year-old gown of deep red muslin with white trim that was too plain to be fashionable these days. But it was comfortable and suited her well, as did her reprieve from Town life and the possibility of encountering Thomas again, before she was ready. Besides, Victoria did not mind, and no one else was there to notice.

She'd made her escape from Town and Thomas days ago, but the distance between them had done little to assuage her longing for the warmth of his company and all their sweet intimacies. Maggie had not missed Julian's touch, because her husband had never been a particularly tender or considerate lover. She'd had no idea how delicious the relations between a man and a woman could be. Not until Thomas.

Maggie set aside her tea. She'd hoped the physical miles between herself and Thomas would help to settle her nerves and put their affair in perspective. She'd been wrong. She missed him. She could close her eyes and smell his scent, feel the rasp of his whiskers on her cheek, hear the deep timbre of his voice. Every night, Maggie had lain in her bed, her body aching for his touch. She yearned for the taste of his kiss and the gentle caress of his hands.

She wondered if he thought of her, or if he'd asked where she'd gone. She knew it had been cowardly to disappear without saying good-bye, or telling him where she'd gone.

But she was a miserable failure as a mistress, unable to separate her emotions from the profoundly intimate acts she'd shared with her lover. Fortunately, Maggie knew her limitations. It had been absolutely essential to break away from him before she lost her heart entirely. One more tender touch, one more kindness to her children, and she would be lost.

She looked outside and tried to think what explanation she could give Victoria for her restiveness. Surely not that she was pining for a man who was not only a foreign royal who was in England only temporarily, but a man who had taken her to bed and shown her the heights of pleasure. A man who would never be her husband.

Zachary and Lily were outdoors with Victoria's

children and their nurses, enjoying the sunshine and the freedom of the estate, without having to worry about roads and carriages and the thick, black air in Town. They'd gotten some pink in their cheeks in the past week, but it would have to end soon, for Maggie could not hide forever. She had made another drawing for Mr. Brown before leaving Town, but it was nearly time for her to produce another.

"I wish you could confide in me, Maggie," said Victoria. "You know I only want to help."

Maggie knew that was true, but it was difficult to speak of her deep secrets to her very staid and proper friend. Yet Victoria had almost come out and encouraged Maggie to pursue something with Thomas. . . .

She took a deep breath. "The Blackmore estate is a disaster," she finally said, shying away from telling her friend about her affair. "Julian gambled away everything that was not entailed. I'm hoping I can keep the manor from falling into complete wrack and ruin for Zachary."

"Oh my heavens," Victoria exclaimed. "I was worried it was something like this."

"You knew?"

"No, not really," she replied. "I only had a vague sense of Julian's character—that he was not terribly dependable. I will tell you now—I was so disappointed when you married him."

"You didn't say anything."

"Maggie, how could I?" Victoria asked. She put her hand over Maggie's and gave it a squeeze.

"Your mother and Shefford pushed you into that marriage so quickly it even caused *my* mother to remark on it."

Victoria's mother was exceedingly circumspect, so Maggie knew it was highly unusual for her to have mentioned it. She wished *someone* had, before it was too late.

"I was a fool," Maggie said. "I think from the first, that Shefford intended for me to be Julian's dupe."

Victoria frowned. "Dupe? What do you mean?"

"I overheard Shefford talking to Robert Kimbridge soon after I came to Town," Maggie explained, her heart stinging with self-derision. She should have been smarter, more wary of her stepbrother who'd pulled any number of nasty tricks over the years, on those he felt were his inferiors. She'd never thought he'd do the same to his own sister, even if she was not his sibling by blood. "It sounded as though Kimbridge has need to marry a respectable woman in order to inherit."

"Ranfield mentioned a rumor to that effect. Kimbridge is a bit wild, and his father insists that his son settle down before releasing his trust."

Maggie stood and went to the window. She pushed the curtain aside and looked out at the well-managed land and the Ranfield sheep grazing on it. "Apparently, his father has specific criteria for his son's wife. Shefford said I would be perfect for the post. A doormat, just as I was for Julian."

"No! He did not say such a thing, did he?"

"Oh yes," she said coldly, "and that I am a good breeder, besides."

"How disgusting."

"I can only think he must have arranged my marriage to Julian in the same way for much the same purpose, although Lord Blackmore did not have any great fortune to pass to his son. I was so naïve it never occurred to me that Julian might want a wife and children to hide away in the country while he did what he pleased in Town. A stupid child of a wife."

"I am appalled at Shefford, although that is nothing new. He is . . ." A worried frown crossed Victoria's brow. She looked earnestly at Maggie. "You will not do it, will you? Marry Kimbridge?"

"Absolutely not. I am through with men."

"Oh, my dear. I am so sorry that things turned out so badly with Julian."

Maggie returned to her chair. "Julian was a handsome charmer with very little character. And I let him pull the wool over my eyes. I let myself believe that we had a normal, comfortable marriage."

"What else could you do once you were married to the man? Divorce was out of the question, of course. And if he did not abuse you—"

"No, never." But he'd never treated her well, either. Not as Thomas did.

"Well then, you were trapped, weren't you?"

Maggie rubbed her arms and nodded. She'd had no idea what her husband had withheld from her—the intimacy of intense lovemaking, the gentle caresses a man should give the woman in his bed.

He'd saved those for his mistresses.

"Perhaps there is something that can be done about the estate," said Victoria. "What does Shefford say about it?"

"That he is not to be held responsible for Julian's debts."

Victoria frowned. "He is the trustee, is he not?"

"There might as well have been no one, for all the good Shefford did since Julian's death."

Victoria pressed a hand to her breast and tried to cover her dismay. "Oh my. When Ranfield arrives, will you speak to him about it? He is very good at investing and I'm sure he would be happy to advise you."

"I'm not sure he can help. There is little left but debt, and the house and lands are in dire need of attention."

"Oh Maggie, I had no idea things were so bad."

Maggie sighed. "Neither did I, until I came to Town and met with the solicitor."

There was far more, but Maggie could not bring herself to speak of Thomas and the confusion she felt about her affair with him.

Escaping London was the best thing Maggie could have done, for she knew she could not resist him, even though further contact with him put her heart ever more deeply at risk. It had been nearly impossible to leave their bed in the cozy cottage in the woods, and she'd tossed and turned that night and every night afterward, longing for the pleasing comfort of his arms.

"Whatever the situation, I feel certain Ranfield can help you," said Victoria. "Please ask him what he thinks."

Maggie nodded. "I will."

"Would you like to walk with me to visit our tenants?" Victoria asked. "It might help to take your mind off your troubles."

"Yes, I would like that very much," Maggie replied.

"The Blackmore estate is in serious trouble," said Mark Saret.

"What do you mean?" Tom asked. He should have felt a good deal more satisfaction in Maynwaring's public disgrace, but all he felt was a cold hollowness inside. He remembered his own ignominious arrest and could not prevent an absurd feeling of sympathy for what the hateful judge was going through.

"The entailed estate is intact, but in poor condition," Saret said. "And some of the properties are mortgaged."

"Do you have details?"

Saret nodded. "No, but I will soon."

Tom dragged a hand across his face. "Let me know what you find out before you do anything."

"Of course," Saret replied. "On a far more interesting—and disturbing—note, Andrew Harland accompanied Lord Shefford and his friends to their S.C.H. assignation last night."

The skin at the back of Tom's neck prickled. "And?"

"The letters stand for 'Seventh Circle of Hell.' The members are daredevils."

"They do what . . . ?" Tom asked, trying to grasp what Shefford might possibly gain from such an association. "They *dare* each other to—"

"No. They perform feats of daring that involve innocents. They put unsuspecting people at risk."

"How?"

"They commit outrageous acts of some small skill and a great deal of daring. Last night, they plucked a young man from the east end and took him to a cellar of the abandoned shop they favor— unwillingly, of course—where they secured him to a wall, spread-eagle. They blindfolded each member of the club, who then took turns throwing knives at the lad. The loser was the one who cut the boy."

Tom's stomach roiled. He could only imagine the lad's terror. "I'd say the boy was the loser."

"Harland says they paid him well and set him free when they were done."

"What, enough to pay a surgeon to stitch up his wounds? How generous of them."

Saret shrugged.

Tom tamped down his disgust. "It's not enough. We'll need evidence of some more serious wrong-doing." Which Tom believed would not be difficult, considering the kind of game Shefford and his gang seemed to enjoy.

"Aye. Harland has arranged to be the foot-man who accompanies Shefford on all his S.C.H. jaunts."

The urge to go down to Hanover Square and throw a few knives at Shefford was nearly overpowering. It was just like Shefford to victimize those he believed were his inferiors, and their death or dismemberment would mean little to the arrogant bastard.

"Any news of my family? Have we heard from Salim?"

"Not yet," Saret replied. "But I expect either a message or Salim himself to appear any day."

"Keep me apprised."

"Of course," Saret said.

Tom should have felt greater contentment. Maynwaring had been put away, and Shefford would soon follow. His family would be found and brought to London. But he felt restless and agitated, his impatience entirely out of character. During his years away, he'd learned to bide his time, to wait for opportune moments and situations. To do whatever was necessary to survive.

But now he knew Maggie Danvers's touch. He knew the taste of her skin, and how it felt to be inside her.

He knew what it was to miss her.

Tom did not delude himself into thinking she'd gone away with Lady Ranfield just for recreation. She'd done it to get away from him. Hell, the last time he'd been with her, she couldn't have gotten out of his bed and away from the huntsman's cottage quickly enough. And yet nothing had gone wrong between them. If anything, it had all been frighteningly right.

Tom knew he should be exceedingly glad that she had seen fit to leave him. All she did was complicate matters, arousing him to a fever with barely a touch of her hand or the whisper of a kiss on his lips.

He wanted to see her. He did not examine his reasons why—he only knew that a week without her was far too long.

So when Lord Ranfield invited Tom to visit his Richmond estate for a small house party, he readily agreed. Even though there were still questions about his family, and he didn't know enough about Maggie's estate in Cambridgeshire, he was settling scores. Events were progressing exactly as he'd planned. But Tom knew he would have gone to Richmond, even if that had not been the case. Maggie was there.

Tom liked Ranfield, a man of reason and good sense, proof that not every English nobleman was a wastrel or a scoundrel like Shefford. The trip to Richmond took only about an hour, and Tom found that he was finally able to breathe easily. He enjoyed the ride, something he'd done too little of since leaving New York. He missed his farm and the freedom he enjoyed in the American countryside. Lying, and playing the role of a prince had started to wear on him.

"Lady Blackmore is one of my wife's childhood friends," said Ranfield as they rode at a trot along the northern road. "They came out together eight years ago."

"Lady Blackmore is lucky to have such a friend.

Your wife is a very welcoming woman," Tom replied, though he found Lady Ranfield altogether too conventional for his taste. She was quite pretty, but possessed none of the fire that he saw in Maggie's eyes, none of the sizzle of her touch. But it was obvious that she suited Ranfield quite well. "You must be very happy."

Ranfield nodded. "Aye. I am a very lucky man. My wife had a great many offers during her first season," Ranfield said. "I am fortunate that she waited a year and finally accepted mine."

"And Lady Blackmore?" he asked.

"I believe she married her husband quite soon after her first season began," said Ranfield, his visage darkening. "If she'd waited, I'm sure there would have been other offers. I wouldn't have wished that bounder Viscount Blackmore on any woman."

Tom felt his bile rise as he imagined every possible abuse. "What do you mean?"

"I should not speak of the dead . . ."

"I shall assume the worst, then," said Tom.

"If by worst, you mean that he was a lying, cheating scoundrel, led around to the darkest corners of London by his old friend, Shefford—then you'd be correct."

Tom guessed Julian would have been a member of Shefford's club, but Ranfield did not mention it. It was likely a man like Ranfield wouldn't know of it.

"He was a prodigious gambler," Ranfield added. "And a very bad one, at that."

"He lost heavily, then?"

"Rumor has it that everything he owned is gone or mortgaged beyond its worth. Except for his entailment, of course."

"Then Lady Blackmore—"

"Is just next door to destitute."

Knowledge of Julian's family's downfall should have given Tom the utmost satisfaction. And yet his mind raced with thoughts of Maggie's straits.

Of course she had said nothing to him. She was a proud woman who would somehow manage to take care of her family, though he could not imagine what she would do, since Shefford would soon be destitute as well.

"Has she any money to invest?" he asked.

"My wife was planning to broach that delicate question this week. If Lady Blackmore is willing to accept my help, I will do what I can to advise her."

"Doesn't her brother oversee her affairs?"

Ranfield gave a laugh. "Shefford is no better than his old chum, Julian. You'd do well to stay clear of him."

"Too late," Tom said, feeling deflated and oddly defeated. *Maggie was destitute.*

"What do you mean?"

Tom managed to speak with a level voice. "He's got a horse he wants to run against one of mine. He and some of his friends have already wagered quite heavily against my ambassador, Mr. Beraza."

"He's got some good racers," said Ranfield. "And some bad friends. They're involved in some sort of club . . ."

"You know about it?" Tom asked, surprised.

"Not much. Only that it's unsavory. I am sorry to say that it's not the only one of its type in London." Ranfield shot him a sidelong glance. "A word to the wise, though. Do not trust him, no matter what the situation."

Tom gave a quick nod. "I don't intend to."

"It's a blessing the man has never married, for his wife would eventually find herself in Lady Blackmore's situation. I'm hoping his peerage will one day fall into more responsible hands."

Tom wondered what effect Shefford's destruction would have on Maggie, and whether she had to rely upon him for her livelihood.

He felt the blood drain from his head. Christ, he'd wanted her ruined, too. He'd intended to have absolutely no regrets when he sailed back to America. And yet it rankled to think of leaving Maggie behind, penniless.

And with that thought, Thomas knew he must be losing his mind.

Victoria's two sons ran ahead with Zachary, laughing and chasing one another as they all walked back from the village. Lily was tired after all their visits to the tenants, so she rode in Victoria's little pull cart among the empty baskets they were bringing home.

The weather was fine and Maggie felt at ease there in the country, with her children. She pulled off her bonnet and smiled happily, for the moment forgetting all her cares. "Thank you for inviting me out here, Victoria," she said. "It's exactly what I needed."

"I know you love the country, Maggie. Why don't you take the children and go back to Cambridgeshire?"

"I wish I could," Maggie said. "But I must stay in Town to . . . to sort things out." Even though Thomas was there, and she wouldn't be able to avoid him forever.

Not that she really wanted to. Every fiber in her body screamed out for him, and some irrational corner of Maggie's mind wished she could ask him to stay in England with her. She had developed a dangerous infatuation, one that was certain to cause her pain. Thomas was going to return to his country one day, and Maggie could not allow herself to think of the wretchedness she would certainly feel when he left.

She had children to raise and an estate to run, and yet just the thought of him made her mouth go dry and her heart race. She became the same weak-kneed dimwit she'd been when Julian was alive.

Maggie raised her face to the sun. She knew she would never again know the kind of passion she'd shared with Thomas. But it had to end. She'd done the right thing by leaving his little cottage the other night. She'd taken the only steps possible to keep him from stealing her very soul.

To keep from handing it to him herself.

"Look," said Victoria, smiling happily as she pointed to her house in the distance. "There's Charles's carriage. He must have arrived."

Maggie liked Charles, and could not help but wish she had waited as Victoria had done, for an equally loving, dependable bridegroom. Though Julian had derided Charles as a pompous prig, Victoria's husband was no such thing. He was a caring, responsible gentleman who took care of his wife and family.

Maggie decided she would do as Victoria suggested, and speak to him about her finances. She couldn't trust Shefford to do any better than he'd already done, and she was waiting to see what Mr. Clements would say about removing him as the children's guardian and trustee of Julian's estate. Perhaps Lord Ranfield would agree to take that post.

The three little boys ran circles around the two women as they walked the path to Ranfield Park, and when they all arrived at the house, Maggie lifted her sleepy daughter from the wagon. Two grooms came around to take charge of the cart and move the carriage away as the butler stepped out of the house and quickly descended the stairs.

He spoke to Victoria. "My lady, we received word that Lord Ranfield will be arriving shortly. He decided to ride, and so sent the carriage ahead."

"I don't blame him," said Victoria. "It's a beautiful day."

"Also," said the butler, "he is bringing a guest. We have made the yellow and gray room ready."

"Thank you Godfrey. Who is it?"

"A prince, my lady," he replied. "A foreign dignitary, I understand."

Maggie barely had time to recover from the news that Thomas was coming to Ranfield Park when they heard horses' hooves on the drive. As she set Lily on her feet, part of her was tempted to flee. The other part wanted to wrap herself up in Thomas's arms and pretend they could remain there together, forever.

As the men cantered to the house, the three small boys went running toward them shouting with glee. "Papa!" cried Victoria's sons.

"Thorne!" Zachary cried happily at the sight of his hero, and Maggie felt a twinge in the center of her chest.

Zac had never run toward his father with such excitement, and when Thomas smiled at Zachary as though he was just as happy to see him, Maggie's heart slid to her toes. She would not be the only one disappointed when Thomas left the country.

The two men dismounted, giving their horses over to the grooms, and Zachary pulled Thomas's sleeve and showed him something he'd collected in his hand. Thomas gave it due respect, then ruffled Zac's hair. A second later, he looked up at her, his dark green gaze cutting through the air between them like lightning.

He was angry.

Maggie wished she could retreat, but she forced herself to stand still. She had done no wrong in leaving so abruptly. There had been no promises between them, and surely he had no expectations beyond their few carnal encounters.

Walking beside Ranfield, Thomas approached Maggie and Victoria. Charles kissed his wife's cheek while Thomas bowed over Maggie's hand with excruciating formality.

Which was exactly as it should be. Chewing her lip, she turned away and started up the steps to the house, trying not to think about spending the night under the same roof with him, about lying alone just a few doors away from his gray and yellow bedchamber.

"Your Highness, it is a surprise to see you," said Victoria, leading the way beside Charles as the children's nurses came for them.

"I could not refuse your husband's gracious invitation," he said, escorting Maggie as they followed their hosts into the house.

Her heart beat a little faster at the possibility that he'd known she was here. That he'd come for that reason.

"You left London rather precipitously," he said quietly.

There was nothing she could say, because it was true. And she'd done it in order to get away from him. "I'm sure London fares well without me."

"How would you know if you are not there to see?" There was an edge of anger to his words.

"Since it has stood for two thousand years, I'll assume all remains well."

"One should never make assumptions."

"Surely there are some givens in life. Certain facts that will always be true." Paramours were temporary, for example. And simple country vis-

countesses needed to be careful around men who
would charm them into bed with a bit of kind
attention.

"No one in England knew of Sabedoria's existence before, so that particular assumption was
not quite true."

He was right, but they were not speaking of geography. "We can only act on what we believe is
true, based on what is known."

He hesitated momentarily. "Though you might
believe London is the same without you, nothing
could be further from the truth."

Maggie's heart stumbled in her chest.

But pretty words did not change the facts. She
would never possess the sophistication she needed
to maintain her affair with Thomas. She was relieved that continued private conversation between them became impossible when they went
into the drawing room where Victoria introduced
her young sons to Thomas.

"Where are the other guests, Victoria?" Ranfield asked.

Victoria looked at him quizzically.

"I thought you invited Lord and Lady Westridge.
And Clarebourne."

"Oh yes. They were previously engaged. All of
them. It's been just Maggie and I all week."

Ranfield covered his discomfiture and took
Thomas to his room. He obviously realized the
awkwardness posed by the presence of the two unmarried guests in the house.

"I'll order tea," Victoria said to her husband as he

left with Thomas, then sat back in her chair fanned her face with one hand, as though she needed a cooling breeze. When the two men's footsteps had receded, she looked up at Maggie. "I don't believe I've ever seen a man quite so . . . so . . ."

"Potent" was the word Victoria was looking for, or perhaps "sensual." But Maggie was not about to supply either of those descriptions to her friend. She looked down at her fingernails and tried to appear nonchalant.

"Can you just imagine how it would be to—" Victoria stopped abruptly, frowning at Maggie. "Margaret Danvers, you *know*!"

Maggie kept her eyes averted. She went to the piano and played a few notes as she stood there, trying desperately to create a diversion from the color in her cheeks. "What are you talking about?"

Victoria came to her. "I recognize that expression on your face. You've done it . . ." She lowered her voice to a whisper. "You've shared his bed!"

Tears burned at the backs of Maggie's eyes. She had no choice but to admit it. "It all happened very quickly."

Victoria laughed. "I knew it! Something besides finances has bedeviled you all week!"

"Hush, Victoria," Maggie said, relieved that her friend knew the secret and did not revile her. "It's over now. As much as I might wish it, I am not meant to be any man's mistress."

"Oh bosh. With a man like the prince, how could you refuse?"

"Let me assure you, it was not easy."

"You actually did it? Refused him?" Victoria asked. "Oh heavens, that's why you came with me to Richmond."

Maggie dropped down onto the piano bench. She'd never wanted anything more in her life, and yet she knew her affair with Thomas was the worst thing possible for her. It ranked alongside her ruined finances and Shefford's manipulations. Destined to cause her anguish.

Victoria looked at her slyly. "Why do you think he came here with Ranfield?"

"To get away from all his admirers in London, I suppose," Maggie answered.

Victoria sat down beside Maggie. "He is here for you, Maggie."

She swallowed back the irrational hope that welled up in her chest, and depressed one of the piano keys. B flat.

"Oh no," said Victoria. "You're in love with him."

"No, I absolutely am not!" She practically flew off the bench. "He is just visiting England, and when his duties here are done, he will make his months-long journey back to Sabedoria, and I will never see him again. I would be a fool to fall in love with the man."

Victoria was quiet for a moment. "I understand."

How could Victoria possibly understand? She was married to a wonderful, decent husband who wouldn't dream of hurting his wife.

"It all started just after you told me about Julian and his . . . his . . ."

"Mistresses?"

Maggie nodded, folding her hands tightly together in her lap. "I was so upset and . . . and felt so betrayed."

Victoria put her arm around Maggie's shoulders. "I don't fault you, dear. After your lackluster marriage and everything you told me about the estate, I think you are entitled to a respite."

"That's all it was," Maggie whispered. "That's all it will ever be."

Chapter 14

Supper was served in a small dining chamber, not far from the library. It was a pleasant, intimate setting, and Tom had to set aside his imaginings of dining there in private, beside Maggie. He would pull her onto his lap and feed her morsels of something sweet, then lick the crumbs from the corners of her mouth.

The restlessness he'd felt during the past week finally eased, though Maggie's very nearness turned it into something altogether different. It seemed to be an attraction that would not be denied, no matter how many miles lay between them.

It did not bode well for his plans.

"How long will you be in England, Thorne?" Lady Ranfield asked. He'd given his hosts leave to call him Thorne, in spite of his cautions to his men. But he'd kept his Christian name private, for Maggie's use alone.

He shrugged, hoping his stay would be long enough to satisfy his thirst for Maggie Danvers.

"I haven't decided. We still have business to transact with Lord Marsden, and Mr. Ochoa has meetings scheduled this week and next with Lord Castlereagh."

"Then you might stay through the summer?"

"It's possible, Lady Ranfield."

She smiled. "I certainly hope so. Your presence has enlivened society this season."

Lord Ranfield turned to him. "There is a rumor that you will soon be dining at Carlton House."

"That is true. In just a few days, in fact."

"The regent has been away in Bristol," Ranfield remarked to his wife and Maggie. "He only returns tomorrow."

"I do not hold the delay against him," Tom jested, "since I arrived in England without giving advance notice."

Ranfield and his wife chuckled, but Maggie was conspicuously quiet, not eating, merely pushing her food around on her plate. Tom pressed his thigh against hers. She did not withdraw, but glanced at him with those clear gray eyes that had glowed with the intense pleasure of their lovemaking. Her gaze sent rivers of steam through his blood, but he somehow managed to keep his expression unruffled. She had spoken earlier of assumptions—but he could not fathom what she'd meant. Had she discovered any of the truth about him?

"It seems quite strange that none of our explorers ever encountered your kingdom in the South Seas," said Ranfield, partially distracting Tom from the considerable arousal caused by Maggie's mere proximity. "How large a country is Sabedoria?"

No bigger than his erection. "Roughly the size of England," Tom managed to say. "But we're well-hidden among a throng of smaller islands. It isn't easy to navigate through our archipelago, which has served us well, I might add. The narrow channels are difficult to navigate, so they provide protection from invaders."

The geography of Sabedoria was a believable fiction, since Tom—and likely the British navy—knew there were many close-set islands north of Botany Bay. English ships hadn't done much exploring in the area in the years since their discovery of Botany Bay less than fifty years before, so Tom's fiction was safe. By the time an English ship could be dispatched to investigate, and then return home with information, Tom and his own crew would be long gone. And they would be nowhere in the vicinity of Botany Bay, thank God.

But all their talk of Sabedoria failed to return his attention to his mission and his sole purpose for coming to England. He was far too engaged by the heat of Maggie's body, so close to his and yet much too far away.

Ranfield acknowledged Tom's remark with a slow nod. "Aye. No telling how our navy would have reacted to finding a civilized country down below the equator. I should hope our commanders would show proper enthusiasm and respect upon meeting your people."

"I'm sure they would."

A few wisps of Maggie's hair had escaped her coif, and curled softly near her ears and at the nape of her neck. Tom remembered the way she would tilt her head and shiver slightly when he put his lips to her ear. He could almost taste her warm skin, and knew that her velvet-soft nipples would pebble when he scattered kisses down her neck.

She was the most incredibly responsive woman . . .

He forced his attention back to Ranfield's questions, even though his tongue felt thick and his brain had turned numb with desire.

"What are your chief crops?" Ranfield asked.

"We grow grains that are very similar to yours," Tom replied, keeping his answer as simple as possible. He wanted the meal done, and the evening formalities finished so that he could seek out his lover in private. To touch her. Kiss her. Slide into her.

Tom did an admirable job of holding up his end of the conversation, answering questions about his fictitious country while he thought of the night to come, of Maggie with her hair down, her body naked and straining against his in a fever of passion.

They discussed growing seasons and the structure of the Sabedorian government. Fortunately, Ranfield did not pursue any detailed questioning. The superficial discussion allowed Tom the opportunity to view and appreciate Maggie's delicate features, the charming freckles that raced across her cheeks and nose, and the endearing scar on her chin.

"Shall we give the ladies a few minutes?" Ranfield finally asked, pushing back his chair and standing while Tom did the same. The earl addressed his wife and Maggie. "Would you excuse us?"

He poured two glasses of brandy, picked up a couple of cheroots and led Tom from the dining room. Walking away from Maggie was the last thing Tom wanted to do, but he recognized the importance of gaining some control over his unrestrained lust. She had complicated his plans and he had yet to figure out what he was going to do about her.

"Don't be ridiculous," Maggie said to Victoria. "He is not."

"I tell you the man is smitten," Victoria retorted.

They went into the drawing room, but Maggie did not sit down.

"I observed him carefully," Victoria said, "and you must believe me when I tell you his eyes never left you. Good lord, the man was consuming you with his glance."

The blood rushed to Maggie's face, heating her cheeks. She'd felt his leg and then his foot against hers and knew the truth of Victoria's assertion. She shook her head, not to deny all that she felt, but to reject the affair that could not be continued. "And when he sails away, what am I left with, Victoria?"

"Sweet, sweet memories," Victoria replied with a sigh. "What if he asked you to go to Sabedoria with him?"

"He won't."

"What *if*?" Victoria repeated. "You wouldn't stay in England for your family's sake, would you?"

Maggie shook her head. Victoria was perfectly aware of the way things stood with her family. "There's Zachary's title."

"Which is practically worthless, if your solicitor's assessment is correct."

"Such conjecture is all rubbish," Maggie retorted. Her heart felt heavy as she put her assessment of the situation into words. "Can you imagine that a man like Thorne does not have a perfectly formed life in his own country? He is a prince with wealth beyond imagining and it is more than likely that there are laws regarding Sabedorian royal marriages, just as there are in England." She did not add the obvious possibility that he might ask her to accompany him as his mistress or concubine.

She did not know what she would do if that came to pass. Perhaps concubines enjoyed greater favor than wives in Sabedoria.

The men rejoined them in the drawing room and Charles took Maggie aside and apologized for putting her in a dubious situation, having invited Thorne on the mistaken belief that others would be present at the house. At the same time, Victoria seemed determined to keep Maggie and Thomas together. She suggested a few hands of whist before they retired, and they had just begun to play their first hand when the nurses brought down the children to say good night.

Nurse Hawkins set Lily on her feet, and as Maggie reached for her, the little girl went to Thomas and started to climb onto his lap. Stunned, Maggie watched as he lifted her daughter and clasped her against his broad chest. "Story, please, Mum," she said.

"Yes, please," Zachary added. "Would you draw a story for us?"

"Oh, I'm sure Lord and Lady Ranfield would rather—"

"Not at all," said Charles, ringing for the butler. "By all means, share one of your story drawings with us."

The butler was sent for drawing materials, and when he returned, the children gathered around Maggie. All but Lily, who stayed on Thomas's lap, her thumb firmly in her mouth.

Thomas did not seem to mind, and the sight of little Lily sitting so contentedly with him filled her with a longing that she knew would never be fulfilled. She could do nothing but turn her attention to the story.

Daniel and Richard were as mad for horses as Zachary, so Maggie began to draw a tale about three young boys who looked remarkably like them, of course. They were English boys who had to capture and tame some wild horses in order to perform the heroic task of rescuing a princess.

Maggie engaged Lily by drawing her likeness and making her the princess who was locked in a tower by a wicked duke. In the meantime, the boys had no end of trouble catching the wild stallions.

She was just about to start drawing a scene that featured the little princess when Thomas spoke. "Do you suppose the princess might find a rope," he asked. "And get herself down from the tower?"

"Yes!" Lily cried out, clapping her hands.

"How did you know that that was exactly what she did!"

An intense, fiery emotion burst in Maggie's chest when Zac turned to Thomas and grinned his approval. She could not allow her children's fondness for Thomas to sway her. If anything, it was her responsibility to protect them from becoming too close and being heartbroken when he left. They might have missed a father's affection, but Thomas was not the one who was going to provide it. No one was.

She started drawing a picture of Lily, escaping the tower quite daringly, dangling from a thick rope that she tied to a spindle in the tower room. She glanced up and saw amusement dancing in Thomas's eyes.

"I think the little princess probably has her own pony, hidden away somewhere," he said. "What do you think, Lily?"

Maggie's heart seemed to splinter a little bit more with each addition Thomas made to the tale, just as a father might do. Their banter in creating the story was far too appealing, and only fueled impossible wishes and desires.

"How lovely!" Victoria said when Maggie closed the drawing pad.

"I never knew how very gifted you were, Lady Blackmore, though Victoria has often remarked on your drawing skills," said Lord Ranfield.

Maggie felt pleased by the compliment, but then slightly concerned when Thomas picked up the drawings to look at them more closely. She hoped he did not make the connection between those quick pencil drawings and the Redbush caricatures.

Victoria collected her sons and accepted a good night kiss from each. "Say good night to your father, and thank Lady Blackmore and Prince Thorne for the story."

The boys bid Thomas good night, and when the nurses arrived to take the children upstairs, Lily turned to him. " 'Night, Torn," she said. "Can we find some ducks in th' morn?"

Maggie saw a muscle in his jaw tighten momentarily, and he answered her earnestly. "I look forward to it."

If Thomas looked abashed by Lily's attention, he was no less so when Zachary came to him and put his small hand on Thomas's knee. "Will you show Daniel and Richard how to make paper boats tomorrow, Thorne?" he asked.

He gave a silent nod, and Maggie's throat thickened with concern. Thomas was more attentive than Julian had ever been, and yet he was not their father. He was merely the man who'd taken their mother to bed, the man who'd just given her a key to understanding what had gone so very wrong in her own life.

All of society would eventually hear that Thomas had gone to Ranfield Park, and everyone would believe he'd made the trip to be with Lady Blackmore. Whether he bedded her or not, it would be assumed that they had become lovers. He wouldn't need to add her to their Carlton House entourage in order to establish her reputation as a woman of loose morals. It was done. He had accomplished part of what he'd set out to do.

So there was no need to go to her now. Absolutely none. The conclusions he'd aimed for would be drawn by his mere presence at Ranfield Court. Besides, she was obviously the artist who put his caricature in *The Gazette* every week, and he really ought to keep his distance. If she ever learned the truth about him . . .

Thomas paced impatiently in his room until the house became completely quiet. Ranfield's house was a large, comfortable residence, its style similar to the house Tom had built on his own estate. Ranfield Court was smaller and far less grandiose than Delamere House, but it still possessed extensive corridors, and the room that had been given to Maggie was only a few doors away.

Dressed only in shirt and trews, Tom walked the short distance to her door and stood still for a moment, telling himself to return to his own bedchamber. There was nothing more to accomplish. He could keep his identity secret, and when she returned to London, her reputation would be in shreds.

Her door opened suddenly, as though she expected him.

Tom's body ached with lust. He hadn't intended to feel such a powerful need for her, for the taste of her mouth, or the slide of her body against his.

Her hair was loose and her feet bare, and she was wearing the same thin chemise she'd worn the last time he made love to her.

"You haven't been to bed," he said, trying to will some control into his wayward hands.

She gave a shake of her head. "I knew I wouldn't be able to sleep." She looked up at him. "Not with you lying so near."

"Christ, Maggie, I missed you," he rasped just before taking her into his arms.

She raised up onto her toes and pressed her mouth to his, initiating a kiss that burned through his veins. Her breasts were unfettered, and Tom felt those soft curves and their hardened tips against his chest. He thought he might have groaned, but when she sucked his tongue into her mouth, he had no sense of equilibrium, and lost his ability to stand. He sat down hard on the bed and she took his face in her hands, kissing him as she straddled him. Tom lowered the small capped sleeves of the chemise down her arms until her breasts were exposed.

The scent of her skin made Tom mad for her

touch. Her capable hands wreaked havoc with his senses. She'd learned just how to touch him, where to kiss and suckle, how to draw out the most amazing sensations.

But it had been far too long since he touched her. When he could take no more, he lifted her onto the bed and pulled her underneath him. He slid between her thighs and entered her slowly, torturously. Rising up over her, he braced himself on his hands and looked into her eyes as he moved within her welcoming body.

"Thomas!" she whispered, grabbing the sheets in her fists beside her.

"All in good time, sweet."

A strange, sweet calm came over him as he withdrew nearly all the way, keeping only the tip of his erection inside her. He was exactly where he belonged, in the one place where it seemed that everything was right with the world.

"You have a spring in your step this morning," said Victoria the following morning as they walked out to a quiet spot in the garden.

Thomas had left her bed early that morning, and she knew that he and Ranfield had planned to go riding just after dawn. They would be back soon.

"I realized something last night," Maggie said.

Victoria shot her a sly look.

"Not *that*," Maggie retorted.

Victoria laughed. "What did you realize?"

"That I have allowed myself to be managed," she said. "For most of my life, I've been controlled

by . . . well, by my family, and the guilt they made
me feel. And then by my husband during our marriage. And now, by convention."

Victoria slid her arm through Maggie's. "I have
a secret to tell you, my dear." She lowered her voice
to a whisper. "We all are!"

"I know," Maggie said. "But I could have—
and *should* have—exerted more control over my
own life. My . . . affair with Thorne is the first
independent act I've accomplished in my entire
adult life. I've been little more than the dupe
Shefford described me to Kimbridge. A doormat.
A gull. But no longer."

A thin crease marred Victoria's perfect forehead.
"What are you going to do?"

"Don't worry. It's nothing drastic," she said.
"But I intend to start making my own decisions.
I've finished trying to please my family. And I plan
to ignore Shefford and his disgraceful demands."

"That sounds like a very good idea," Victoria
responded. "Your sisters have been pure poison for
as long as I've known you, and Shefford always
had a mean streak."

"There were times when I was embarrassed to
admit he was my brother," Maggie said, remembering several unpleasant incidents that took place
when she was just a girl.

"There was a boy once," she said, "who'd
brought horses from Suffolk to my stepfather. I
was only ten or eleven years old, and still walked
with a crutch."

"I remember."

"I went out that morning to see what all the excitement was about. I tripped . . . and this boy caught me and kept me from falling into a muddy puddle."

"Good lad," said Victoria.

Maggie shook her head, the memory becoming clearer with every word she spoke. "It had rained heavily the night before, and the path to the stable was a mess. The boy had just come out to gather up some of his tack when I tripped. Shefford was there with Julian. They saw the incident, and Julian taunted Shefford, asking if he was going to allow a stable boy to manhandle his sister."

"Oh no." Victoria placed a hand against her breast. "I daren't ask what he did."

Maggie remembered the boy had been handsome in a young, strapping way, and she'd felt flattered by his attention.

"Those two rascals put a couple of extremely expensive silver bowls from the house into the boy's pack and then accused him of stealing them."

"Oh dear God, what happened to him?"

"I didn't hear of it until weeks later . . . The boy was convicted by some horrid hanging judge. No one believed his pleas of innocence."

"They hanged him?"

"No," she said, feeling all over again the shame of having been a part of it. The cause of it, really. "He was transported."

Victoria clucked her tongue. "Shefford should be flogged for such a low trick."

"No doubt that is true, but who would dare to thrash a marquess?"

Something was different about Maggie. Tom observed her as she waltzed with Zachary to Lady Ranfield's accompaniment in the drawing room, both of them laughing happily as they moved, in spite of the bad weather that had forced them to retreat indoors, interrupting a lively game of cricket on the lawn.

While it rained heavily outside, Maggie created their own sunshine inside.

He'd seen her dance at the Waverly ball, and knew she was self-conscious about her lameness and the scar that marred her thigh. But no weakness was evident now. Tom saw no flaws in her movements.

Nor had he experienced any awkwardness in her movements the night before. On the contrary, her sudden dominance in the bedchamber had been enormously arousing. She'd become the princess in the story they'd told the children the night before—taking control and ravishing him, it seemed, within an inch of his life.

"Thorne!" cried Zachary, but Tom was so deeply immersed in thoughts of his interlude with Maggie, he didn't really hear the boy until Zac called his name a second time.

Zachary released himself from his mother's grip. "It's your turn!"

"My pleasure," he said, more than happy to take the boy's place. Even outside of the bedchamber, Maggie had enticed him and enthralled him all morning long—while they played cricket on the lawn, and later, when they came inside to make paper boats for the duck pond if the weather cleared.

He found he did not mind having the children with them. It was an extremely rude awakening, realizing that he held no animosity for Julian Danvers's offspring, understanding that Julian had played little part in his children's lives, merely providing the seed.

As Lady Ranfield played on, Tom took Maggie's hand in his and placed one hand quite properly at her waist. He pulled her improperly closer, aware that the children would not notice, and hoping that Lady Ranfield would keep her eyes on her keys.

Had they been alone, he would have dipped down and kissed her plump lips. Instead, he slid his hand down to forbidden territory, allowing it to rest on her hip.

Maggie looked at him with awareness and promise, her eyes never leaving his. She licked her lower lip in a deliberately seductive action and Tom reacted immediately. He leaned forward and put his lips beside her ear. "You will have to stand in front of me when our dance is done, love, or everyone will see your effect on me."

Her laugh mirrored the gentle patter of the soft rain, washing over him, cleansing him. He pulled her closer, wishing he could draw her into his arms and take her upstairs now, rather than waiting for night.

He forced himself to concentrate on the dance, leading her away from the children, who were playing quietly together near the piano. "Tonight, Maggie," he whispered.

She squeezed his hand in response, and when the music ended, Lady Ranfield applauded. "You should dance more often, Maggie! Don't you agree, Thorne?"

"I do," he said, releasing her reluctantly. He'd allowed himself to think a few days with her at Ranfield Court would allay the attraction he felt.

He couldn't have been more wrong.

Maggie rejoined the children and Thomas excused himself. He knew better than to foster his fascination for his enemy's sister, but could not stop thinking about the surprises that were in store for him tonight.

Chapter 15

Maggie felt wildly powerful. For the first time in her life, she was in charge of it. She could do as she pleased, within the constraints of her stressed finances. But even those circumstances might actually improve with Lord Ranfield's advice. She didn't tell him of her venture with Mr. Brown at *The Gazette*, but he listened attentively to her assessment of Blackmore's financial difficulties, and offered a few suggestions that she intended to follow.

It was late afternoon, and the children were in the nursery with their nannies. Victoria was napping, Charles was in his study with his steward, and Thomas was . . . Maggie did not know where he was, but she had not seen him since their dance in the drawing room. She smiled as she climbed the stairs, marveling at the effect she could have on him. Last night, she realized that her short tenure as a mistress had taught her a great deal about men and their deepest desires.

She went up the stairs and started for her bedchamber, noticing that Thomas's door stood partly open. A flash of heat ran through her at the thought of accosting him in his own territory, but she dismissed the idea immediately. No respectable woman would dare think of . . .

But she was no longer respectable. And she had taken charge of her life. She could be a mistress in truth, not just in action, and use Thomas for the pleasure he could give. And perhaps she could manage not to miss him when he sailed for Sabedoria.

She did not think that would be possible, though perhaps there was a way to avoid being devastated by his departure.

She stopped outside his room and saw the glimmer of a fire in the fireplace. Taking a deep breath, Maggie braced herself and slid her hands down the front of her dress, not exactly sure how to proceed.

The door creaked when she pushed it open. Thomas looked up from the journal he was reading and Maggie closed the door behind her. She turned the key in the lock and bit her lip.

"I hope I'm not disturbing you." Turning to face him, she reached for the pins in her hair and pulled them out.

"You always disturb me, Maggie." His voice was hoarse as he watched her.

"Is that a bad thing?" she asked in a flirtatious tone, in spite of what her sisters used to say about her flirting skills. Because of Thomas, she was no longer self-conscious about her hair, and allowed it to drop in long waves down her back. She started to unbutton her bodice as she moved toward him and he set his journal aside, swallowing thickly.

Awareness of her own potency bolstered her. She could do this. She could act the harlot and pretend she felt no connection to him.

"Not at all." He sat still and watched avidly as she slipped her gown from her shoulders and bent seductively to lower it past her hips. She knew her clothing was not particularly enticing, but saw that its removal tempted him.

Standing in her corset and chemise, she put one foot on a boudoir chair and raised her chemise to expose her unscarred leg. She unfastened her garter and lowered her stocking slowly, then pulled it gently from her toes. Then she repeated the action on the other side. "I'm very glad you don't mind."

She could hear his breathing, harsh and intense, and turned to gaze at him seductively over her shoulder. His mouth was slightly open, his nostrils flared, and Maggie felt very powerful, indeed. She put both feet on the floor and faced him as she reached behind her and pulled the laces of her stays, loosening her corset, letting it fall to the floor.

"Christ, Maggie!" Thomas rasped when she allowed the neckline of her chemise to drop down her shoulder. Thomas started to stand, but she went to him and put one hand on his shoulder, keeping him in his chair.

"As long as I'm here . . ." She knelt before him and he spread his legs wide as she reached for the placket of his trews. His knuckles were white on the arms of his chair, but he did not interfere while she opened the placket and drew out his thick, hot erection.

Looking into his eyes, she bent down and touched her tongue to the tip of his rod. He let out a slow breath and Maggie swirled her tongue around it, fondling him at the same time. She felt his thighs tighten when she sucked him fully into her mouth, and tasted a faintly salty flavor.

She sensed that she was driving him mad, but had no intention of stopping.

"Maggie, I'm dangerously close . . ."

Ignoring his warning, she closed her fist around the base of his shaft and licked its sensitive underside, feeling more aroused with every stroke. She heard his breath catch as he struggled for control. She slid her teeth along his hard length, and when he shuddered, she felt an answering throb between her own legs. As much as she wanted to continue her gentle assault, she was desperate to feel him inside her. Wanted the astounding climax he could give her.

She released him and pulled her chemise over her head, then stood and lowered herself onto his lap. He closed his eyes as Maggie slid down his manhood, inch by torturous inch, shuddering at the wondrous sensations.

Thomas braced his hands on the arms of the chair and let her have her way. His jaw was clenched tight, and a light sheen of perspiration appeared on his forehead. Maggie held on to his shoulders and moved down, then up, in a cadence that became more intense with each second that passed. She let her head fall back as every tendon, muscle and nerve in her body seemed to gather and tighten and then burst into flame. She heard his sharp intake of breath as her body stretched and squeezed around his.

Maggie felt him then, contracting and spilling his seed, groaning with satisfaction as he cupped her bottom and pulled her close. Maggie fell forward against him, and he slid his hands up her back, raising goose bumps as his gentle touch trailed up to her shoulders.

He framed her face with one hand. "So . . . I see the little princess has decided to climb down her rope and make her own escape."

Two long, dreary days after Tom's return from Ranfield Court, Mark Saret found Tom in Delamere's library. "I've a bit of bad news."

"What?" Tom asked. He'd been working with Arrendo and catching up on business while trying to avoid thinking about future assignations with Maggie. And failing miserably.

"But at least there is some good news to go with it." Saret did not take a seat, but stood before the fireplace and clasped his hands behind his back. "First of all, Foveaux is leaving the country. He sails for India tomorrow."

Disappointment churned in Tom's stomach. "And the good news?"

"I bought up all the outstanding loans at Thatcham's Bank."

"Dare I hope that Thatcham's is Foveaux's bank?"

Saret nodded. "We called in his debt yesterday. He is having a devil of a time finding a way to raise enough blunt to cover his house and other properties before he goes. He has his orders, and I don't believe even a general can refuse them."

The wheels of Tom's mind turned. "Is there a way to inform him of who caused this trouble?"

Saret smiled broadly. "Aye. He sails on the *Manchester* at noon tomorrow. Lucas Reigi has a connection—a midshipman who will deliver a message to Foveaux for you, whenever you like. Perhaps when they've arrived in India."

Perfect. By the time Foveaux had a chance to send word back to England, Tom and his party would be long gone. "I'll have it ready within the hour," he said as Edward Ochoa came into the room with more news.

"I thought you would like to know that Lord Justice Maynwaring is fully cooked," Ochoa said as Saret took his leave. "He and one of the city aldermen have had an ongoing feud that's lasted for years. As it happens, the complaint against your judge was brought to that particular alderman."

Tom gave a nod of satisfaction, but Ochoa's report put him on edge. So far, everything had played out too well for him to feel entirely comfortable.

Perhaps it was because he knew that when Maggie returned from Ranfield Court, she would likely feel the repercussions of their assignation in Richmond. All of society would soon learn they'd been together for several days. Certain suppositions would be made. And they would be correct.

There was a time when Tom would have felt some satisfaction in tearing down her respectable reputation . . .

"Thomas . . ." Ochoa said, taking a seat.

"What is it?" Tom asked, wondering if there was some important detail that Ochoa had not yet mentioned.

The American's brows gathered together and he rested his elbows on his knees. "I want you to know that I entirely respect your purpose here. There was no justification for what Shefford and Blackmore did to you. Or for Maynwaring to sentence you so harshly."

Tom looked into the older man's clear, dark eyes and wondered if Ochoa was thinking of trying to talk him out of his plans.

Ochoa cleared his throat before speaking. "I once killed a man."

Tom listened intently.

"He was my daughter's husband," Ochoa said, looking down at his hands. "The bastard struck her once too often. I arrived unexpectedly one day and saw her bruised eye and split lip. When he took his horsewhip to her, I decided it would be the last time."

"You were convicted of murder, then?" Tom asked.

Ochoa shook his head. "It was ruled self-defense. He nearly killed Ruth, and then he turned on me."

"What were you convicted of, then?"

"I helped a runaway slave escape," said Ochoa. "I was compelled by law to turn him over to the authorities, but I did not."

"What happened?"

Ochoa turned his gaze to the library window. "He was a huge man, with arms as thick as tree trunks. He was obviously a farm worker, and on the run. I caught him attempting to steal one of my horses, and managed to capture him."

"But you let him go?"

"Not at first. I'd planned to take him to the authorities. But then . . ." He frowned thoughtfully. "You know, he was just a man. His skin was different from yours and mine . . . but no man has the right to own another."

After Tom's years trying to survive under the mercy of the authorities who thought they owned him, his respect for Edward Ochoa grew immeasurably. Tom nodded, but Ochoa wasn't through.

He hesitated for a moment. "After I killed Roger . . . There was little satisfaction in it. He'd hurt Ruth, to be sure. But there was something . . ." He shrugged and stood. "I never hated anyone the way I hated Roger. But his death didn't sit well. I'm still haunted by the look in his eyes when he realized he was a dead man."

"What about the slave?" Tom asked quietly.

"I never regretted releasing him."

Maggie had hoped that by taking charge of her affair with Thomas, she would be able to keep her feelings out of it. She repeatedly told herself that their liaison was just a temporary amour, a superficial merging of bodies that had nothing to do with hearts and souls, or creating a life together. But when she closed her eyes, she saw him patting Zachary's head. Or kneeling behind Lily while he "helped" her bowl a game of cricket. Cheering when Zac hit the ball. Putting up with her awkward dancing.

Their intimate relations were only a part of what she'd experienced with Thomas, a small piece of the man she'd come to cherish. He had charmed them all.

And yet it was more than charm. He'd managed to draw out a side of Maggie that she hadn't known existed. With Thomas, she felt calmer and far more confident than ever before, and found that she possessed an untapped well of strength and courage.

But he would soon be gone.

Maggie did not know how to contend with that surety. Continue their affair and have her heart broken? Or end it and suffer the same result.

She returned to London, aware that she still needed time to think, to sort out the emotions that choked her whenever she thought about life without him.

Maggie and Nurse Hawkins settled the children into the nursery for a nap after their long carriage ride, and when she went down to the study, Mathers sought her out to give her a note that had been delivered the day before. It was from Thomas.

The butler left the room and Maggie sat down

at the desk and opened the missive. She read it, and then pressed it to her breast, willing her heart to slow. He wanted her to come out to the cottage.

Dear God, it was what she wanted, too. She craved the deep connection she felt when they were together. And she feared the horrible emptiness she would feel when he was gone. It was bad enough, knowing he was only a few miles away. And yet he would soon be oceans away from her. Perhaps it was better to retreat now, while her heart still had a chance to recover.

Mathers returned to the room before she could curb her emotions and gather her thoughts.

"My lady, Lord Shefford is here to see you." Her stepbrother pushed his way into the study past Mathers, who looked aghast at the marquess's rudeness. "My lord!"

"Stow it, Mathers. I need to see my sister."

Maggie looked at him blankly for a moment, then remembered herself. As she stood and faced him, all her years as a second-rate member of the family fell away. Shefford was a bully and a manipulator, the bungler whose incompetence had put the final nail in Blackmore's finances. He did not deserve her deference.

"To what do I owe this visit, my lord? Have you figured some way to repair the leaking roof at Blackmore Manor? No?" She knew she was goading him, but in her present mood, could not help herself. "How about a solution to the flooded fields in the southeast quarter of the estate?"

"Be serious, Margaret."

"Oh, but I am," she said. "I'm very serious. In fact, I wrote to Mr. Clements while I was in Richmond, asking him to petition the court for a new trustee. Because it is quite clear that you have not carried out your responsibilities very well."

"Neither did your husband," Shefford said derisively, "but you never petitioned anyone to remove him."

It was amazing how composed she could be when she believed in herself, and did not allow him to intimidate her. "If I knew then what I know now, I might have found a way."

"Don't be impertinent, Margaret. I've come here with a solution to all our problems."

"I assume it's some scheme that has nothing to do with vigilant monitoring of property or careful investing?"

He squinted at her as though seeing her for the first time. "I'm serious here, Margaret." He started to pace. "There is a huge opportunity here, and I intend to take it."

Maggie started for the door, intending to point the way out. No doubt he was going to reiterate his demand that she somehow intervene with Thomas. Fortunately, Thomas could take care of himself. He would never fall prey to any of Shefford's schemes. "I have no intention of becoming involved. Do what you will, but leave me out of it."

"Everyone knows you're the Sabedorian's whore. You can find out which horse is his champion. And how well-guarded he keeps his stable."

She refused to feel embarrassed or guilty. "No, Shefford. You will win or lose on your horse's merit, not on whatever evil you can do to your opponent."

He flushed deeply and grabbed her arm before she could step away. "It's about time you did something for your family, Margaret."

"Let go, Shefford, you're hurting me."

"You will feel a whole world of hurt if you do not hie yourself out to Delamere House and wheedle your way into the prince's stable."

Maggie tried to yank her arm away, but he had a solid grip. She gritted her teeth and told herself she was imagining the ominous gleam in his eyes. "We are at an impasse, Shefford. I will not help you."

The reception at Carlton House was full of pomp and pageantry, and deadly dull. Thomas sat at a long, sparkling table among various lords and ladies, and three of his own men, listening to some surprisingly dull repartee. He had expected more from the prince regent.

At least there were no pretty young maidens in pastel here, batting their lashes and smiling coyly to gain his attention. Only the wives of Prince George's chief friends and advisors were in attendance, dressed in their finery and bedecked with jewels. The Countess of Bennington was seated beside him, and took every opportunity to turn to him and brush her bosom against his arm.

It wasn't that the lady was unattractive. Her hair was as black as night, and she had dark, seductive

eyes to go with her fetching smile. Her deep cleav-
age flowed over her low-cut neckline. Her assets
should have enticed him.

And yet they did not. While she flirted openly,
giving him more than what was a proper view of
her bounty, his thoughts turned to Maggie. To her
loose gait as she danced in the Ranfield drawing
room. Watching her laugh when Zachary and Ranfield's sons played a trick on their parents. Sooth-
ing her weepy daughter in her arms.

He hadn't asked her to accompany him tonight,
for the damage to her reputation had been done.
Countess Bennington had already hinted at some
knowledge of his fondness for widows, suggesting
that he try the charms of the more sophisticated
ladies of the ton.

Tom cringed at the thought of bedding one of
the women he met in Prinny's ornate, gothic dining
hall, far preferring the sweet, unpretentiousness
of Maggie Danvers. He hadn't seen her since his
return from Ranfield Court, but not because he
hadn't tried. He'd sent her a note of invitation, but
received no reply.

Tom's mood darkened, her lack of communica-
tion a burr against his skin. He wanted to see her.
Needed to touch her. And yet she had not agreed to
meet him at the cottage.

She'd given no clear indication that she wanted
to end their affair, though Tom had noted a subtle
change in her demeanor during their last day together. Her lovemaking had been as fiery as ever,
but her intensity almost seemed a kind of farewell.

As though she knew his departure was nearing and she could not bear . . .

He gave himself a brisk mental shake and forced his attention toward that very departure. A great deal was still unsettled. The date of the horse race was fast approaching, and he had yet to hear anything from Sebastian Salim regarding his family.

He had always planned to abandon Maggie without a word of farewell. By the time he gathered his family and left England, it would be clear that Shefford was ruined, and Maggie would know exactly who had done it to him, although she would never know why. Tom doubted she would remember the long-ago incident in Hanover Square that had precipitated Tom's incarceration and transportation. In the grand scheme of life in London, it had been an insignificant event.

But his stomach burned at the thought of the future Maggie would face in London. Alone.

Then he reminded himself that it had been Maggie herself who'd instigated the episode that had ripped Tom's life from him. If she hadn't wandered into the stable yard at exactly the moment Tom had gone back to pick up the bridles the other groom had left there . . .

The thought of continuing his liaison with her should not even cross his mind. He'd done the damage he'd intended to do and now he could get on with the final components of his plans.

Then he would quickly get his family and himself onto one of his ships and safely away, before anyone could figure out how completely they'd been duped. He was quite certain the regent and his ministers would not be pleased.

He glanced over at Edward Ochoa, who was conversing quietly with Lord Perceval, and reflected on the American's earlier remarks. Words of wisdom, perhaps . . . and of caution. A warning to Tom that he might regret his actions one day. That it might be better to let the thief get away with the horse than inflict an extreme punishment.

He slid a hand across the lower half of his face, then realized that the countess at his side was speaking quietly—discreetly—to him. He tipped his head slightly and gave her his attention.

"Our house is in Upper Grosvenor Street," she said, leaning close enough to whisper in Tom's ear. "Number twenty-one, not far from the park. And my husband will be at his club most of the night, playing cards."

"I am quite flattered, Your Ladyship," Tom said, feigning an affability he did not feel. "But I . . . ah . . . I promised that very man that I would join him later for cards."

When supper was done, Tom sent the others home in a hired carriage. He allowed them to believe he was going to spend some time in Upper Grosvenor Street with the countess, but as soon as his men were out of sight, he did not have to think twice about his true destination. He wanted to know why Maggie hadn't responded to his invitation to come out to the cottage.

At least, that's what he told himself. It was a perfectly legitimate reason to call.

The house was completely dark, but that was no deterrent to his intent. He picked the lock quite easily, and let himself inside. In the shadows, he located the staircase and began his climb to Maggie's bedchamber, the location of which he remembered very well.

It had been so much simpler at Ranfield Court, spending enjoyable days together, making love throughout the night, and leaving Maggie's bed early in the morning before the servants came around. He felt a distinct desire for the same relaxed bond they'd shared there, and could almost imagine waking with her every morning at Thorne's Gate.

The thought of it gave him pause.

Her door was ajar, and Tom stepped inside, inhaling deeply of the familiar, faint aroma of roses. The moon cast a brilliant glow across the room, catching Maggie in its dim light, sound asleep in her bed. She lay on her back, her face turned toward him. Her lips were slightly parted, and Tom's entire body clenched in anticipation of tasting her.

One of her hands had found its way out from under the blanket and was resting haphazardly beside her head. It lay upon a loose braid of her thick, dark hair. She looked young and beautiful, and far more innocent than his mistress ought.

Tom forgot all about asking why she hadn't replied to his letter. He wanted to touch her, wanted to kiss her lips as he slid into her. He could think only of holding her in his arms through the night, just as they'd done at Ranfield's country house, and making love again in the morning, before anyone in the house stirred.

Tom untied his neck cloth and leaned forward with the intention of waking her gently, by tracing one finger down the length of her arm, curling his fingers with hers, then touching his lips to her mouth. But something stopped him all at once, some deep, internal warning signal that caused him to wait.

He listened intently for some noise or some cautioning undercurrent that would cause him to hesitate. But there was nothing, only a low pressure behind his eyes, and an insistent urge to reflect on what he was doing. All through the evening, Maggie had been a presence in the back of his mind, an insistent need that had beckoned to him unrelentingly. And yet . . .

She had known it was over, while he had assumed they would continue their affair in Town.

Tom unclenched his jaw and dragged a hand across his mouth as he tried to reconcile what he *wanted* to do with what he *must* do. He could change her mind. A few kisses and they would melt in each other's arms.

He had to be a fool to complicate matters now. He needed to put Maggie Danvers and their affair into some reasonable perspective. She was the sister and widow of his enemies. *That* was what he had to remember, not the incredibly delicious hours they'd spent together.

He slipped out of her bedroom and let himself

out the way he'd gone in, engaging the lock behind him. He took the long way back to Delamere House, so as not to arouse any questions about his activities after the fete at Carlton House. Because he had no answers. No answers at all.

Maggie had difficulty sleeping. She'd awakened some time during the night, missing the comfort and warmth of Thomas's arms around her. She could almost feel his presence in her bedchamber, but knew it was pure longing that made her think he was near. No doubt he'd been in attendance at Carlton House until all hours of the morning.

She had trouble falling back to sleep, wishing he was there to soothe her jangled nerves. It was surprising how quickly she'd become accustomed to sharing her bed with him, sleeping together, when she'd never done such a thing with Julian. Her husband had come to her bed on occasion, but never stayed after his duty was done. Clearly, he had not understood—or perhaps hadn't *wanted*—the sweet intimacy that was possible from a night spent in each other's arms.

He had not realized what he was missing, and might not have cared for it, even if he had. Her husband had been nothing but a weak, pampered nobleman who'd merely done what he was told for his entire life. First his nanny, then his parents, then his friends. He hadn't once entertained an original thought. She pitied him, and all at once knew that she had forgiven him, too.

She got out of bed and pulled on her wrapper. Shefford was not quite as easy to forgive. His threats were not going to persuade her to deceive Thomas. What could he do to her? Destroy the Blackmore estate? Expose her affair with Thomas? Both of those had already been done, so she had nothing to fear.

In any event, she would never take part in an underhanded plot that would give him an undue advantage. What he wanted her to do was wrong and she hoped he was not foolish enough to attempt some kind of sabotage, because she was sure that Thomas would not take such a thing lightly.

She sat in the chair near the fire and sketched Shefford's face, and the cruel twist she'd seen when he'd grabbed her arm. Her return to Blackmore Manor could not come soon enough, and yet she knew that by the time she went back to Cambridgeshire, Thomas would be gone. Her eyes burned at the thought of his leaving, but she pressed her cool fingers to them and forced herself to pay attention to purely practical matters.

She still had to deal with Julian's debt and try to come up with a theme for the next drawing she would make. She couldn't allow herself to weep over what would never be. Nor would she allow herself worry over Shefford's attempt to intimidate her. She had a drawing to complete, and she suddenly knew exactly what it would be.

When morning came, she went to Mr. Brown's office and delivered it. Much to the editor's delight, it depicted a short, corpulent Prince George in one of the gaudy military uniforms he was known to favor, dining with the handsome, stately Sabedorian prince. An empty money cask sat open on the floor behind the regent in his opulent dining chamber.

"I sincerely hope Randolph Redbush's identity remains secret, especially after this," Maggie said dryly to Mr. Brown. "I cannot imagine that the regent will appreciate this caricature."

"Oh, but there have been many inquiries about Mr. Redbush," said Mr. Brown.

Panic caught Maggie by surprise, but Mr. Brown reassured her immediately.

"Not to worry, Lady Blackmore. Redbush's anonymity works in our favor. The mystery makes him outrageously popular." He laughed as he held up the drawing to the light at the window and admired it. "Besides, Rowlandson has done far worse to the same subject, but not quite so well, if I do say so. Your drawing of the Sabedorian will sell papers as usual. Tell me, did you attend the reception for the prince?"

She shook her head. "No. Th-there is no reason why I would have been invited."

Everyone in Town would soon know that the Prince of Sabedoria had not gone out to Richmond merely for the purpose of consulting with Lord Ranfield on agricultural methods.

Maggie knew her reputation was compromised. Ruined, actually. Nothing was ever going to be the same.

"Well, my lady, your drawing gives every appearance of authenticity," said Mr. Brown, handing Maggie her payment in cash, wrapped in a sheet of fine vellum, as he'd done before.

She looked inside through a sudden blur of tears, then blinked them away, shocked. "My word, Mr. Brown!"

"Aye, it's a pretty penny you've earned to date. I say, my lady, it ought to take you a long way toward . . . er, correcting your financial situation."

Every rational part of Tom's being knew that Maggie was right to let their interlude at Ranfield Park mark the end of their affair. But the thought of seeing her again only in the company of others . . . the idea that he could never touch her, never kiss her again . . . caused a spear of longing to pierce through his chest.

"You're going to develop permanent lines in your forehead if you keep that up," said Nate.

He and his friend had spent the morning watching six of the horses race, though Tom had been too preoccupied to fully appreciate Arrendo's performance.

Seeing his Thoroughbreds compete had always been a balm for his nerves. Except that it wasn't working now.

"I wish I could see Foveaux's face when your note is delivered," said Nate as they walked away from the race course.

"Aye," Tom replied absently.

"He's going to boil over when he realizes why you looked familiar at Lady Sawbrooke's musicale, and he discovers who was responsible for his financial disaster."

Tom should have been more satisfied with his success, but he felt a disturbing hollowness all along his spine. And Mrs. Foveaux's certain distress troubled him. Strange that it would, but the woman did not know the kind of brutality her husband had committed, nor did she have any control over him. She was not the one who was at fault. "His wife was left to deal with it," Tom said. "They *both* pay."

Nate hesitated in his step. "Aye," he said quietly. "It doesn't seem quite fair, does it?"

Tom gave an almost imperceptible shake of his head as he looked at his friend, surprised that Nate shared his insight. "She was no part of his history at Norfolk Island."

"And Lady Blackmore?" Nate asked. "She had no part of the accusations against you, did she?"

"No." Tom glanced at Nate, puzzling over his change in attitude.

Nate met his eyes. "Well, she's not exactly what we expected when we arrived here, is she? Even her children. You'd never know they were the offspring of a rotter like Julian."

"No."

"She, er . . ." Nate cleared his throat, as though embarrassed to concede that Maggie was not the enemy. "Ollie speaks well of her. He says she's not like the others."

"She isn't."

"What are you going to do?" Nate asked.

Before Tom could form any kind of answer, they

heard a shout and saw Andrew Harland and Mark Saret riding toward them.

The two men arrived at the paddock and dismounted. Harland still wore Shefford's livery, and he appeared upset and shaken, even after the long ride to Delamere House.

"What is it? What's happened?"

"I believe I have what you need, sir," said Harland, his voice raw and brittle. "Information to use against Shefford."

Saret whistled for one of the trainers to come and take the horses, then the four men started back toward the house.

"His club met last night. The Seventh Circle men."

"Go on." They went into the house and Harland sat down on a bench, while the others remained standing, watching his agitated movements.

"They met as usual, in the east end," Harland said, "at their broken-down building in Hounds Ditch. Then Shefford had his driver take a few of them into Whitechapel and help him steal the first unattended child he saw. She was a filthy little thing, hardly more than an infant, begging in the street. She bawled her lungs out when they grabbed her, but nobody came out for her."

Tom's stomach turned. "What happened then?"

"We drove a long way, down to Waterloo Bridge. One of them bribed the turnkey to go away for an hour while they played their game."

"I hate to ask what it was," said Nate.

Harland rose abruptly to his feet and started to

pace. "They were to lower the girl from the center of the bridge on a rope. Then each member was to climb down and try to rescue her."

"Good Christ."

"She screamed the whole while, but of course, no one was near enough to hear." He shuddered and scrubbed one hand across his face. "It was all I could do not to shove them all into the drink and go for the chit myself."

Tom trembled with rage while Harland continued. "Shefford was to go first. He's quite strong, and he had no trouble shimmying down the rope, a separate rope, of course, and he was securely tied." He returned to the bench and covered his face in his hands.

"What happened then, Andy?" Tom asked quietly.

"He grabbed the child, but it was dark, so we couldn't see exactly what was happening. We heard a sudden shout, and a splash, and I—I saw a flash of white in the water."

There was silence as the men absorbed the words.

"He dropped her," Harland said, brushing a tear ruthlessly from his face. "The bloody bastard took her and then dropped her into the river. And there was nothing I could do."

Chapter 16

When Maggie received a summons to her mother's house, she considered not going. No doubt Beatrice wanted an explanation for—

No, Beatrice's way was usually to accuse Maggie of some offense, and then berate her for it. This time it was probably about the incident with Charlotte in the park. Or perhaps she wanted an accounting of her trip to Ranfield Park . . . with Thomas.

Maggie girded herself for what needed to be done. She had decided it was time to set matters straight.

She arrived at Beatrice's residence in Berkeley Square, and was ushered into her mother's sitting room. Charlotte happened to be there, but when Maggie entered, her sister stood and exited the room in silence.

Maggie watched her go, deciding not to engage in a petty exchange of words that would most certainly turn angry, and accomplish nothing. But when she looked at her mother, she knew their encounter was unlikely to be civil, either. Her mother's color was high and there was a sharp, blue fire in her eyes.

"It is unconscionable that you have not yet sent an apology to your sister," Beatrice said.

"Are you referring to the incident in the park?"

"Have you committed some other dreadful slight that I should be aware of?"

"Nothing I say matters, does it, Mother?" Maggie asked quietly.

"You have never cared for this family, Margaret. From the time you were a child. You destroyed a perfectly good man, just on a—"

"All these years, you and Charlotte have blamed me for Chatterton's disgrace," she said, her voice trembling with regret as well as anger. "When you know perfectly well it was *he* who should have borne the blame. A man his age—"

"*Do not speak disrespectfully of your poor, deceased cousin!*"

Maggie crossed her arms over her chest, appalled that her mother would still take Chatterton's part. "You do realize he would have raped me if I had not screamed and carried on as I did." It was the first time those words had been said aloud, at least between Maggie and her mother. "Would you have preferred that?"

Beatrice pursed her lips and turned away in disgust, but Maggie knew the answer to her question. She supposed she'd always known.

"If you and the others would only stop for a moment and consider the kind of marriage Charlotte would have had with Chatterton, I doubt you'd continue to blame me for exposing his perver—"

"My nephew was a perfectly decent, charming young man. He would never have—"

"Mother, he hurt—he *raped*—several young girls in his village, and who knows where else! His father paid their families to keep quiet. You must know this! Why do you persist in denying it?"

"Those chits were despicable liars," Beatrice said, leveling her ice blue gaze at Maggie. Her mother knew the truth of it, even though she would not acknowledge it. But far too much had ridden on Charlotte's betrothal to Chatterton. And it had all been lost.

"It's clear that we have nothing more to say," Maggie said quietly as she started for the door. "I will be in London for several more weeks, but you and the others need not—"

"You know you could redeem yourself in the eyes of your family."

Maggie stopped in her tracks as a wave of hurt and revulsion came over her. She had a feeling about what was coming before her mother spoke.

"You have culled some special favor with the Sabedorian prince," Beatrice said, "though only God Himself knows how or why—and yet you refuse to use your influence to benefit your own family."

Maggie clenched her teeth, her defiance obvious. She counted to ten in Latin. Then in French.

"First Charlotte, and now Shefford." Beatrice's pulse thrummed in her neck. "I did not raise my daughters to eschew their responsibilities. And I will not tolerate—"

Maggie had had enough. "No, Mother."

"What do you mean, *no*?"

"I mean that you have no idea what you're talking about, and even less—"

"How dare you!"

"She dares because she's a fool," said Shefford, strutting into the room. Maggie had not expected to see him there, and when he tossed her a look of pure malice, she shuddered, wondering how far he would go to get her cooperation. His earlier aggression had been frightening, and she had a bruise on her arm to remind her of it. She would not care to be alone with him in his present state of mind.

Beatrice turned her back to Maggie and stalked away to the settee. "I understand you are in dire straits, Margaret," she said in a rather superior tone, as though Maggie was somehow at fault for her financial troubles.

Maggie turned to glare at Shefford. Her finances were no one's business but her own and the estate's trustees, from which position Shefford would soon be removed, if she had any say over it.

"You must give Shefford the information he needs about the Sabedorian prince and his stables," Beatrice said, her posture stiff, her voice still full of quiet fury.

"Ten thousand of my winnings would be yours, gel," Shefford interjected, slapping his newspaper down on a table, her drawing of Thomas with Prince George laid bare. "And time is running out to assure our win! Find out if he has sentries in his stables. And which horse he's betting on. Those are the kinds of things I need to know."

"You would have me help you cheat the man," Maggie said flatly. Her stomach burned as she looked at her mother and stepbrother, thinking of the many ways they'd bullied her through the years.

"He's not even one of us," Beatrice said, and Maggie knew that she wasn't one of them, either. She thanked God for it. "And he has more money than Croesus. He won't miss—"

"I've lost a good deal of blunt in some recent investments, Margaret. My estates are at risk," he said, and Maggie heard an unfamiliar edge of desperation in his voice. "I am stretched far too thin to risk losing this horse race."

"Then perhaps you should not have made that ridiculous wager," Maggie said.

"Margaret," Beatrice interjected, "if you have some . . . *personal* . . . influence with the prince, then—"

"The irony is just too much, Mother," Maggie retorted pointedly, turning her gaze to Beatrice. "You would have me use *my wiles*? Use my admittedly paltry charms to gain some information about the man's horses?" She directed her disgusted gaze to the marquess. "And my reward would be a very generous *one quarter* of the winnings. You are unbelievable, Shefford."

"More, then. Another five thousand."

Maggie could not get away fast enough. She craved Thomas's solid presence and the serenity she'd known in his arms, even though she knew better than to rely upon such fleeting comfort.

She left her mother's house with a sinking feeling that Shefford would somehow figure a way to use her against Thomas, in spite of her refusal to take part.

"Tom!" Nate shouted. "It's Salim riding up the drive! And he's followed by a carriage!"

They hurried down to meet Salim's party as it arrived at the front of the house. Tom realized that his family must be inside the carriage, else Salim would have come to Delamere House on horseback. And there would be no carriage behind him.

Feeling more nervous than ever before, Tom waited as the footmen opened the carriage door and his family descended the steps. Four of them, all told, including a man he did not recognize.

"Pa?" Tom asked, slipping into his Suffolk dialect.

His father had aged twenty years, but he was still nearly as tall as Tom. His pate contained more gray than black, but his jaw was still square and his eyes the same deep, clear green as Tom remembered.

"Tommy," George Thorne croaked, clasping Tom to his chest. His pa hugged him tightly, then let go with one arm, drawing Tom's mother, Rebecca, into his powerful embrace.

She looked so good to him, even though she wept quietly, and his father's eyes welled with tears, too. Then Jennie came to him and patted him on the shoulder, embracing them all. "We couldn't believe it when Mr. Salim came to us."

Tom's throat felt so thick he knew he could not trust himself to speak. Not yet. He held on until the intensity of the moment eased, and still, his parents were loath to release him. They kept their hands on him as though they could not believe he was really there.

"Seventeen years," said his father, his voice gravelly with age, his Suffolk accent bringing back memories. "Seventeen years we've not known what ever happened to you."

"Pa wrote to you every week," said Jennie.

"I never received any letters," Tom said quietly. "I thought . . ."

"What, lad?" his father asked. "You thought what?"

"After years of hearing nothing, I was afraid you'd . . . disowned me."

"Never!" his mother cried clutching him even tighter. "We know what happened. You were an innocent lad." She was still the pretty farmer's daughter Tom remembered, though she seemed more fragile now, her skin as thin as delicate linen.

His father finally eased his grip and Jennie drew the fourth of their party closer. She put her hand through the crook of his arm.

"Thomas, do you remember John Markham?"

"From Newmarket? Aye. I do, but you were just a boy when I . . ." He put out his hand and shook Markham's as he looked at his sister, a woman now, amazingly enough. "I take it you and Markham . . ."

"Yes. He and I are of an age. We married two years ago."

"I'm glad to meet you, then," Tom said, leading his family into the house. He took them to a small parlor, where he thought they would be most comfortable, and ordered refreshments.

As Tom told them a much diluted version of his years in Botany Bay, he noted they were wearing what must have been their best clothes, and yet they were nearly threadbare in spots. The years had not been kind to the Thornes, and Tom could not help but think how much better they would have prospered had he been present to take up the family trade and ease his father's burden.

Tom left out the worst parts of his story—the brutality he'd known on Norfolk Island, and the horrors he'd experienced as a slave on Butcher's pirate rig—focusing his narrative on the immense wealth bequeathed to him by old Duncan Meriwether. His family was duly incredulous, even though they could not possibly conceive of the extent of Tom's wealth. They had trouble grasping the reality of Delamere House . . . and that Tom owned it. That he was a wealthy man.

"Are you a horse breeder, John?" Tom asked.

"No. The Markhams were farmers," John said. "But after my pa died, yours has been teaching me what he knows."

"John's developed a fair eye for horseflesh," said George. "I'd hoped he could take your place. And then Mr. Salim arrived—"

"I'm so glad you've come back to us," his mother said, her eyes watery with emotion. "And yet I can hardly believe . . ." She sat close to her son and kept a tight grip on him, as though she feared he might slip away if she released him.

Tom swallowed hard, hugging her close. "Ma. I missed you and Pa every day."

He enfolded his mother into his arms as she wept, and he was not above shedding a tear of his own.

Tom had thought of a hundred different ways to make his proposal to his family, and only one answer that would be acceptable. But now that Jennie was married . . .

"Ma, Pa . . . I won't be staying in England. I've only come back to find you, and to take care of some pressing business."

His father visibly composed himself. "You've settled somewhere, son? With . . . with a family of your own?"

Tom shook his head. "No family but you. But I've got my own horse farm in America now. It's a beautiful place, and . . . I want you to come back with me. All of you."

A heavy silence descended upon the room. "Leave England?" his father finally asked.

Tom nodded.

George stood and clasped his hands behind his back. A deep crease appeared above his eyes, but when he looked at Rebecca, he said, "Times haven't been good in Suffolk of late."

Tom had seen that, and not just by their threadbare homespun. It was written all over his father's aging face and his mother's fragile features.

"Things are grand in New York," Tom said quietly. "I've got five thousand acres, and I'm not far from the city. You'll have every—"

"Five thousand acres!"

Tom nodded, grinning as the coil that had been so tightly wound inside him for seventeen years began to loosen. "And the most spectacular stables you could imagine. Far better than what you've ever seen up at Lockhaven Stables. And just wait until you see my champion, Arrendo. You won't believe how that horse can run."

George skimmed a hand across his face, and Tom recognized it as his own gesture of uncertainty. "I never thought . . ."

"There is plenty of land to be had, Pa," said Tom. "I'll build you a house anywhere you like, on my land or nearby. I want Ma to have every comfort. Servants to wait on her, frocks made in town."

"Oh!" his mother whispered.

"But I'd like you to help me run my stables, Pa." He swallowed. "I want you both close."

"It's unbelievable, Tommy," Jennie said. She was so pretty with her dark hair and hazel eyes, just like their mother. Tom had pictured her as a little girl for all the years he'd been away, unable to imagine her all grown up. "And such a surprise. Can you give us a night to sleep on it? It's such a decision to make."

"Of course," he said, nodding, trying to mask his disappointment. He couldn't expect them to jump at the opportunity to board a ship and take a possibly perilous journey across the Atlantic, never to return home again. He wondered what Maggie would say if he asked her to go away with him.

He might have laughed at the absurdity of that. He couldn't even get her to respond to his note. Besides, she was a viscountess, and had a place here in England. She would never consider leaving, would never deprive her son of his title.

"I've naught to think about," said his father. "Your mother and I will be coming with you." He looked at Jennie and her husband. "You and John will have to make your own decision, of course. But think of the past few years in Suffolk. Brutal weather and bad crops. And next year, more of it."

John gave a curt nod. "Your father is right, Jennie."

Tom felt a wave of relief, and smiled broadly. "You can do anything you wish in America. Farm the land or raise horses. Start a business. It's a new country, open to any venture you might want to try."

"Aye," said John. "If you can put us on track—"

"Of course," Tom said. "Whatever you need."

"Then I think we'll be joining you, Tom," John said. "What do you say, Jennie?"

His sister smiled at her husband. "Aye."

And the coil came close to being completely unfurled.

Maggie left her mother's house and directed her driver to take her up to Hampstead Heath, to the little cottage hidden away behind Delamere House. She needed to give Thomas fair warning. Shefford was not to be trusted.

She had not responded to Thomas's request that she meet him at his cottage, and yet there she was. She'd come back to the place where they had made love, from where she'd fled that day, before she could risk her heart.

It was too late for that now.

She hadn't come for any romantic purpose. On the contrary, her business was utterly serious. She had to tell Thomas that Shefford most certainly intended to harm his horses, but she could not merely send a messenger. She would never know if Thomas had received it—or if he'd taken it seriously. She had to be sure he understood the danger her brother posed.

She waited impatiently inside the cottage while her driver went to Delamere House for him. Her heart beat significantly faster when she heard his footsteps on the path. Maggie clasped her hands together, mastering her intense desire to run out to meet him. All she wanted was to feel his capable arms around her.

She was obviously the fool Shefford had called her.

The door opened and he ducked slightly to enter. "Maggie?" He wore the same horseman's clothes he'd had on the last time he'd come to her here. Maggie's hands tingled with the memory of the texture of his trews and the heat of his body, and how quickly he'd shucked those trews and climbed into the bath that had been made ready for him.

He started for her, but when she closed her eyes and took a deep, bracing breath, he stopped. She *could* talk to him without reaching for him, even though her heart was crumbling inside. "I need to talk to you, Thomas."

He took hold of the back of a chair and Maggie saw a muscle in his jaw clench tightly.

"I—I apologize for not responding to your note . . ." She bit her lip.

He stayed perfectly still, and when he shuttered his eyes, she knew he understood. They had no future together, so it had to be over between them.

"I came to tell you . . ." she started quietly. "Shefford is going to do something. He's going to try to affect the outcome of the race."

"Go on." His voice was hard, and she sensed something very different about him. . . . She'd been a coward not to respond to his oh-so-tempting invitation. But she was not being cowardly now.

"I don't know what his plan is. H-he asked me to use my . . . my . . ." Her voice quavered and she stopped to compose herself. She hadn't realized how difficult it would be to face him and know that he would never again touch her. "He wanted me to use m-my influence with you to find out . . ."

"Find out what, Maggie?" he asked, his voice low and impassable.

She shrugged and tried to summon the same kind of righteous might she'd felt when speaking to her mother and Shefford. But her heart was splintering and her knees buckling as she faced Thomas. She knew she couldn't have what she wanted, even though he stood no more than three feet from her.

"He wants to know which horse is your champion. And whether you have sentries guarding your stable."

"Anything else?"

She shook her head, looking directly into his eyes. "I don't know. I refused before he could say any more."

He started to speak, but gave a her a quick nod instead. "We assumed he would try something."

Her eyes widened. "You did?"

"Aye." He watched her reservedly, as though a huge chasm lay between them. They were perfectly civil, the heat and passion of their earlier assignation nearly impossible to imagine.

Maggie wished he would ask her to go away with him. She didn't care if Sabedoria was at the farthest corner of the earth. Their parting was going to damage her heart irreparably.

He remained silent.

"There is a great deal of money involved in Shefford's wager."

But it was about more than the money. She knew Shefford, and knew it went against his grain to allow anyone, especially this foreign prince, to best him. "I fear my brother has done some terrible things in the past . . ."

"I am not surprised," he said. He tapped his fingers against the back of the chair. "His reputation here in London is not exactly sterling."

Maggie could easily believe that, if he went about making forty thousand pound wagers while he neglected his management of Julian's estate. And it upset her to know that the rest of her family was hardly any better.

Tears burned the backs of her eyes, but she refused to let them fall, aware that once Thomas was gone, her only sanctuary would have evaporated.

She reminded herself once again that he could not be her refuge. She'd stood up to her mother for once, and she was correcting the damage Julian had done to the estate. "I do not excuse him, Thomas. I'm just glad that you are prepared for whatever he might do. My family wants me to . . . they are not the most . . ." She looked down at the floor to say her next words. "I hope you understand I am no part of them."

Tom did not move as Maggie went past him, and holding on to the chair was the only way he managed to keep from reaching out to her. He'd seen the sheen of tears in her eyes and hated not being able to pull her into his arms. But it was clear she'd made her decision. When he heard the carriage door close, he let go of the chair and jabbed a hand through his hair while he cursed under his breath.

Her carriage drove away, and Tom walked outside. He took a long, shuddering breath as he watched her disappear, fully aware that he would always want her.

She'd been far more sensible than he, ending

the affair before it could progress any further, any deeper. But Tom had never understood how painful their separation would be. She possessed a depth of character he'd known in few others, and, in spite of her connection to Shefford and Julian, he realized it was too late to protect his heart. She had already taken a piece of his soul.

Resigned to what he must do, he walked through the woods back to Delamere's stables and made sure his guards were fully alert. Whatever Shefford tried to do, at least they would be prepared for it.

Chapter 17

Maggie had an abysmal day. The children were out with Hawkins, leaving her feeling unbearably alone, but unfit for company. She swallowed the miserable loneliness that welled up in her throat, and picked up her sketchbook. She sat down in the drawing room and pressed the pages to her breast.

With the money Mr. Brown had given her, the servants' wages both at Blackmore Manor and the London town house were now up to date. She'd paid several of Julian's outstanding bills, and had a list of his unpaid debts. She hoped to earn enough by the end of the season to resolve those. Then she could concentrate on Lord Ranfield's recommendations for some steady, sensible investments and things that could be done to improve the estate, although it was hardly a prize for Zachary to inherit.

In spite of her relief that Shefford might soon be removed from the oversight of Zachary's inheritance, Maggie could not let go of her anger with

him. It wasn't just the money. It was his expectation that she should be just as willing to try to trick
Thomas as the rest of her family seemed to be. Just
as Julian had always done. And his good friends,
Kimbridge and Ealey, no doubt.

At least she'd made sure Thomas knew of the
threat, though their encounter had given her little
peace of mind.

She took out a sheaf of foolscap and started
to draw her next caricature for Mr. Brown,
but her pencil seemed to have a will of its own.
Thinking of Shefford's unscrupulous demands,
she started drawing him as she remembered him
years ago, when she'd first had an inkling of his
true character. He'd falsely, cruelly accused the
young horseman of thievery, and when Maggie
had learned of his deceit, he and Julian had
laughed at her tears.

She started sketching the poor, accused boy, his
features coming back to her as she drew. Remembering that horrible day, the scene came easily to
her. She recalled how her heart had tripped in her
chest at the attention paid to her by the handsome, strapping boy, with his nearly black hair
and his . . .

Maggie's hand stopped. She closed her eyes and
pictured his broad shoulders and capable hands.
He'd had bright, green eyes and a strong, square
jaw, and a smile that . . .

Oh God. It was Thorne. Thomas Thorne.

And yet it could not be. Her memory had to be
playing tricks on her. She'd been only ten or eleven

years old at the time, far too long ago for her to recall—

She got up from her chair and went upstairs to her bedchamber. Pulling open the doors of the armoire that stood in the corner of her room, she knelt down and reached into the shelves at the bottom. She dug through all her old sketchbooks, the ones she had stored and forgotten over the years.

They were not marked in any particular way, but Maggie remembered each one from the drawings within. She quickly found the book that she sought, and began turning the pages that were a record of that fateful summer.

When she came to the picture she'd drawn of her young hero, she knew it was true. It was Thomas Thorne. Her prince.

She squeezed her eyes shut against the sure knowledge that somehow the innocent boy had become staggeringly wealthy and returned to England. He had to know it was Shefford—and Julian—who had accused him, resulting in his unjust conviction. Oh lord, how he must hate them for what they'd done.

The scars she'd felt on his back—he'd dismissed them as a childhood accident. Maggie cringed at the realization that they were very likely scars from floggings. She could not imagine what he'd gone through.

Shefford and Julian had callously accused him, an innocent boy, and even *she* had played some part in his destruction. She wondered if he realized that she was the girl he'd helped in the stable yard.

He would be completely justified in exacting retrib—

Dear God, the horse wager . . .

Maggie pressed one hand against her mouth. Thomas had allowed Shefford to make his ridiculous wager, and she knew now that her brother would not win, no matter what mischief he might try. She was as sure of it as she was of her own name. And she was equally certain that the loss would ruin him. *Exactly as Thomas intended.*

Maggie felt shaken to her core, but she had to admire Thomas's audacity. He'd come into England with a flourish, fielding invitations and courting ministers at the highest levels of society and government while he lured Shefford into his trap. No one would ever suspect that the lauded Prince of Sabedoria had once been a humble stable boy from England's horse country, a former convict who'd been transported to . . . to God knew where. They would never guess that his purpose here was to lure his enemy into . . .

A sudden thought struck her. Shefford was not the only perpetrator of Thomas's downfall. Julian was equally to blame.

She felt light-headed at the implications of that. If Thomas was out to wreak vengeance on Shefford, he must feel the same about Julian. Or Julian's family. *Herself, and even her—Julian's—children.* A hollow chill came over her at the thought of having been used, and betrayed yet again. First Julian, and now Thomas.

Could her time with him have been nothing

more than a master manipulation? While she'd been falling in love with him, had he been making his enemy's wife—and sister—pay for their misdeed of years ago?

She left her bedchamber and returned to the drawing room, feeling dazed and upset. Everything she thought she knew about Thomas was erroneous, and even their affair had been contrived.

Maggie sat down again and started sketching, quickly drawing Thomas's features, portraying him in his Sabedorian finery, but putting him in shackles. Then she drew a grim prison hulk in the background, his obvious destination.

Maggie knew that if she added a pointed caption and exposed the Sabedorian prince for who he really was, Mr. Brown would be beside himself with joy. And, considering how much money her previous work had earned, such a drawing would bring in enough to absolve her debt and allow her to begin improvements on Zachary's estate.

No one would care that Thomas had been unjustly accused and convicted. His ruse as the Prince of Sabedoria—did such a place even exist?—would be over. No one would welcome him into their drawing rooms or ballrooms any longer. Maggie didn't even know if it was legal for him to return to England or if he might be arrested again just for coming back.

She could not believe how well he'd duped society. His money and regal bearing had fooled everyone. And his English . . . She had actually believed his nonsense about learning the language from some pirate—but so had everyone else, apparently.

Maggie wondered where he'd been sent. She had no doubt that it had been an unspeakable place, and that he'd been consumed by a very justified hatred for the two callous boys who'd put him there. Why wouldn't he despise the two rascals who'd torn him from his family and his country on a cruel whim?

Tears of confusion and hurt rolled down her cheeks, but she dashed them away as she picked up the old sketchbook and looked once again at the drawing she'd made so many years before, of the boy who'd kept her from falling in the puddle. He'd been so sweet then, telling her that she was not clumsy, but that anyone might have tripped on the uneven cobbles. Maggie had held him in her heart for months, savoring thoughts of him as the handsome hero who would return for her one day, fall in love with her, and take her away from her hateful family.

It had all been a young girl's foolish fancy, and yet some perverse version of it had come to pass. He'd returned, and seduced the poor lame girl who'd been a part of his terrible downfall.

How pathetic was it that she still loved him? That she still ached for his touch?

The front door slammed shut, startling Maggie.

"Lady Blackmore!"

She set her drawings aside and rose abruptly from her chair, alarmed by Nurse Hawkins's panicked voice.

"It's the children!" the nurse bawled, meeting Maggie halfway to the drawing room. "He's taken them! Grabbed them from me!"

Disbelief, and then horror stabbed through Maggie, worse than anything she'd ever felt before. "Who, Hawkins?" she cried. "*Who* has taken the children?"

Hawkins sniffled and wiped her tears, but she could not keep herself from wailing in distress. "Lord Shefford. He said to tell you that you'll see them after you find out what he wants to know!"

The Thornes were settling in at Delamere House, and Tom ought to have felt content. His parents were older, but still in good health. It pleased him to know that he could provide them a life of ease in America. His wealth assured that they would never again face the hardships they'd known at home. They would all be together again, finally, after all these years.

But as satisfying as it was to think of his parents and sister at Thorne's Gate, it was not enough. He needed more.

He needed Maggie.

The vengeance he sought felt hollow now, especially without her. He'd known it at the cottage, but her demeanor had made it quite clear that she did not wish to continue their liaison. He'd felt the wall she'd put up between them, a self-imposed barrier that defied any attempt to pass through it.

Tom swore quietly. He was a blockhead. Of course she'd ended it. She was a respectable woman who'd never expected to be seduced, and he had taken advantage of her innocence and her vulnerability. He'd promised her nothing beyond a few weeks' pleasure, when he knew he wanted nothing less than a lifetime.

He did not care that she was Shefford's sister or that she'd been Julian's wife. None of that mattered.

The only thing that did matter was that he loved her. He'd seen the sheen of tears in her eyes at the cottage, and hoped it meant there was a chance that she cared for him, too. Cared enough to leave England and sail with him to Thorne's Gate.

It was a great deal to ask of a viscountess whose son would be a member of England's elite. But he had to try.

He sent Andrew Harland to get the carriage ready for a trip down to Hanover Square to collect her and the children, then he went in search of Nate.

"I've decided to call off the race," Tom said when he found his friend in the library, conversing with Edward Ochoa and Mark Saret. "Have the men take the horses to the ships."

Saret grinned, and Nathaniel nodded. Ochoa sat quietly, with a knowing expression on his face. He'd been right. Vengeance did not necessarily equal satisfaction. Taking his family home, winning Maggie . . . that was the satisfaction Tom needed.

"Aye. There's no point in running the race now," said Nate. "One word from Harland and Shefford hangs. There isn't a judge in the country who would let him off with a witness to his crimes."

"You don't mind, then? Giving up the race?"

Nate shrugged. "I wouldn't mind going home. You've accomplished everything you wanted— there's no need to risk discovery now."

Tom agreed. It should have been a letdown after all his meticulous planning, but he didn't need to be the one to destroy Shefford. The scheming bastard had done it to himself.

"It's been quite a lark," said Saret as Ochoa gave a slow nod. "But we're finished here."

"Send word to Lucas that we'll be leaving the day after tomorrow." Two days would have to be long enough for Maggie to tie up her affairs in Town, or appoint someone to do so. He intended to have her and the children home, at Thorne's Gate, within the month.

He started for the door. He should never have let Maggie leave the cottage without telling her how he felt, but his stupidity was not going to continue.

Turning as he left the room, he looked at his old friends and begged one last request. "See if any of you can find me a dog somewhere. A pup."

"Where would he have taken them?" Maggie asked, trying to control her alarm. She realized she hardly knew Shefford at all, and his behavior the past few days did not garner her confidence. He could be mean and violent, and—

"I don't know!" Nurse Hawkins whimpered. "He just yanked them away before I knew what he was about. They knew him, of course, but Lily was wailing and Zachary fighting him, and so he had to force them into his carriage."

"Mathers." Maggie tried to remain calm as she pulled on her coat. Dissolving into a panic would not serve her now. "Go to Berkeley Square and see if my mother has any idea where Shefford would have taken the children. Hawkins, send Tessa to Lady Ranfield and tell her what's happened. I'm going over to Shefford House to see if he's there."

She pulled open the door and her knees buckled when she saw Thomas standing on the other side. All at once, he swept her into his arms and kissed her deeply. "I'm not letting you go, Maggie Danvers," he said when he released her. "You're mine."

Maggie's heart clenched in her chest, her joy at seeing him tempered by dread. "Thomas, Shefford has taken Zachary and Lily!"

"Where?" he asked, pulling her tightly to him.

Maggie didn't care that they stood in plain sight of everyone in the square. The security of Thomas's arms and her confidence that he could recover her children were all that mattered. She looked up into the kind, green eyes that she should have remembered for all these years. "Hawkins had them in the park and he took them from her. We don't know where they are!"

He let her go, but kept her hand in his and

squeezed it as they went into the drawing room. "Why did he . . . What did he say?"

Hawkins answered Thomas's question. "He said we would see them only when Lady Blackmore told him what he wanted to know."

"The horse race, Thomas."

"Aye. You warned me, but I never thought—"

Maggie had forgotten the drawings until that moment. Thomas looked at them for an instant, then seemed to dismiss them. Moving quickly, he returned to the front door. "Harland!" he called.

His footman jumped down from the carriage and came to the house. "Yes, Your Highness?"

"Do you know where Shefford might have taken Lady Blackmore's children?"

"I have a fair idea," the man said.

"Let's go, then."

"Hawkins," Maggie said as calmly as she could, "please wait here for Tessa and Mathers to come back. I'll get word to you as soon as we know anything."

"Maggie," said Thomas, "it would be best if you stayed—"

But she hurried past him to the carriage, wholly uninterested in waiting for word of her family. Fortunately, Thomas did not argue.

Tom felt stunned, not just because of the situation with the children.

Maggie knew who he was. And yet she had not exposed him. Perhaps his true identity was the reason she had decided not to continue their affair.

Ollie jumped down from the carriage and let down the steps for her. She climbed into the carriage, and the sight of her tear-streaked face exposed the triviality of Tom's schemes and plans. Nothing mattered but Maggie, and getting her children back from Shefford.

Tom took his seat beside her and pulled her close as the carriage began to move. He pressed a kiss to her temple. "We have no reason to think Shefford will hurt the children."

"You haven't seen him these past few days," she said. "He's desperate. And it's made him ruthless."

"Aye. I'm sorry. I'm at fault."

She gazed up at him, and he wiped a tear from her face. But she did not contradict him.

The carriage picked up speed, and as Tom looked out the window, he was relieved to note that they were going in the opposite direction of the Waterloo Bridge. At least there would be no repetition of Shefford's previous depravity.

"Where are we going?"

"I'm not sure. But Harland knows Shefford well."

"I don't understand. How would your footman—"

"Maggie, you know who I am. You know why I've come to England."

She gave a shaky nod.

"Harland is one of my men. He took a post as one of Shefford's footmen and learned all his haunts." He didn't want to say anything more, for Maggie's face was pale enough, and her features tight with worry. He didn't want her to know what he'd already learned about her brother.

He felt her shudder. "Where? Where are they?"

"We'll be there soon." They were heading east, so he assumed it would be Shefford's club's meeting place, somewhere near Whitechapel. Maggie would certainly never know to look for him there.

The ride was interminably long, and Maggie said nothing more. It was no time for any further explanations, and Tom had to content himself with holding her as they rode at breakneck speed through the busy streets.

The carriage finally slowed and Tom opened the door before it even had a chance to come to a complete stop. Harland jumped down and came to Tom while Ollie tied the horses.

"I had Ollie stop a ways back from the building," said Harland as Tom exited the carriage. "Shefford's meeting place is just there."

Maggie stepped down behind Tom, and started in the direction of the five-story building Harland indicated. Tom grabbed her.

"Wait."

"If my children are there, I'm—"

"Maggie. Sweetheart, it's not going to work," said Tom. His heart felt as though it was about to burst. He hadn't felt this kind of fear since he'd been arrested seventeen years before. And Shefford had been responsible then, too. "Shefford isn't going to listen to you. He went far past that point when he took Zachary and Lily."

"But I—"

He took her hands in his. "Please trust me. You must believe you can't, but . . ." He swallowed. "It means more than anything to me to get the children back. Let me handle this."

He did not breathe until she gave a slow nod, her eyes watering and her mouth quivering in anguish. He pulled her close and gave her a quick hug, then released her and handed her into the carriage. He started to move quickly, with Ollie and Harland behind him, in single file. They stayed close to the shop fronts so that Shefford wouldn't be able to see them if he happened to look out one of the grimy windows.

He didn't like leaving Maggie alone, but he hoped it would not be for long.

"Here, lad," he said to a youth passing by. He showed him a coin. "I've got another just like it if you will find a constable and bring him back here."

"Yes, sir!" said the boy as he ran off to do Tom's bidding.

"Ollie, you take the back. Harland, you and I will go in through the front."

As they got closer, Tom heard the familiar wailing of a small child. *Lily!* It was all he could do to keep from storming the front door and pulling Maggie's daughter from Shefford's contemptible possession.

"That cry sounded like it was coming from an upper floor," said Harland.

Ollie entered the vacant building next door and made his way to the back, while Tom and Harland went to Shefford's front door. Getting inside was going to be easier with Shefford on an upper floor, but Tom didn't know how they could possibly get up the stairs without alerting him to their presence. With any luck, Lily would keep up her crying and mask any sound they made.

"Is he likely to have a weapon?"

Harland stilled. "They do like their pistols," he said, "but I never knew Shefford to carry one except during his club jaunts. A knife, perhaps."

Tom swore under his breath. It should have been relatively simple to rush the stairs and grab the children. Now he had to worry that the bastard might shoot somebody. "Come on. There's nothing we can do about it."

There was a sudden crash far above them, and then a mad scrabbling on the stairs. Tom hurried to the staircase when he heard Zachary's scream, and started his race up the stairs. Shefford must be carrying Lily and somehow dragging Zac up the steps in order to move so quickly. But they were not on the second floor.

"We've got to get to them before they reach the roof!" he said to Harland as they took the steps two at a time. He didn't want to think about the danger if he managed to get the children up there.

A door slammed on the topmost floor, and when Tom reached it, he was unable to open it.

"Shefford, I know you're inside. Send the children out!"

"You!" called Shefford's voice from within.
"You're the cause of all this—"

"Thorne!" Zachary screamed. "We're in here!"

Tom felt his heart beating in his throat. "Don't
worry, Zachary, I've come for you."

Tom signaled to Harland, and on the quiet count
of three, they threw their shoulders into the door
and smashed it open.

Zachary ran to him instantly, but Shefford held
Lily in one hand. And a half-cocked pistol in the
other.

Chapter 18

Maggie could not spend another moment sitting blindly in Thomas's carriage. Of course she trusted him to rescue her children. She'd seen his heartfelt distress over his part in their abduction, and knew that there was something more. Something she was afraid to define.

But she could not sit still a minute longer. She clambered out of the carriage without assistance, and hurried to the derelict shop Thomas's footman had indicated. The door of the building was open, but Maggie saw no one inside. She crossed the threshold and heard some distant sounds from above.

When she realized it was the sound of Lily's crying, she forgot all caution and hastened up the stairs, praying all the while that Shefford would not hurt her little girl. Lily was not at fault . . . nor was Thomas. If Shefford had not been such a scoundrel all his life, he wouldn't have left his swath of justifiably angry casualties. He deserved everything Thomas had planned for him.

But not at the cost of her children's well-being.

Lily suddenly stopped crying, and there was complete silence at the top of the stairs until she heard Thomas's voice. It was tense, edgy. "Put down the pistol, Shefford. Don't make your situation any worse than it is."

Shefford had a pistol? Maggie's heart stopped. Somehow, she managed to creep up the last few steps and saw Thomas standing in the doorway with his footman, with Zachary right behind him. Protected. Safe.

But Lily! *Where was Lily?*

Maggie held her breath. As much as she wanted to grab Zachary and take him away, she was afraid that any move might distract Thomas, or make Shefford act rashly.

And she couldn't flee without Lily and Thomas!

She moved stealthily up to the landing, and managed to see into the room without alerting Shefford to her presence. But the sight of her whimpering daughter struggling to get out of Shefford's arms was nearly too much. Her little daughter was so close to that pistol.

Maggie clamped her hand over her mouth to keep from crying out. Tears filled her eyes as Thomas took a step forward.

"Put the gun down, Shefford. It's over."

"You might be some potentate from God knows where, but you have no power here!" Shefford ground out through gritted teeth.

"And I will be leaving soon. You don't have to put your horse up against mine. I concede."

"What? You concede the race? The forty thousand pounds?"

"For Lily? Of course. Do not endanger the child, Shefford." His voice was so calm, so even, while Maggie's knees were knocking and her hands trembling with fear. *The gun was pointed directly at the man she loved.*

"Think of it. Forty thousand pounds, just to hand her over to me."

"Why should I believe you?"

He moved forward another step. "Because I'm no rogue. I'm a man of my word."

"Fifty," Shefford said, and Maggie nearly screamed. "I'll need fifty."

"Hand over the girl, Shefford." He took another step closer and Lily lunged just then, grabbing for Thomas, and setting Shefford off balance. Thomas took her and lowered her to the ground so quickly, Maggie could hardly see what happened next.

Thomas moved suddenly to the right, his footman to the left. Shefford had a moment's confusion, giving Thomas an opportunity to take hold of his wrist. At the same time, he smashed Shefford back against the wall as the footman tried to seize the gun. But it discharged, the ball shattering the window behind him.

The children shrieked and Maggie gathered them in her arms while Thomas drew back his fist and punched Shefford's face, bloodying his nose.

Shefford sank to the floor.

"I'll swear a warrant against you within the hour, Sabedorian!" Shefford rasped, his eyes tearing.

"Not before you are indicted on murder charges, Marquess. Your life is over."

The satisfaction Tom felt in seeing an outraged Shefford in shackles was outweighed by the precious weight of Lily in his arms and the tight clasp of Zachary's small hand in his. Nothing mattered more than the safety and well-being of Maggie's children.

It took an interminable length of time, and was quite late by the time the warrants had been sworn and it had been decided what to do with a murderous marquess. The charges against him were so heinous that the lord mayor himself had been notified of the situation. There was little doubt that Shefford would hang for his part in the murder of the poor child whose body had been found earlier in the day.

The children were asleep when they arrived at Delamere House, and as Tom carried Zachary inside, Nurse Hawkins brought Lily. They found a suitable set of rooms for the children and their nurse, and once they'd settled in, Tom took Maggie to his own bedchamber.

He'd barely shut the door when she collapsed in his arms. He carried her to a chair and sat down, keeping her in his lap. She clutched him desperately, and he felt her quake as she wept, her tears drenching his shirtfront. "Hush, love. It's all right. Everything is all right now."

She looked up at him through her tears. "They were so horrid to you. All those years ago, Shefford and Julian . . . And all because of me, because of my clumsiness."

"Don't think of it now. It's behind us."

"How can you say that?" she whispered. "You helped me, and they decided to punish you for it."

He took hold of her hand and pressed a kiss to its palm. "God, I've missed you."

Still, she wept quietly. "I didn't know what they'd done until weeks later."

"And now? When did you recognize me?"

"Just this afternoon." She wiped her eyes and looked up at him. "I was thinking about how hateful Shefford could be, and I remembered the incident." She covered her mouth as though she felt ill. The evening had surely taken its toll, but Tom could see that she was far from settling down.

"Was *Redbush* going to expose me in the newspapers?"

She shook her head. "No. I would never do that to you."

He let out a long, deep breath. He hadn't believed she would, but it felt good to hear her say it.

"You ought to despise me."

"Despise you?" He pulled her close and held her tightly. "I'm in love with you, Maggie. I could nev—"

"Oh Thomas, I love you, too," she cried, looking up at him. "I was a fool to think I could ever end it . . ."

He kissed her then, and Maggie slid her hands up his shoulders, then twined them into the hair at his nape. He groaned and deepened the contact.

He'd had no idea how full his heart could be, and how little his revenge mattered, compared to what he felt for this woman.

"You know then, that nothing is as I told it," he said when he could force himself to break the kiss. "Not Sabedoria, not my royal blood . . . All of it is a sham."

She nodded. "It doesn't matter. I love you, Tom Thorne."

He touched his forehead to hers. "Come home with me, Maggie. Marry me. Be my wife."

"Oh yes," she said. "There's nothing I want more."

Tom smiled at her tears. He would make sure she had no reason to weep once they departed for Thorne's Gate.

Maggie awoke in stages. Hardly aware of the cozy softness of the mattress under her or the warmth of the room, she felt Thomas's arms tighten around her and the press of his long, solid body behind her. She felt his breath on her shoulder, ruffling her hair, and his firm erection against her bottom.

She turned in his arms and looked at him, at the perfect green of his eyes and the thick lashes that bracketed them. *Good morning* was far too pallid an expression for what she felt.

She skimmed her hands up his chest, and slid one of her thighs between his legs. He made a low growl and kissed her, sucking her lower lip into his mouth and nipping her lightly. "I want you," he rasped.

She was more than ready for him, and when the kiss turned more demanding, Maggie moved over him, taking control. Impassioned, she pinned him beneath her, even though she knew he could change their positions in an instant.

His fingers wandered down her back, and cupped her bottom as she raised up and lowered herself onto him. She closed her eyes and savored the sensation of his hard length inside her.

"Maggie, sweet Maggie," he whispered, and began to move, sliding in and out in a slow melding of their bodies and souls.

She looked at him then, their eyes locking as her body gripped his intimately. "I love you," he said.

The intensity of his gaze matched the strength of his movements. He stroked her, grinding against her in a primal rhythm that marked her forever. He moved slowly, teasing her by entering and withdrawing at a purposeful pace. She writhed toward him, needing, feeling— Wanting more.

Her heart was about to burst. "Fast, Thomas. Take me fast!"

All at once he obliged her, causing her abrupt release, an unending spasm of sensation, of pleasure so intense she felt tears building in her eyes. Their bond was sealed when he flexed within her at the same time, tightening his grip on her as he came. Maggie trembled, her mind and body a tumult of emotion.

Still joined, she lay against his chest as their hearts slowed and their breathing returned to normal. The top of her head fit just below his jaw, and she shivered when he skated one hand up her back and cupped the back of her head.

"We will marry today," he said, turning them so that they faced each other, resting on their sides.

Maggie's heart could not have been more full. But there were complications. She touched his mouth, then ran a hand down his whiskered jaw. The law would not allow them to marry on such short notice, but it did not matter. She would wait until they reached their destination, the home she would share with him.

After Thomas met with his solicitor, Maggie met his parents. They were a fine, gracious couple from Suffolk, who seemed genuinely pleased when Thomas introduced her as his fiancée, and delighted by her children. She cringed at the knowledge of all they must have gone through when Shefford and Julian ripped their innocent son from them. It had been unconscionable.

Thomas's sister was sweet, and clearly eager to embark on their journey to America.

America. Thomas squeezed her hand, instantly calming her nerves. He'd promised her that Zachary could return to England to claim his inheritance if he ever decided to do so. But Thomas did not think he would. He'd told her about Thorne's Gate, and insisted that once Zac saw it, he wouldn't want to leave it. None of them would.

There was to be no horse race. Maggie learned that Thomas had already sent his horses to his ships, and would be ready to sail the next day. She had little to pack, but Randolph Redbush had one last drawing to make.

As Thomas's amused family looked on, Maggie drew a caricature of herself and Tom, standing together inside a wreath of spring flowers, and St. George's Church in the background. Not that they would wed at the popular Mayfair church, but there would be no mistaking the meaning of this picture. She drew their hands clasped together, with wedding rings distinctly drawn. All of London would know that Lady Blackmore had wed the Sabedorian prince.

The ink dried and Maggie penned a note to Mr. Brown, telling him that this would be her last caricature for *The Gazette*. She sent the picture and the note to London with one of Tom's men, asking that Mr. Brown send her earnings to Lord Ranfield. Victoria's husband would use them to reconcile the rest of Julian's debts.

When she and Thomas were finally alone, he drew her into his arms. "I've been waiting for this all morning," he said, brushing a melting kiss across her lips. "I have a surprise for you and the children."

She pulled back slightly. "What?"

"It's out in the barn. Let's get them and we'll go out together."

Maggie did not let him go, but cupped his face in her hands. "Have I told you how very much I love you?"

He grinned. "Aye. But I'll never tire of hearing it, Maggie, sweet."

Maggie didn't think she'd ever known such happiness, or simple contentment. Nothing in the world mattered besides the life she had begun with Thomas.

She started for the front staircase to fetch the children, but encountered Thomas's butler, opening the door to callers.

Maggie's heart sank. It had been unrealistic to hope she could leave England without seeing her family, but there was Beatrice, entering the house with Charlotte, Stella, and her husband, Lord Horton.

"There you are!" Beatrice said in a low, odious tone. "You traitorous girl. Do you know what you've done?"

Charlotte sneered. "Exactly what you did to Chatterton. Have you no sense of loyalty? Of responsibility?"

Maggie felt the blood rush from her head as they crowded around her.

"You can never leave well enough alone, can you?" Stella snapped while Horton merely looked on. "You are a menace."

Beatrice grasped Maggie's arm and squeezed hard. "I told you to help Shefford, but inste—"

"*Enough!*"

Abruptly, Beatrice released Maggie's arm at the sound of Thomas's harsh voice, but she leveled her coldest gaze at him. "It's your fault, you . . . you . . . *foreigner!*"

Thomas positioned himself between Maggie and her family. No one had ever taken her part against her mother before, and she nearly wept with gratitude at his intervention.

"Mr. Mickles, open the door, if you please." Thomas turned to Beatrice. "I suggest you take your leave while you still can, Lady Shefford, before I decide to lodge a complaint against you as an accomplice to your stepson's schemes."

Beatrice blustered with indignation. "Why, I have never been—"

"And the rest of you," he said, shifting so that he could slide his arm around Maggie's shoulders. "You are not welcome in our home."

"*Our—*"

"Aye. Our home when Lady Blackmore becomes my wife." He allowed no more conversation, but drew Maggie away as two footmen joined Mr. Mickles to ensure that there was no delay in her family's exit.

Her knees felt weak, but Thomas supported her as they went into the drawing room. He bade her to sit down, and then went down on one knee before her. He raised her hand to his lips. "It's over now. We've dealt with Shefford, and you need not have any contact with those vipers ever again. Once we leave, they never need know where you've gone."

For the first time in years, Maggie felt as though she could breathe freely. "After all this time . . ." She gave him a watery smile. "It doesn't matter anymore. None of it."

He pressed a kiss to her hand and stood. "Wait for me here. I'll go get the children."

* * *

Tom didn't think he'd ever seen such a shaggy cur, or bigger paws on a pup. But Zachary squealed with glee when he saw it, and the delight seemed to be mutual. The dog took to Zac like a long lost friend, and Maggie looked up at Tom as though he'd just given her a mountain of riches.

Her sweet gratitude humbled him. "I would give you the world if I could, Maggie."

"I don't want the world, Tom. Only you."

Zac laughed. "Look! He can do tricks!" The dog was running after a stick Zac had thrown. "That shall be his name! Trick!"

Lily stood next to Maggie, clapping her hands happily, uncertain how to approach the exuberant pup. Tom wasn't sure how they were going to manage Trick on the ship, but he'd gotten more than a dozen horses across the Atlantic. Surely they could deal with one small dog on the trip back to New York.

For the first time in years, he was not thinking about plans and schemes to bring Shefford and Danvers down. There had been something in Edward Ochoa's story. Tom knew that he was not the one to mete out justice, and it was a surprising relief to relinquish that task. He felt complete.

He had his family now. And the possibilities for them in America were limitless.

Unforgettable, enthralling love stories,
sparkling with passion and adventure
from Romance's bestselling authors

ONE RECKLESS SUMMER   *by Toni Blake*
978-0-06-142989-7

DESIRE UNTAMED   *by Pamela Palmer*
978-0-06-166751-0

OBSESSION UNTAMED   *by Pamela Palmer*
978-0-06-166752-7

PASSION UNTAMED   *by Pamela Palmer*
978-0-06-166753-4

OUT OF THE DARKNESS   *by Jaime Rush*
978-0-06-169036-5

SILENT NIGHT, HAUNTED NIGHT   *by Terri Garey*
978-0-06-158204-2

SOLD TO A LAIRD   *by Karen Ranney*
978-0-06-177175-0

DARK OF THE MOON   *by Karen Robards*
978-0-380-75437-3

MY DARLING CAROLINE   *by Adele Ashworth*
978-0-06-190587-2

UPON A WICKED TIME   *by Karen Ranney*
978-0-380-79583-3

At Avon Books, we know your passion for romance—once you finish one of our novels, you find yourself wanting more.

May we tempt you with . . .

- **Excerpts** from our upcoming releases.

- Entertaining **extras**, including authors' personal photo albums and book lists.

- Behind-the-scenes **scoop** on your favorite characters and series.

- **Sweepstakes** for the chance to win free books, romantic getaways, and other fun prizes.

- Writing **tips** from our authors and editors.

- **Blog** with our authors and find out why they love to write romance.

- **Exclusive content** that's not contained within the pages of our novels.

Join us at
www.avonbooks.com

AVON

An Imprint of HarperCollins*Publishers*
www.avonromance.com